of the

Summerhouse

Also by Elise Darcy

The Living Apart Together Series

Living Apart Together

It Takes 2 to Tango

Dear John

Love on the Rooftop

Standalone books

Lola & The Man

A Mallorcan Affair

The Villa in Sicily

We'll Meet Again

The Sunrise Coast Series

New Beginnings at the Harbour Inn

The Secret of the Summerhouse

The Cottage by the Sea

The Secret of the Summerhouse

A Novel

ELISE DARCY

Penny Lane Press

ISBN 978-1-913147-09-9

"A secret remains a secret until you make someone promise never to reveal it." –Fausto Cercignani

1

Lili heard the tinkle of the bell above the shop door. She'd put the *Open* sign in the window and had just nipped upstairs to the flat to put the kettle on. She thought everyone who came would want a drink. She'd bought biscuits too and had tried her hand at making a cake. She looked at the chocolate sponge, which she had cut into slices and put on a plate. The sponge had sunk a bit in the middle, but it had turned out okay considering that baking wasn't really her forte. *Neither is running an antique shop*, she thought as she laid out the cups and saucers on a tray.

'They're here!' Maisie called out, poking her head up the stairs.

'Okay, I'll be down in a minute.' A feeling of déjà vu swept over Lili as she stood in the small kitchenette of the two-bedroomed flat above the old antique shop in Cobblers Yard. The last time she'd made tea and coffee for her guests downstairs, it had been an impromptu gathering of the owners of the shops in the cobbled square, and she'd made do with a hastily bought selection box of biscuits.

Cobblers Yard was located off the main street in the seaside town of Aldeburgh on the Suffolk Coast, where Lili had gone for a holiday. Lili hadn't meant to stay in a flat above a shop for her holiday – and certainly not with everyone in the little community of shops under the impression that she was a good friend of the owner, Joseph, who had ended up in hospital after a fall. It was all a bit of a misunderstanding that Lili had failed to correct.

Lili sighed as the kettle boiled, wondering again how she had got herself into this fix. Her holiday, which had been planned as a romantic break away from London with her boyfriend, Alex, had turned into anything but romantic. It hadn't been her fault, though. She reminded herself of this, thinking of her best friend, Hannah.

Footsteps thumped up the stairs, interrupting her thoughts. Hannah's daughter, Maisie, whom Lili had brought with her on holiday, ran into the kitchen. 'Sarah and William have arrived.'

'Okay, sweetheart. I'll be down in a minute.'

'Hurry up. We're waiting to get started.'

'All right, all right. Tell them I'll be down in a sec.' Lili stared after her. The situation wasn't Maisie's fault either. She was the innocent party in all this. Maisie was eight years old, and Lili had been looking after her, on and off, since she was born. She had looked after Hannah a great deal too. Lili's boyfriend, Alex, had put up with Lili's wayward best friend for several years as Hannah flitted in and out of relationships, crashing on their sofa with her little girl when things did not work out. A fortnight earlier, though, it had all come to a head.

Lili poured boiling water into cups, wishing she could put that day out of her mind. The trouble was, she couldn't. Alex had barely been in touch since the massive row they'd had before she'd left London. Little wonder. He must have been looking forward to the week in an atmospheric hotel, The Harbour Inn on the Suffolk coast. Lili sighed. The trouble was that Hannah had chosen that day to stage another one of her impromptu appearances. She had dumped Maisie on Lili before jetting off with her boyfriend to Barbados on what she had called a 'make-or-break' holiday. As usual, things hadn't been working out with her current beau.

And, as usual, Lili had not had it in her heart to refuse her. Unfortunately, for Alex it had been the final straw. He had thrust the train tickets and hotel booking details at Lili, telling her to take Maisie instead – and hinting that she shouldn't bother coming back.

They had been together for six years. During the week at the hotel, Lili had eventually phoned Alex. She hadn't planned to, but Hannah had been in touch to tell her she had extended her trip. Lili hadn't been all that surprised; it had happened before, when she'd ended up looking after Maisie for the entire school holidays. This time around had been different. At the point when Hannah had called to say she'd extended her break, Lili had had nowhere to go. All the holiday rentals in the vicinity had already been booked for the summer, and she hadn't thought that Alex would have her back with Maisie in tow.

That was when serendipity had stepped in, and she'd met the lovely people from Cobblers Yard.

Lili poured milk into two cups of tea, and a dash into the coffee for Ray. She added two tall glasses of juice to the tray, along with the cake and biscuits, and headed out of the door. Carrying the tray with both hands, Lili carefully walked down the stairs and entered the antique shop, smiling at Sarah and William, who were already seated on stools at the old-fashioned wooden counter.

'Tea for you, Sarah.' Lili handed her the mug.

'And a juice for William.' She smiled at Sarah's six-year-old grandson as she passed him a glass of orange juice.

Maisie took the other glass before taking a seat too. Lili picked up her tea and glanced at the coffee. 'Where's Ray?'

Sarah frowned. 'I expect he'll be along in a moment.'

Lili caught the frown. It wasn't because he was late. It was because he was coming at all. Sarah and Ray were meant to be getting divorced. They'd had the papers for five years – or so the story went, according to the resident rumour mill in the shape of two widowed sisters next door in the charity shop. Sarah and Ray still hadn't got round to finalising it.

Lili had heard that Sarah and Ray had previously lived in London but had split up when they retired. Ray had followed Sarah to Aldeburgh and had even leased an art shop in Cobblers Yard – right opposite the flower shop that Sarah ran – just so that he could be near her. Ray was Sarah's biggest customer; he went in to buy her flowers every day. Lili thought it was incredibly romantic.

She glanced at Sarah's face and knew she saw it differently. Lili guessed Sarah felt Ray was being a nuisance, and she could tell Sarah didn't want him to turn up at the antique shop that day. He was not going to be there for Sarah, though, but to help Maisie with her amber jewellery, which had become a bit of a hit with the tourists. The necklaces, rings and brooches were being snapped up as souvenirs from The Amber Coast – perhaps because people didn't expect to see jewellery in an antique shop. Lili thought it might also have to do with the prices. There was an amber jewellery shop up the road in another coastal town. Their pieces, although made with much more expensive materials, were also much more costly. Maisie's were handmade and individual but were a fraction of the other shop's price.

Lili and Maisie had met Sarah and her grandson, William, at a little café in Aldeburgh on the first day of their holiday. They'd visited the café after spending time on the beach amber-hunting.

Maisie had discovered several pieces while foraging along the pebble beach. In the café, Sarah had noticed them and directed them to Ray's art shop so they could buy a jewellery-making kit and Maisie could turn her little amber pieces into something that could be worn.

That had marked Lili and Maisie's first visit to Cobblers Yard and the start of a chain of events that had led them to rent the little flat above the antique shop and to run Joseph's business while he was in hospital.

2

Lili looked at Sarah and asked how her father, Joseph, was.

'Still not quite with it, I'm afraid. They said it's expected, at his age, after a fall.'

Delirium. That was what Lili had heard. It could take days or weeks for Joseph to come out of it – if he came out of it at all. Of course, Lili didn't say what she was thinking. 'I hope he feels better soon.'

'Well, he has to go through a hip operation first.'

Lili had learned about that too. It had turned out that the old fool had been suffering in silence. If it hadn't been for their chance encounter, he might never had taken a tumble and then had to have the x-ray that had revealed his worn hip. Lili still felt responsible. The first time she had visited Cobblers Yard, she had intended to go into Ray's shop, but it had been closed. It had been raining at the time, so on the spur of the moment she'd walked into the antique shop instead, where she'd had the strangest of encounters. The old man there had called her Alena, as though he recognised her from somewhere.

Lili had been looking for a rental to stay on in Aldeburgh, as her week in the hotel was coming to an end. Joseph suggested that she could rent the flat above his shop, which was vacant. She hadn't wanted to commit. He'd offered it to her for such a cheap price that she'd felt the whole situation was a bit odd.

However, with rental cottages in the area all booked up, and no availability at the hotel, Lili had returned to the shop, only for Joseph to have a fall, right there in front of her. She'd reached out to try to stop him, and he'd taken her down too. They had both ended up in the local minor injuries unit at the hospital in Aldeburgh – Joseph initially with concussion and Lili with a hairline fracture in her wrist. When she'd returned to the antique shop with his keys and had moved into the flat, everybody had assumed she was a friend of Joseph's. The other shop owners had had an impromptu get-together to welcome the young lady who was looking after Joseph's shop while he was in hospital.

The trouble was that Lili wasn't Joseph's friend. She'd only just met him, but because she needed somewhere to stay with Maisie, she hadn't corrected the misconception. It had worked in her favour that Joseph was still disorientated. He didn't know she was running his shop. Lili didn't have the first clue about how to manage a business, although she had sold some items. She also put his peppercorn rent, in cash, in his till. No one could accuse her of taking advantage of a man of advancing years. She didn't have to run his shop, but she thought it was the least she could do.

That wasn't the only thing she'd kept from Sarah, Ray and the other residents of Cobblers Yard. None of them knew that Maisie wasn't her daughter. It had not been intentional; they'd just assumed she was Maisie's mum, and she hadn't corrected that either. Some of the shop owners in Cobblers Yard, along with Joseph's relations, had voiced their thoughts: w*e didn't think*

Joseph had any friends. Lili thought he sounded quite the curmudgeon – the same initial assessment she'd made of his grandson, Nate.

Ray still hadn't appeared, but just as she was thinking of Nate, he turned up instead. Lili smiled when he walked in – although that hadn't been her reaction when she'd first met him.

Nate was the new locum doctor in the hospital, and Lili had met him in the minor injuries unit when she'd broken her wrist during Joseph's fall. Nate was a good-looking guy but had come across as taciturn and short-tempered; his bedside manner had left a lot to be desired. However, she remembered he redeemed himself when he spoke with Maisie. It was as though someone had flicked a switch and he was a different person, kind and thoughtful; the Nate she saw now. She'd found out later he was a single parent and a widower, and a new arrival in Aldeburgh. He'd had a promising career at one of the prestigious London hospitals; he had given it up to take a position as a locum doctor at Aldeburgh's cottage hospital so that his parents, Sarah and Ray, could help with his six-year-old son, William.

It was through Maisie's friendship with William, amber-hunting on the beach together, and Lili's acquaintance with William's grandparents, that she had started to get to know Nate. She'd even accepted a dinner invitation.

It hadn't been her intention to get involved with someone new – and she hadn't; not really. It was all very innocent. The children had been there, along with Joseph's dog, Bella, who had interrupted the meal too. She had accepted the invitation to dine with Nate because of Alex and what she had received from him through the post.

Alex had asked for her forwarding address when she'd called

him to say she was moving from the hotel and extending her holiday with Maisie in Suffolk. Lili still hadn't been sure what was going on with Alex, and whether they were splitting up for good. Then she had received a package from him in the post. Alex had sent a large box. She had been shocked when she'd opened the box to find it contained all her stuff from the flat they had shared in London. That was when she'd accepted Nate's invitation to dinner, even though she wasn't ready for another relationship. She didn't know when she would be ready, but she told herself that it didn't mean she couldn't make new friends.

Lili had then received an unexpected call from Hannah, who had extended her sojourn abroad, yet again – this time, island-hopping in the Caribbean for a month. Lili hadn't really been surprised.

As much as she would have liked to stay in Aldeburgh for the rest of the summer, Lili had decided she'd outstayed her welcome in Cobblers Yard and that it was time to return to London. She had good friends she was sure would put her up. They were two couples whom she and Alex had often socialised with at their favourite pub at weekends.

There was also Connie, whom she could always rely on. She had known Connie nearly all her life. It was Connie who had accompanied her back from the island of Corfu when she was a toddler, where she'd been found wandering along a beach alone. Lili's parents had never been traced.

As it happened, Lili hadn't had to worry about asking to stay with her friends or Connie; Nate had persuaded her to stay on at the flat. And Sarah had wanted her to continue minding Joseph's shop. And then there was Maisie's burgeoning side-line in amber jewellery; her creations were flying off the rack and earning

Joseph a nice little percentage commission. In fact, they appeared to be the only things that were selling.

Lili stared at Nate. He'd never had the time or inclination to join them all in the shop. She wondered what he was doing there. Wasn't he meant to be on a shift?

'Daddy, what are you doing here?'

Lili looked at Nate's son. He'd taken the words right out of her mouth.

'Ah, I didn't expect to see you here, Mum, with Will.'

'We're busy making jewellery. I don't want to go home yet, Daddy.'

'I'm not here to take you home.'

Nate was holding something behind his back. At that moment, the bell above the shop door tinkled as it opened. Ray walked in, took one look at Nate, and said, 'Nice flowers.'

Nate rolled his eyes. 'Thanks, Dad – you just ruined the surprise.' He brought out an enormous bunch of flowers from behind his back.

Maisie sniggered into her hand.

'What are you doing here, anyway?' Ray asked Nate.

Nate frowned. 'I might ask you the same question.'

'I came to help with the amber jewellery.'

Nate looked at him askance. 'Oh, really,' he said sarcastically, aware that it was a ruse. Ray found any excuse he could to see Sarah.

Ray raised his eyebrows, catching the sarcasm in his son's voice. 'Well, I don't think you're here to help either.' He eyed the flowers and glanced over at Lili.

Lili felt her face flush when she realised that they must be for her. She had felt that this could be a fresh start, a new beginning, when Nate had convinced her to stay for the rest of the summer. But the reality of her situation and the untruths she'd let remain soon resurfaced and burst that bubble. He was still under the impression that she was a single parent, like him.

Then there was the other thing. Lili fingered the ring she wore on a chain around her neck. It was the only item, apart from the clothes she'd been wearing, that had been in her possession back when she was found alone on the beach in Corfu. It was Maisie who had spotted that Joseph had a ring just like it. Lili wanted to discover why Joseph had the same ring. Was it just a coincidence? Were they ten a penny? Had Joseph holidayed on Corfu once, and had the rings been something you could buy from any street vendor? Lili's ring had an inscription on the inside of the band. Did Joseph's have one too? Lili had yet to speak to him and find out.

Nate walked up to Lili and held out the bunch of flowers. Her face turned crimson; this was not what she had expected when she'd agreed to stay.

She was just reaching for the flowers when the door opened again, and Mabel and Marjorie walked in. Lili had to restrain herself from rolling her eyes and sighing heavily. Of all the people to see her taking flowers from Nate, it had to be the resident gossip girls.

The widowed sisters who ran the charity shop in the yard were in their early eighties, and they adored a bit of scandal. Lili could see their eyes home in on the flowers that Nate was passing to her. Their timing couldn't have been better. She saw them exchange a glance, smiling at one another. She knew everyone would hear about this and think that she and Nate were an item.

Sarah looked at the flowers and joked, 'I hope you bought those in The Potting Shed, Nate.'

He rolled his eyes at his mother. 'Yes, I purchased them in your shop. I still have the receipt if you want to check.'

'That won't be necessary.'

Ray took his place on a stool behind the counter at the back of the shop and picked up a necklace. He looked at the flowers, then at his son. 'So, what's all this in aid of?'

Lili cringed. Wasn't that just like Ray? Direct and to the point. She saw Mabel and Marjorie exchange another glance before Marjorie said, 'We'd like to stick around and help out making the amber necklaces.'

Lili glanced at them. She knew that wasn't the only reason they wanted to stay. She caught them looking at Nate as they walked over to the counter.

3

'I'm going upstairs to put these in water.' Lili had one foot on the stairs when Nate came over and whispered, 'Sorry if I embarrassed you. I didn't realise this lot would be here.'

Lili glanced over at them all. When the shop was closed, they had started to catch up on creating the jewellery. It had started with just her and Maisie, but then Sarah and William had volunteered their help. They planned to come along on the Sundays that they were together, when Nate was doing a shift at the hospital.

Ray had soon found out about these little jewellery-making sessions from William, and he had started coming along too. This was the first time Mabel and Marjorie had joined them. Their charity shop was normally open on Sundays. Lili suspected that the sisters had spied Nate with the flowers and hadn't been able to resist putting the *Closed* sign in the window and scooting across the yard to find out what was going on.

Still, Lili liked that they were getting more help. The fact was, they weren't keeping up with demand. Even so, she would have preferred that Nate hadn't brought the flowers to the shop for the two gossip girls to see. She whispered back, 'Why didn't you wait until you saw me at The Summerhouse?' Lili and Nate had an arrangement whereby Lili took care of the plants and did some gardening at Joseph's house. It had all arisen from a misunderstanding over a home delivery of groceries. Lili could laugh about that episode now. But she hadn't found it funny at the time.

Lili threw a glance over at Bella, a big old German shepherd dog. She was wandering up and down by the counter, getting pats on her head and fusses from everybody. As if she knew Lili was thinking about her, she padded over and nudged Lili's hand for a fuss too.

Lili noticed that Nate took a step back. 'Nate, she is friendly.'

Bella was still a little wary around men. Or perhaps it was the men – Ray and Nate – who were still wary around her. Lili still thought they needed convincing she was a big softie.

Nate said, 'I know. But it wasn't that long ago that things were different. Remember that episode in the conservatory?'

'How could I forget?' she replied.

When she and Maisie had found some dog food in Joseph's shopping, Maisie had insisted they take the tins of dog food to The Summerhouse and feed Joseph's dog. Judging by the quantity of cans, Lili had guessed Joseph had a big dog. She hadn't been all that enthusiastic to meet it, let alone feed it.

Lili looked down and patted Bella's head. Their first meeting had not got off to a very auspicious start. Lili had given in and visited the house with Maisie – the keys to Joseph's house had been with the shop keys. At first, she hadn't been able to find the dog. That was when she'd made the mistake of venturing into the conservatory, which she could see was full of plants; she'd decided to see if they needed watering. And that was where she'd found Bella, who was growling. She had ended up hiding behind a large potted plant, afraid of Bella, who had been a guard dog for most of her life.

It had been Maisie who had saved the day. Hours spent around the television at home – because her mum didn't have time or couldn't be bothered to take her out – had paid off. It turned out that one of Maisie's favourite programmes was *Dogs Behaving Badly*. She'd learned a thing or two about animal behaviour, and soon had Bella under control and eating out of her hand.

Nate tentatively reached out and gave Bella a cursory pat on the head. Bella's brown eyes looked up at him as if to say, *is that the best you can do?*

'What are you thinking?' Nate asked Lili, noticing she was lost in thought.

Lili glanced at the flowers, and said again, 'Why didn't you bring them to The Summerhouse?'

'I don't always see you there. Sometimes you're gone before I finish my shift and collect William from his grandparents.'

Lili looked at him sheepishly. It was true. She'd been locking up Joseph's shop early and spending more time at The Summerhouse. She had not only been watering the orchids; she'd been enjoying working on the garden too. But she had been ensuring she left before Nate arrived home, just to avoid this sort of scenario.

Nate looked at the flowers. 'I shouldn't have bought them.'

Lili felt guilty for avoiding him after he had gone to so much trouble to persuade her to stay. As a surprise, he'd booked and paid for a hotel room back at The Harbour Inn for one night just for her. Maisie had stayed with him and William at The Summerhouse so that she could have an evening to herself to think things through.

She'd made her decision. It had been influenced by a phone call that she made to a good friend in London – one of the group that she and Alex had often met up with at the weekends. Abigail had been the first of their friends to marry.

Lili had been so shocked to find out from Abigail that her husband Toby had died suddenly. They were only in their early thirties, and that year would have been their tenth wedding anniversary. The funeral arrangements were being made.

That was why Lili was standing there, looking at the flowers, thinking about Abigail and deciding that life was too short not to live for the moment. If a handsome young man was going to buy her flowers and ask her out, she knew what Abigail would say – don't waste a precious minute.

Lili smiled at Nate, and despite the gossip girls she could see staring at them, she decided to give them something more to talk about. She stood on tiptoes and kissed Nate on the cheek. 'They are gorgeous, Nate. Thank you.'

He beamed at her. His smile, which she rarely saw, gave her goosebumps. 'Will you come out with me?' he asked. 'There's somewhere I'd like us to go, together.'

4

'Daddy, I'm busy. I don't want to go now.'

Nate and Lili turned to look at William, who was listening in on his dad's conversations. Lili eyed Maisie. She was the same; always attuned to what was going on with the adults in her life. There was a reason for that. Lili understood. She knew that when a childhood wasn't straightforward, when a child suffered a loss, like William, or grew up feeling responsible for their parent, acting more like an adult than the adults in their life – as in Maisie's case – then they would always have one eye on what was going on. Lili sighed. They were children. They should be living in the moment, not worrying about what was going to happen next.

Nate looked over at his son. 'I was thinking of just Lili and I popping out. Would that be okay with you?'

William shrugged his shoulders. 'I want to stay here and finish my necklace.'

Nate smiled.

'What about Maisie?' Lili whispered. She couldn't impose on—

'Mum, do you mind …?' Nate asked Sarah.

Sarah looked at her watch. 'When I'm finished here, I've got a date.'

'Oh.'

Ray swivelled on his stool to face her. 'What did you just say?'

Marjorie and Mabel exchanged a glance, stopped what they were doing and stared at Sarah.

'I said, I've got a date.'

'What do you mean – you've got a date? With whom?'

Sarah raised her eyebrows at him and motioned at the children, not wanting to start an argument in front of them. 'That's none of your beeswax.'

William looked at his grandad. 'It's none of your beeswax, Grandpa.'

Maisie giggled. 'What's beeswax?'

William shrugged and continued threading his necklace with beads.

Nate glanced at his dad. 'Dad, have you got anything planned later this afternoon?'

'No, I'm free.' He looked at Maisie and William. 'How would you like to see my houseboat?'

'Yippee!' William turned to Maisie. 'I can show you Grandpa's houseboat. It is *so* cool.'

Lili couldn't help smiling. Wasn't that Maisie's catchphrase? Everything was so cool since she'd arrived on holiday. It had clearly rubbed off on William.

Sarah rolled her eyes. 'No war movies, Ray.'

'I don't know what you mean.'

Sarah eyed him for a moment until he turned away. He knew very well what she meant. She remembered the episode when she had been in The Potting Shed and had caught William going off with his grandpa for the afternoon. He had looked so happy. She'd wondered what Ray was intending to do that had got his grandson so excited. During the holidays, she'd spent a lot of time planning days out so that her grandson would have some cultural experiences at the theatre and museum visits, as well as activities like swimming and exercise out in the fresh air in the park or at the beach.

She had not been amused to discover that William had spent his time with his grandpa sitting around an enormous flat screen TV on Ray's houseboat, scoffing popcorn and watching old black and white Second World War B-movies. Worse still was that William had enjoyed it as much as his lazy grandpa had.

'That's settled, then,' said Nate, smiling.

'So, when are you picking me up?'

He checked his watch. 'Er, now.'

'Now?' Lili had assumed he was intending to take her out for a meal that evening. 'As in – right now?'

Nate smiled. 'I was on an early shift this morning, so I have the afternoon off. I thought it would be nice to spend some time together.' He glanced at William. He was showing Ray how to thread some beads, which Ray appeared to be finding difficult. Nate guessed he was preoccupied with Sarah's hot date later. He could tell by the way Ray kept glancing at her.

Maisie was explaining to Mabel and Marjorie how it was done; showing them the amber and the additional beads they used to make the necklaces and bracelets pretty. 'This is our production line,' said Maisie, sounding quite grown-up. She pointed at the small sanding wheel used to shape the amber, the cotton buffing wheel used to polish it, and the Dremel tool used to drill a hole right through the amber for threading. 'Children have to be careful using those tools – that's why we need an adult to help us. Isn't that right, William?'

William was in the middle of threading some beads. He nodded.

Nate smiled at the children. He turned to Lili. 'I thought it would be nice to have some time on our own without … distractions.' He eyed her. 'Don't you think?'

Lili knew what he was getting at. So far, the only times they had been together were with the children – and Bella the dog.

Lili nodded, staring at the large bunch of flowers. 'Have you got a minute? I just want to take these upstairs and put them in a vase of water.'

'Sure.'

Lili was about to head upstairs when she had a thought. What if they were going somewhere posh for lunch? Although Nate hadn't dressed up – he was wearing dark chinos and a pale blue shirt, with a navy jumper flung over his shoulders – his smart-causal outfit would get him into a restaurant. Lili, on the other hand, had just slipped on a pair of light blue jeans, which were a bit threadbare around the knees – not because it was fashionable, but because she'd spent a lot of time in them, outdoors, gardening. The checked red and white shirt she was wearing had seen better days too. It had been through far too many washes, which had stripped some of its colour.

'Um, I have no idea where we are going. Do I need to change?'

Nate looked her up and down and grinned. 'No – not at all.'

Lili eyed him. It was a stupid question to ask a guy. It didn't matter where they were going, she'd get the same, *yeah – you're fine,* with no clue how humiliated she'd feel if she walked into a posh restaurant feeling like a scarecrow.

As if guessing what she was thinking, Nate said, 'No, really, you're fine. In fact, I'd suggest bringing a warm jumper or jacket, and perhaps a scarf and hat.'

'A scarf and hat?' Was he joking?

Nate caught the look on her face. He grinned. 'No, I'm not joking.'

Lili had a worrying thought. 'I hope you haven't planned something ridiculous, like jetting off to the North Pole?' It was one thing Maisie spending an afternoon with Ray and William, but she couldn't go away on an extended trip. That just wouldn't be right, leaving her for any length of time. Hannah suddenly came to mind. She wondered how she could leave her daughter for weeks on end. Hannah knew Maisie was in safe hands – but didn't she miss her?

Lili glanced at Maisie happily getting on with the job at hand. She knew why Maisie didn't miss her mum. She guessed it wasn't really her mother she didn't miss, but all the crap in her life; her mum's boyfriends and being ignored, and essentially looking after herself. Lili realised that when Maisie was with her, she didn't have to act like a mini adult; Lili took care of the adult stuff, so Maisie could concentrate on the business of being a child. Sometimes, although she acted as though she didn't like the rules; bedtime at seven and teatime at five-thirty, she knew Maisie secretly relished the routines she didn't get at home.

'No, we are not going to the North Pole. If you must know, I'm taking you to Southwold.'

'Southwold – as in the town up the road?'

'Yes.'

'So, why on earth would I need to bring—?'

Nate put a finger to her lips.

Lili caught sight of Mabel nudging Marjorie, two sets of eyes on her.

Nate dropped his finger. 'So, I'll wait outside in the car.'

5

As Lili headed upstairs to put the flowers in water, she overheard Nate saying goodbye to William and telling his son that he'd see him at teatime. She was a little disappointed that, by the sound of things, they would not be having an evening meal together.

Lili sighed as she walked into the kitchen and found a vase. Perhaps it was just as well. She tried to put Alex out of her mind, but he kept turning up in her thoughts like a bad penny. She recalled their argument over the move to Washington he'd planned for them both, which she'd known nothing about. She didn't think she'd been unreasonable when she'd told him that he should have discussed it with her first – even though he'd assured her that he hadn't formally accepted the position he'd been offered there.

Part of the reason she had been upset was to do with his comment about how tough their move thousands of miles away would be on him and his mum and dad. It was as though, just because she didn't have parents, her feelings didn't matter. She had Maisie and Hannah – what about them? She'd asked him that question. He'd shrugged and told her that perhaps it was time her friends stopped ruling her life. But they were like family to her. Why didn't he get that? But it was more than that. Lili finished arranging the flowers in a vase. As she walked into her bedroom to find a jacket, scarf and gloves from the box of her possessions Alex had forwarded by FedEx, she couldn't help but think about Hannah. Lili felt she owed her; always had. That was why, while Hannah was living it up in the Caribbean, she was with Maisie rather than on a flight to start a new life in Washington with Alex.

Lili was thinking about her school years. She had been lucky. At eight she'd left the care home where she lived in London to take up a government-funded place at an expensive fee-paying boarding school, located just up the road from Aldeburgh. Her social worker, Connie, was the person who had put her forward for the scheme that helped children from disadvantaged backgrounds reach their potential. Lili thought she must have scored top marks in the entrance exam to secure one of the coveted places.

However, her first few years had been miserable. She had been bullied. Everything changed, though, when she moved out of the prep at twelve and Hannah joined the school. Hannah had also been a boarder. Like Lili, she'd had abandonment issues, although she hadn't been abandoned on a beach in Corfu at three years old like Lili had. Hannah's parents hadn't been able to cope with her behaviour and had been planning to put her into care – until Hannah's maternal grandparents had stepped in and paid for her to go to private boarding school instead.

Loud and confrontational, Hannah was the opposite of quiet, thoughtful Lili. But they hit it off and became best friends. Lili tempered her friend's challenging behaviour, and Hannah gave Lili the confidence to be more forthright and assertive.

Hannah also provided Lili with something else. Lili smiled as she walked back to the window where she'd placed the vase of flowers and rearranged them slightly.

She recalled how her school holidays had changed from lonely days spent in a near-empty building to vacations at Hannah's grandparents' farmhouse in the Kent countryside with their dogs, cats and chickens. Their house had been chaotic, as had they, but Lili had loved that doting old couple to bits. She had always thought Hannah was so lucky – she couldn't have asked for nicer grandparents. And Lili couldn't have asked for a nicer couple with whom to spend the holidays.

Hannah and her grandparents had made Lili's remaining years at their private school special. And her life since wouldn't have been the same without little Maisie either.

Lili strode back down the stairs with her coat. She had put a woolly bobble hat and a pair of gloves into her bag, thinking how odd it was that at the height of summer she'd need to wrap up warm.

She walked over to Maisie. 'Now, are you sure it's okay that I go out with …' Lili stopped short, catching Mabel and Marjorie staring at her. 'That Nate and I …' No matter how she tried to phrase it, there was no getting round the fact that it would sound like a date.

Maisie let out a huge don't-ask-me-again sigh. 'I'm fine. I can't wait to see Ray's houseboat. It sounds cool.'

Lili smiled at her and gave her a hug. 'Okay. You be good.'

'I will.'

Lili reached over and ruffled William's hair. 'Have a lovely time.'

He turned and wrapped his arms around Lili's waist.

Lili hugged him. He was such a sweet boy. She was surprised how attached she'd become. It was so sad that he'd lost his mother.

'Bye everyone.'

Lili reached the shop door and felt something brush against her leg. Lili looked down to find Bella by her side. 'Oh, you can't come, Bella,' she said. She knew she really should have left her in The Summerhouse the day before when she'd finished watering the plants. The trouble was that the dog didn't do as she was told when Lili wanted to go home. Bella had been quite content in the garden, having a snooze in the afternoon sunshine in between games of fetch with Maisie. But when their taxi had arrived, no amount of cajoling or doggy treats, or pushing her rump, had been enough to get her back into the house.

When the taxi driver had opened the car door, Bella had had no problem jumping inside, on to the rear seat next to Maisie.

'Look, she wants to come home with us,' Maisie had said, delighted.

Lili had been less enamoured at the thought of taking Bella back to the shop with them, but she'd had little choice. She couldn't leave the dog alone in the garden. In any case, she'd got the impression that if Bella hadn't been able to go with them, she would have followed the car all the way to Aldeburgh. Luckily, the taxi driver didn't have a no dogs policy.

And so, the previous night Bella had had her first sleepover in the flat. She had been as good as gold and had slept in the lounge. Lili had texted Nate and told him where Bella was. That morning, Lili had expected to wake up and find her asleep on the sofa. She had been wrong. Bella had been fast asleep on the end of Maisie's bed.

'I'm sure Nate won't mind if you take the dog with you,' Ray said. Lili looked over at him. She could tell that, like Nate, he was still wary of the German shepherd.

'I don't know about that, Ray,' she replied, patting the dog's head affectionately. She wondered if, when the others left, they could they leave Bella alone in the shop without her getting up to mischief or howling.

Maisie looked up. 'Bella could come to the houseboat too.'

Ray was already shaking his head. So was Lili, worried about Bella falling overboard. Lili was as attached to the dog as Maisie was. 'I don't think that's a good idea, sweetheart.'

Ray was quick to second that.

Sarah glanced over at Lili. 'I'm afraid I can't help.'

Lili didn't expect her to, or Mabel and Marjorie.

'I'm sure she'd be fine in the shop on her own,' said Sarah. 'Or Ray could run Bella back to The Summerhouse on his way to the houseboat.'

Ray frowned at Sarah for making that suggestion. 'I don't want dog hairs in my car.'

'Are you serious? I've seen your car; it's not exactly spotless. I'm sure a few dog hairs will be hardly noticeable.'

Everyone knew it wasn't the dog hairs that were bothering Ray.

Lili felt Bella's wet nose nuzzling her hand. She rolled her eyes and sighed at the sad puppy dog expression looking up at her. Nate would not be pleased, but she knew that Bella wouldn't be any trouble. Lili glanced at the coat in her hands and thought of the hat and gloves that Nate had said she might need. It sounded as though whatever they were doing together would be outside. She couldn't see an issue with taking the dog. Besides,

Ray had agreed to look after Maisie; two children was enough without a dog to take care of too.

'Come on,' Lili said, reaching for Bella's lead dangling from the antique coat rack in the corner by the door.

Bella did a couple of excited spins when Lili reached for her lead. Lili didn't bother attaching it to Bella's collar as they stepped outside. She knew Bella would walk to heel; she was taking the lead with her just in case.

Closing the door behind her, Lili paused for a moment in the cobbled yard. With shops on three sides, the yard was reached from a short walkway between buildings in the main road through town, High Street. There was a street sign for Cobblers Yard pointing down the lane. Without that, Lili suspected no one would realise the shops were there; a passer-by could easily blink and miss it.

Lili glanced at Ray's art shop on the left and the charity shop run by Mabel and Marjorie next door. She waved at Reggie, another baby boomer who ran the music shop next door to The Potting Shed on the other side of the yard. The only unoccupied place was the bookshop next door to Ray's shop. It sat there with cobwebs in its window, the books on display forlorn and forgotten.

Lili loved the things that the shops all had in common: the old-fashioned shop fronts with bowed-front leaded windows and the paintwork in vintage greens, browns and blacks. It all harked back to another era. There was even an old-fashioned streetlamp in the yard that Lili guessed had once been a gas lamp.

She smiled. It reminded her of the scene from the movie *Singing in the Rain* – the one with Gene Kelly singing the iconic song while dancing around a lamp post. Although it had been converted to electricity years earlier, unlike the modern street-lamps which gave off a harsh bright white light, this lamp was subtle, casting a soft yellow glow in the centre of the yard at night. And the light wasn't intrusive in her bedroom in the flat upstairs; it didn't keep her awake at night, but it was comforting when she did wake.

Lili continued through the yard and down the little lane. She could see Nate sitting in his old Saab, which he'd bought second hand when he moved from London. He was looking down the street, so he didn't see her until she'd walked right up to the car. Nate grinned when he saw her, making her wonder what he had planned.

He looked incredibly pleased with himself – but less pleased when he leaned across to open the passenger door for her and spotted the dog.

Lili opened the rear door and Bella jumped inside. When Lili sat next to Nate, she caught him looking over his shoulder at the occupant on the back seat. He turned to Lili. 'Couldn't Ray pop the dog back to The Summerhouse on his way to the houseboat?'

Lili frowned. 'But that would mean he'd go out of his way. Thorpeness is in the other direction to Walberswick.'

'Yes, I know that.'

Lili caught Nate rolling his eyes. They both knew it wasn't the real reason Ray didn't want to do it. She imagined he just didn't want to be stuck in the confined space of a car with a dog he still didn't trust.

'It's also in the other direction to Southwold, which is where we're heading.'

'I know.' Lili smiled. 'That's why we won't drop Bella at The Summerhouse first. She's coming with us.'

Nate's smile evaporated. 'I thought it was just going to be the two of us.'

'It is.' Lili was still smiling. 'Ray has got the kids.'

Nate cast an eye at Bella sitting on his black leather upholstery. He hoped the hound behaved herself and didn't chew his upholstery or dribble everywhere. Still, that wasn't what concerned Nate. 'But it isn't just the two of us,' he said.

Lili turned to Nate. She didn't see what he was getting all het up about. She tried to keep her sarcasm in check but failed. 'Bella is a dog,' she reminded him. 'I can assure you that she won't ruin your plans.'

6

Nate and Lili had reached their destination, and Nate felt like being sarcastic and asking Lili to repeat what she'd said earlier about Bella not ruining his plans. But he knew that at the time, she'd had no idea what they were going to be doing. It did not surprise him that Ray had opted not to have the dog, even just to take her back to The Summerhouse. Despite Maisie and William's obvious affection for her, and Bella's for them, Nate knew his father was still a little afraid of her – as was he. That was the reason he couldn't object when Bella insisted on sitting or standing between them at every opportunity.

Nate could see that his plan to slip an affectionate arm around Lili's shoulders was hopeless. He was sure that Bella had just growled at him, but Lili didn't appear to have heard anything. Perhaps it was just his imagination.

'This is an amazing view, Nate. I feel on top of the world,' Lili said. They were standing several storeys up, on a metal wraparound balcony. Nate didn't know how many flights up they were, because it wasn't a standard building. He had imagined it would be different, and quite romantic – and it would have been, if it hadn't been for the dog muscling in between him and Lili, paws up at the railings to share the view. 'Seriously?' Nate said when he saw Lili put her arm around the dog. When she asked what he meant, Nate thought up something on the hoof. 'Um, what I meant to say was, seriously nice view.'

'I'll say,' Lili replied. As she walked around the narrow circular platform, she looked out over Southwold Harbour, then the beach and pier in the distance. She could also see a bird's-eye view of Southwold and the village of Walberswick. The countryside beyond looked like a patchwork quilt of browns, yellows, and greens. She'd seen nothing quite like it.

She tore her eyes away from the views and glanced at Nate. 'How did you get access to this place? Is it a holiday let?'

'Ah, no. A friend of mine, Joss – his uncle lives here.'

'He lives here?' Before they'd stepped foot inside, Lili had seen the living quarters through one of the little windows as they made their way up the outside staircase of the building. It stood on the headland but was within walking distance or a short drive to town. Lili had never seen a lighthouse up close, let alone been inside one.

No longer a working lighthouse, this one had been decommissioned and converted into living accommodation. Lili was impressed by the first oval room they entered from the outside staircase, which was a cleverly organised kitchen diner and lounge. Because the walls were curved, the kitchen units were in the centre of the room, dividing the dining area from the lounge. In an ordinary house it might not work. But this was no ordinary dwelling.

The upstairs mezzanine room she could see from the lounge was a double bedroom.

'I love it,' Lili exclaimed, holding on to her woollen hat so it didn't blow away. She had her gloves on too, and her coat; she was thankful that Nate had suggested she bring them.

'Do you want to climb up and see the old light?'

'Can we?'

'Yes – there's a wooden flight of stairs over here.' Nate glanced at the dog. 'I think we should leave Bella down here.'

'Oh? She's managed the stairs so far.'

'No, it's better if she sits this one out.' *Better for me*, thought Nate.

Lili stroked the dog. 'Yes, I think you're right.'

Bella sat at the foot of the interior wooden stairs and watched them walk up the stairs. Lili could hear her whining. She paused halfway up and glanced over her shoulder. 'No, you can't come too.'

Bella put one paw on the bottom step.

'No!' said Nate, firmly.

He got a growl in response.

'Bella, lie down!' Lili said. That worked. She found Bella responded better to commands and positive reinforcement than being told off. She'd learned that from Maisie. 'Good girl.'

Nate cast a glance over his shoulder and frowned at the dog.

Lili climbed the wooden open-tread stairs with Nate following. They stepped into the small room enclosed by floor-to-ceiling windows on all sides, the massive light that had once shone out to sea in the centre. Lili stood by the window, looking out to the ocean. Nate walked up beside her. She felt a tentative arm around her shoulders.

'It's very peaceful up here, Nate. I bet the sunrises from here are incredible.' Lili knew this stretch of coastline was renowned for its spectacular sunrises.

'I wanted to bring you up here at dawn, but as someone lives here, that wasn't possible.'

Lili cast her gaze down to the left. A whitewashed cottage stood next to the lighthouse. Lili pointed. 'Was that the lighthouse keeper's cottage before it was decommissioned?'

Nate followed her gaze. 'I should imagine so.'

'Who lives there now?'

'I don't know. I heard it was a holiday let.'

'This is a lovely spot to stay on vacation.' She turned to Nate. 'Your friend's uncle could charge to give people tours of the lighthouse.' Lili glanced at the cottage; she was thinking of the holidaymakers who stayed there. 'I bet people would pay good money.'

Nate raised his eyebrows at Lili. 'Would you let people tour your home, even if they paid you?'

She smiled. 'You've got a point. Probably not.'

Lili moved around the glass windows, looking down at the patchwork countryside again. Nate joined her. She could feel his arm around her shoulders again. Although she was enjoying the unexpected tour of the lighthouse, and Nate's company, Alex was still on her mind. How could he not be? They'd been together for six years. He had been her first long-term boyfriend. She still hadn't got over how quickly things had fallen apart.

Her thoughts drifted to Maisie. It wasn't her fault that Hannah had left her with them. It had been going on for years, throughout her relationship with Alex, since Maisie was tiny. If it wasn't both Hannah and Maisie sofa-surfing at their house, then it was Hannah leaving Maisie with them during the holidays because Hannah just didn't want to entertain her child or spend money.

There had been many times that she and Alex had rowed about it; Alex had called her a soft touch and asked her to say no – just once. *Why was I so surprised when things came to a head?* Lili wondered. It had always been inevitable that Alex would ask her to make a choice at some point. She had begged him not to make her choose between her best friend and him, but he had, and Lili had made her choice.

In hindsight, he hadn't been speaking out of turn when he'd said she couldn't keep putting her life on hold for Hannah. But she'd done so again.

Lili glanced at Nate's profile. He was drinking in the views. *Why couldn't Alex have been more like him?* she thought.

Nate looked at her, catching her earnest expression. 'What are you thinking?'

Lili thought that however much she didn't want to be on her own – and Nate had an awful lot going for him – this was way too soon to get involved with someone else. Lili couldn't imagine having a holiday romance. She knew that Nate had lost his wife to cancer when his son was a toddler. By the sound of things, he'd had a few short-term relationships, but nothing serious, and she expected that he wasn't after a holiday romance either. She saw the way he looked at her. He was after something more. A commitment.

She was just thinking that the outing had been a mistake and was wondering how to extricate herself from having his arm around her shoulders without offending him when she felt a wet nose against her hand. She flinched.

Nate moved his arm from her shoulders. 'What is it?'

Lili looked down at Bella. 'You naughty dog. I told you to stay downstairs.' She wasn't frowning, though. She was smiling at

Bella, who had just saved her from an awkward scenario. What if Nate had wanted to kiss her?

Had Bella saved her from embarrassing Nate, or had the dog saved her from herself? Lili had a feeling that if he *had* attempted to kiss her, she would have kissed him back. *So, what's the problem with that?*

Lili knelt and gave Bella a fuss. *This isn't real*, she thought. *One day soon I've got to return to London and take Maisie home to her mother when she returns from the Caribbean.*

Lili stood up. 'Nate, there's something—'

'Oh, crap!'

Lili looked at him wide-eyed. 'What is it?' By his expression, she imagined that something horrendous was about to happen, like the floor beneath their feet was going to give way. She had wondered if they should they be up here, the two of them. And Bella, who was not a small dog or a light dog, had joined them too.

'Look.'

Lili followed his outstretched arm; he was pointing at something down below. She spied an old, dishevelled-looking man climbing out of a car that had arrived near the cottage. 'Is that the man who lives here?' she said. She'd heard a noise a moment earlier but had thought it was just the wind.

The man down below stopped and eyed Nate's car.

Lili smiled. 'It will be nice to meet him.'

'Er, I don't think so.'

Lili's smile faltered. She turned to Nate. 'Please don't tell me he has no idea we're here.'

7

Nate avoided eye contact as he grabbed her hand. 'Come on, let's get out of here.'

'Oh, my god!' The last thing Lili wanted was an altercation with the old man. As they made for the stairs, Lili said, 'Wait!' She let go of Nate's hand. 'Bella!' The dog was still sitting by the window. Bella ran over.

Lili looked down the wooden staircase, hoping the dog could climb down. She started down the stairs, calling to her. Bella put a tentative paw on the top step and made her way down behind Lili. Nate brought up the rear.

Lili looked about her. They were back in the open-plan living space. 'Now what?'

Nate stood there listening before he whispered, 'There are two entrances. We came in up the outside metal fire escape straight into this room. I wonder which way he's going to come in?' He'd just hurried over to the door through which they'd entered the property when they heard a door opening below.

They both exchanged a glance. 'That answers that question,' remarked Nate in a whisper. 'Come on.' He opened the door to the outside stairs. They'd just stepped out on to the small metal landing area at the top of the stairs, when Nate said, 'Where's the dog?' He was about to close the door and lock it.

'Bella!' Lili called in barely a whisper. She could see Bella moving towards the internal stairs, ears standing on end. The dog had heard the movement downstairs. She growled.

They heard footsteps starting up the internal stairs, and a man's voice calling out, 'Joss – is that you?'

Bella was creeping towards the stairs, head low, looking as though she would pounce if the old man appeared. Nate launched himself inside, grabbed her collar, and dragged the surprised dog outside, shutting the door a little too hard. They heard the old man calling out again. Nate fumbled with the key to lock the door and dropped it.

Lili looked at him. 'Never mind that! Just put it back where you found it!'

Nate put the key under the mat by the door and clambered down the stairs, wincing at the noise their shoes made on the metal tread stairs. They'd just reached the car when the old man appeared at the door, calling out, 'Who's there?'

He stepped out and look down at them as they climbed into the car. Nate sped off, the tyres skidding on the gravel as he swung out on to the road.

'That was a close thing,' Nate exclaimed, grinning.

Lili folded her arms and frowned. Her heart was still thumping in her chest.

Nate glanced at her. He caught the unamused look on her face.

Lili turned to him. 'I wouldn't have come if I'd known we were trespassing. It's not right, walking around someone's home without their permission.'

Nate looked contrite. 'Sorry. I wanted to show you the lighthouse. The guy I know said his uncle wouldn't be back for hours.'

'That's no excuse, Nate. He should have checked with his uncle that our visit was okay. You should have told me.'

'Sorry.'

They sat in silence as Nate drove along the coast road that led into Southwold. Looking down at the beach, Lili saw the rows of pastel-coloured beach huts, some sitting on the beach, others on the long promenade that led to Southwold pier. She glimpsed the pier in the distance. It had been restored to its former glory. Lili liked that it had lost none of its charm and character from yesteryear when the Victorians would stroll up and down its long wooden promenade. There were no tacky shops along the whitewashed pier, just lovely tearooms and cafés. Lili had visited in the past, but she never once stopped for tea and a scone in one of the little establishments that had views straight out to sea.

Nate caught her staring in the distance. 'What are you looking at?'

'The pier. I've heard the cream teas in the café are delicious.'

Nate smiled. 'Look, I want to make it up to you. Let's go there now and have—'

'No thanks.'

Nate's smile faded. He'd blown it.

Lili sat looking out of the car window. She'd known the outing was a bad idea. She hadn't thought of it as a date, but when they'd got to the lighthouse, she'd realised that was what it was. Nate had wanted to take her somewhere memorable for their first date. What had she been thinking? She was on the rebound from Alex, but the problem was that she was attracted to Nate.

She knew he wanted her to stay. She remembered the shop festooned with bunting and the *Welcome home, Lili* banner that Nate and William had put up, hoping that after breakfast at the hotel, she and Maisie would return to the flat above Joseph's shop.

Lili was intending to hang on for the rest of the summer, but what would happen after that? A return to London was inevitable.

They drove on in silence for some time, before Nate said, 'How about dinner?' He knew what she was going to say, so he hastily added, 'Look, I want to make it up to you, so please let me prepare dinner for you and Maisie. No strings attached, I promise.'

Despite her best efforts, the offer of someone cooking her supper was too good to refuse.

Nate must have caught her expression as she turned from the window. 'Is that a *yes*?' He grinned at her.

'Oh, all right,' Lili said, trying not to appear too keen. How could she resist that smile?

8

'So, you might not be an orphan?' Nate ventured.

Lili wanted to change the subject. They had just finished dinner, and the children – who had been dropped off by Ray earlier that evening when Nate was busy cooking – had left the table to play with Bella in the garden, catching the last of the summer sunshine.

She was about to tell Nate that she didn't want to talk about it, when he asked, 'So, how did you come to be a boarder at Saint Vincent School? Did a relative pay for your schooling?'

They had realised soon after meeting that they both attended the same private school. In answer to his question, Lili shook her head. 'Nobody came forward; no relative or family friend who claimed to know me.'

'Didn't the authorities try to trace your extended family?'

'Yes, but with no luck. Don't forget there was no social media back then.'

'Then how come—?'

Lili knew what he was asking. How had she come to be in an expensive, fee-paying school? He obviously thought she might not be an orphan if she had an absent relative who had paid for her schooling. But nothing had been further from the truth.

Lili smiled. 'I was so lucky to have the most amazing social worker who has been there for me all my life. I was a bright child. There was a scheme for poor children from disadvantaged backgrounds to go to top boarding schools, so I sat an entrance exam and got a scholarship.'

'You got a scholarship at eight?'

'Uh-huh.' Lili nodded and smiled.

'You know, my parents looked into funding for me to go to that school. In the end, my grandfather paid for me to go. All the assisted places and scholarship schemes are for children who start in the secondary school, not the preparatory school.'

Lili was still smiling. 'I'm afraid you're wrong, Nate.'

'I'm afraid I'm not. Ask my parents.'

Lili's smile faltered. 'What are you saying?'

'Whatever you've been told, it's just not true. Somebody paid for your schooling, Lili.'

Lili stared at Nate.

'Look, why don't you pop into the school and find out?'

'I left almost ten years ago. Why would they still have my records?'

'I imagine they have to keep them for several years, for tax reasons at least.'

Lili's mind was racing. If she hadn't got a scholarship, if someone had paid her fees, why would her social worker – the lady who had been the one constant in her life, and the person she trusted implicitly – lie to her?

❖

Nate glanced in the rear-view mirror and frowned. 'Remind me why we had to bring the dog?' It was the following day, and Nate had persuaded Lili to pop along to their old school.

Lili looked over her shoulder. Bella was sitting on the back seat, muzzle resting on the headrest, looking as though she was enjoying the ride. Lili turned to the front and glanced at Nate. 'I didn't like the thought they would shut her up in a room all on her own.'

Nate wasn't keen on her being shut in the car, in such close proximity.

'Besides,' Lili continued, 'I feel Ray wanted to steer clear of Bella. I bet the children would have let her out of the conservatory.'

Nate sighed. He knew it was true. Ray was looking after the children at The Summerhouse, although he drew the line at Bella.

They both stared out of the window in silence as the red-brick Victorian property came into view at the end of the drive. 'It seems … smaller,' Nate commented.

Lili turned to him. 'I was thinking the same thing.'

They hadn't made an appointment to see the headteacher, but as former pupils, they were both hoping that held sway when they showed up unannounced.

Nate pulled the car to a stop in a visitor's parking space in front of the school. He turned to Lili. 'Who knows – old Mr Galbraith might remember us,' he said.

Entering the building brought back such vivid memories of their school years that they both felt as though they had been there just the day before. Five minutes later, they were sitting in the headteacher's office.

The headteacher they remembered, Mr Galbraith, was long gone. In his place was a woman much younger than Lili expected for a school headteacher. Lili guessed that she was not even thirty. She was very pretty and neatly turned out in a grey pleated skirt, crisp white shirt and suit jacket. Model-thin, she had straight blonde hair and expertly applied makeup.

Lili glanced down at the dress she'd bought from Debenhams. Although Lili was not overweight, she knew she didn't have that sort of figure and didn't buy those sorts of clothes – she imagined they came with a designer label. There was nothing wrong with the department stores she shopped in, she told herself. Like most people, she was not earning the sort of salary a headteacher of a private school could command, so she couldn't afford expensive outfits and pricey accessories. Lili stared at the young woman's silver necklace and fingered the ring on her chain.

'Welcome back,' the woman said warmly. Lili noticed that her gaze settling on Nate a little too long. She leaned forward and planted her hands on the solid oak desk in front of her. 'It's lovely to have old boys and girls come and visit us.'

Lili cast her gaze about her. The head's office resembled a study, with bookshelves lined with books and two high-backed chairs in front of a giant oak table, behind which the young, diminutive head sat; she almost looked funny, like a pupil had dressed up and was pretending to be the headteacher. Lili expected the real headteacher to walk in at any moment and tell her to stop larking about and go back to class. She tried not to grin at the thought.

Lili had rarely ventured into the inner sanctum of the headteacher's office herself while she was at school. That privilege was reserved for two kinds of students – the ones receiving awards, and the ones who were getting a ticking off for doing something bad. Lili only remembered visiting the room once, and it hadn't been for an award. She glanced at Nate. It had been his fault. If he hadn't thrown the party, then she and Hannah wouldn't have got into trouble for leaving the school grounds without a pass. Lili sighed. Although the young woman couldn't take her eyes off Nate, she was glad it wasn't the old head – even though she imagined there were many, many students who passed through this room, over the years, so it would have been doubtful he'd remember her transgression.

The young woman wiggled her nose in consternation and glanced out of the window. 'Do you hear that?'

Nate and Lili exchanged an innocent glance, pretending they couldn't hear a dog howling. Nate said, 'Nope, I don't hear a thing? Do you?'

Lili threw Nate a conspiratorial smile as she shook her head, denying all knowledge of a dog called Bella making a god-awful racket from Nate's car. She sounded like the Hound of the Baskervilles. It was something Lili hadn't factored in when they had decided to leave the dog.

Luckily for them, Bella fell silent. The head shrugged. 'It must have been the wind,' she said. She turned from the window and glanced at them. 'Why do you two seem so familiar?'

Nate said, 'Well, we *are* former pupils. Perhaps you saw some yearbooks from way back when.'

'Or perhaps I was in one too, way back when.'

Nate looked at her in surprise. So did Lili. 'You were also a student here?'

'Oh, yes. I left in …'

Nate and Lili exchanged a glance. 'You were in our year,' they both said in unison.

No wonder she was staring at Nate, Lili thought. Perhaps she'd fancied him years earlier, and they'd been friends. If she was single – Lili didn't see a ring – maybe she rather fancied her chances with the young, single doctor.

'God, it's Laurie, isn't it?' Nate exclaimed.

'Yes, I was wondering when you'd remember me.'

'You were friends with …'

Lili zoned out at that point, not interested in listening to this. She stared at Laurie, trying to picture her from their school days. Then she recognised her. She had been one of the popular girls who had often thrown disparaging remarks at Lili and Hannah. She'd hardly changed a bit. It was the makeup that had thrown Lili. She looked even prettier than Lili remembered.

Lili was feeling uncomfortable, like a third wheel, but it wasn't just that. She was having second thoughts about being there. She got out of her seat, interrupting their conversation.

Nate looked up at her. 'Where are you going?'

Lili wanted to leave. 'You know what? I think this is a waste of time.'

Laurie looked from Nate to Lili. 'What's a waste of time? How can I help? I'm sure you're not here for a social call.'

Lili glanced at Nate. *I bet he wished he was*, she thought. Her attention shifted to Laurie. 'I don't think you will have the information I need,' she said. She frowned. Perhaps she'd prefer it if Laurie didn't know that she'd been there on a scholarship and that her parents weren't rich, like Laurie's.

Laure smiled at Lili. 'Why don't you let me be the judge of that?'

Nate reached for her hand. 'Sit down, Lili, please.'

Lili relented and sat down. Nate was still holding her hand, she noticed. She saw that Laurie had noticed too.

Nate turned to Lili and raised his eyebrows, motioning for her to ask the question.

Lili sighed. 'What I want to ask is if assisted places or scholarships are ever offered to younger children who want to start in the preparatory school?'

'Yes, all the time.'

Lili let out a sigh of relief. 'Great. That's all I wanted to know.' She was about to get out of her seat again, when Nate asked, 'What are those scholarships for?'

'Music.'

'Music?' Nate glanced at Lili. 'So, there isn't a scheme for children from underprivileged backgrounds to get scholarships here at that age?'

'There is a scheme, but not for children that young – only those of secondary school age.'

This wasn't what Lili wanted to hear. She leaned forward in her seat. 'This is probably a big ask, but do you keep records of former pupils?'

'Ah, you want to know if we still have *your* school records.'

9

'Will you slow down?'

Lili was striding back to the car in double-quick time, leaving Nate behind. He caught up as she got to the car. Bella was sitting in the front seat, barking, excited to see them.

Nate made a grab for her arm. 'Lili?'

She whirled around. 'Why did my social worker lie to me?'

Nate shook his head. 'I don't know.'

'All those years I was at this school, how could she not tell me it wasn't a government scholarship paying my fees, but an anonymous benefactor?'

'I'm sorry.' Nate shrugged. 'Perhaps she was trying to spare you from, er …' Nate trailed off when he realised that his train of thought would not help matters.

Lili frowned. She knew what he was about to say. 'She was trying to spare me from the possibility that there is someone out there, a relative, a parent perhaps, who paid for my expensive schooling, but didn't want to know me.'

'They must have cared about you to pay for all this.' Nate flung his arm around, looking at the expensive school set in acres of grounds.

Or cared about people not finding out about me, thought Lili. After Laurie had told her what she would have preferred not to hear, they had all sat there, a heavy silence permeating the room. She'd stared at the paperwork that Laurie had found and had said, 'There must be records of who paid the fees.'

All Laurie had known was what was in front of her. 'BACS transfers, I'm afraid. The money with your name as a reference appeared regular as clockwork.'

Lili realised that all this visit had done was to raise more questions than it answered.

Lili opened the car door and was greeted by an excited dog. She couldn't help but smile as Bella nuzzled her hand, angling for a fuss. 'Good girl.'

'She wasn't good,' Nate grumbled as he walked round the vehicle and sat in the driver's seat. 'I suggest that if you want to find answers, you'll need to return to where it all began.' He started the engine.

'What do you mean?' asked Lili.

'Where they found you in Corfu.'

Lili sighed. 'Now isn't a good time.' She couldn't just jet off abroad – there was Maisie to consider. And there was the fact that Lili's life had fallen to pieces; she needed to put it back together somehow and work out how to start over.

'If you're thinking about who would look after the antique shop, I'm sure we can figure something out.'

Lili sighed. That was the least of her concerns. 'I told you, Nate, I won't be here for much longer.'

'Why not? Your boyfriend has dumped you. There's a local non-feeing paying school here for Maisie. I send William there. Why return to London?'

Because all this is built on a lie. Lili couldn't look him in the eye. She should have come clean from the outset. This was just a holiday. She didn't expect to make friends, get a job, find somewhere to live, or find someone else with whom she felt such a strong connection even though she barely knew him. Lili cut that thought short. She was on the rebound from Alex – that was what all this was. Besides, she wasn't ready for a relationship. The problem was that she wasn't ready to leave either.

Although Hannah was flying home that day, Lili didn't think she'd mind if they stayed on in Aldeburgh just for the weekend. She hadn't told her they were on holiday in Suffolk. Lili was sure Hannah wouldn't object to having an extra couple of days before they returned. It would be time enough for her to see Joseph, and to explain to Nate, his parents, and the other shop owners in the yard that she didn't really know Joseph, and that contrary to assumptions, Maisie wasn't her daughter.

She knew she couldn't leave without them hearing it from her first, but not on the day she'd discovered everything she'd thought about her life, her past, was a lie.

Lili sat there as they made their way down the drive. She fingered the ring on the chain round her neck and thought again about Joseph's identical ring. Was he her secret benefactor? Or was it just a coincidence?

Nate pulled the car to a stop at the end of the drive, waiting for a gap between passing cars so that he could join the main road back into Aldeburgh. He turned to Lili. 'There is someone who could straighten all this out.'

Lili knew. A single phone might be all it would take. But right now, Lili wasn't ready to talk to the one person she had trusted all her life – Connie.

Nate stared at her. He understood. There was nothing worse than discovering the people closest to you had lied to you, let you down. 'Look, my father, he runs a business as an heir-hunter.'

Lili knew that already. She turned to Nate. 'I'm not looking for an inheritance.'

'He finds people.'

Lili knew that too. 'But you're talking about finding descendants of someone who's died.'

'Yes, I know that's what heir-hunting means, but he still finds people. Perhaps he can locate the person who has been paying your fees.'

'I don't have the money to pay for his services.'

'I get the idea, from what he's said, that you've made quite the impression. He counts you as a good friend, and he wouldn't take money from his friends. Besides, he works for a commission.'

'But he won't get anything …'

'Ah, but you have no idea who you are yet. You might be descended from someone extraordinarily rich.'

'Or famous.' Lili didn't know why she'd said that.

'Or infamous.'

Lili frowned. Although they were larking about, she said, 'Why did you say that?'

'It was a joke.'

'Oh, okay.' Lili didn't find it funny. That was the problem with knowing nothing about your past; who knew what skeletons hid in her family's closet?

Nate guessed what she was thinking. 'You could be the skeleton in someone's closet.'

That's likely, thought Lili. Who would want to pay her school fees unless it was someone who wanted to keep her out of the way. Maybe she was a secret love-child. Was there a family out there with half-siblings who did not know she existed? It was possible. Right now, *anything* was possible.

'Can I ask a personal question, Lili? You can tell me to shut up.'

'What is it?'

'Why didn't you do this before – search for your parents?'

'Who said I didn't?'

'Have you been back to Corfu?'

Lili fell silent for a moment. 'Look, if they'd wanted me, they would have found me. When I reached sixteen, I filled out the paperwork and went on the register, but no one came forward.'

'Perhaps you need to go in search of them?'

Lili shook her head. 'Connie always told me that you should only ever look back to see how far you've come. She told me nothing good comes from …' Lili stared at Nate.

'… from?'

'Looking in the past,' Lili said slowly.

'Especially if there's something in your past that she has been hiding from you,' observed Nate. He glanced in his rear-view mirror and saw a car approaching from behind. He flicked the indicator light and turned onto the main road.

'You should speak to her, Lili.'

Lili shook her head. 'Not yet.' If Connie had been lying to her all these years, then who was to say she would tell her the truth now?

'Then you have to go back, Lili, to where they found you.'

'I know, but first I need to visit Joseph.'

Nate didn't get what that had to do with anything. He

shrugged. 'Okay. Shall we go and see him now?'

Lili stared at Nate. She wanted to go and see Joseph, but not with Nate. 'It can wait.' Lili fingered her ring. She needed to see Joseph alone. 'I'd like to go back to The Summerhouse and collect Maisie.'

'Sure.' Nate noticed her fingering the ring she wore on a chain. He'd noticed it before but hadn't asked its significance. There were things she wouldn't tell him – not yet, anyway. He hoped she would, in time. He sensed she wasn't ready to start another relationship. Perhaps he wasn't either, but he couldn't sweep aside the instant attraction he had to Lili. It was her personality too, her openness, her honesty that was so refreshing. She didn't seem to walk around with a giant chip on her shoulder, like him. She had plenty of reasons not to be upbeat, considering her background.

It made him wonder what he had to complain about. His parents *had* got rid of him, sent him away to stay with his grandfather, but they hadn't disappeared from his life completely. And his father had come back for him. He'd changed his mind. Not straightaway. It had been several months later when Ray had told him they'd made a mistake, but by then it had been too late. That silly young boy who had thrown his easel and paints in the back of his cupboard in a fit of temper had told his dad he was remaining where he was; that he didn't want to live with them anymore.

It had been a half-truth. Of course, he had wanted to return to London with them, but even at that age he had realised they couldn't keep shifting him from one place to another. He knew he'd be back. Their careers had come first. Nate had understood that finding lost art would always come before him. It was what they did. It was who they were. It was the legacy of what had happened to his grandfather; losing his mother when they escaped the Nazis. Through unearthing artefacts that were stolen from the Jews, Ray and Sarah thought, somehow, that they could right the wrongs of the past.

Nate glanced at Lili as he drove along the country road into Aldeburgh. He understood what her social worker, Connie, had meant with her advice. Sometimes, it was better to leave the past in the past. Now, it concerned him what Lili might uncover. He regretted bringing her here. What skeletons might she find, and how would it impact her life? Nate hoped it would be a positive impact, because the Pandora's box had been opened. And whatever Lili discovered, there would be no going back. He just hoped she wouldn't blame him for setting the wheels in motion.

Nate pulled the car up at the house and switched off the engine. He took the keys out of the ignition and turned to Lili, resting a tentative hand on her shoulder. He didn't want to ask if she would be ok after what they had discovered, but he wanted to know if she would consider remaining in Aldeburgh. He craved more time to get to know her and would like to accompany her to Corfu. However, arranging an absence from work and leaving William just then just wasn't an option.

Nate looked up at the house. He'd only known Lili a short time, but he couldn't imagine her not being around. The same went for Maisie. William would miss his new friend.

Bella barked.

Lili and Nate turned in their seats, and said, 'Indoor voices, please!' They exchanged a smile at their reaction, treating Bella like one of the children.

They got out of the car. Bella ran ahead, barking. William

opened the front door and rolled on the floor with Bella licking his face excitedly as though she hadn't seen him in years. Ray appeared next, rushing down the stairs. 'Nate,' he said breathlessly.

'Dad?' Nate took one look at Ray's face and blurted, 'Bloody hell, what's the matter?'

Lili noticed it too. There were tears rolling down his cheeks. Lili stopped dead. 'Where's Maisie?'

'I'm here.' Maisie was standing at the top of the stairs, a paintbrush in her hand.

William sat on the floor with Bella, and said, 'What's wrong with Grandpa? He's been crying.'

Nate looked from William to his father. The last time he'd seen him like this was when he'd told his dad he would not paint ever again. He'd stayed true to his word. Nate replied. 'I don't know.'

But Lili did. She looked up at Maisie. 'Did you show Ray your paintings?'

10

Maisie hung back as Ray, Nate and William walked into the bedroom. She whispered to Lili, 'Am I in trouble?'

Lili put her arm around her shoulders and gave her a hug. 'Not a bit, Maisie. You, my sweet girl, are amazing – do you know that?'

'Why was Ray crying?' Maisie looked worried. 'Was it something I did?'

'Oh, yes,' Lili said, 'but in a good way, Maisie. He loved your paintings so much that …' Lili was going to say it had moved him to tears. 'He is crying for joy. Not because he is upset. Do you understand?'

Maisie shook her head. 'Not really.'

Lili smiled. 'It's a grown-up thing. You'll find out one day.' They walked into the room. Nate and Ray were standing together, staring at the painting on the easel. Nate turned to his father, wide-eyed. 'Did he—?'

'What about mine?' William said, going up to Ray with a piece of his own artwork. Lili noticed that he avoided Nate.

'That is exceptionally good,' Ray said, smiling at his grandson. He glanced at Nate, shaking his head in answer to his question – no, it wasn't William who had painted the masterpiece sitting on the easel.

Lili spotted William's picture. It was just what any normal six-year-old would paint. Her eyes drifted to the painting Nate and Ray were staring at, open-mouthed. Her mouth dropped open too. 'Maisie, you copied the painting hanging in the lounge?'

Maisie nodded. 'Am I in trouble?' she asked again.

'Oh, dear me, no,' Ray managed.

Maisie grinned at Ray. 'I had to go downstairs a few times to get the … *technique* right.'

Ray looked as though he was going to burst into tears again.

Nate stared at Maisie, astonished.

'You told me she had talent,' commented Ray, remembering that conversation over fish and chips on the beach. 'You even offered for me to come and look at her paintings, but I assumed you were just another parent who thought their child was special.' He shook his head, still dumbfounded. 'I have only encountered one other person like Maisie with this sort of genius.'

'Who?' asked Lili.

Nate put a hand on his father's shoulder.

Maisie was listening too. 'Did they go to art school and become a famous painter? Are their paintings hanging in galleries?'

'No, Maisie,' Nate replied. 'He put his easel in the back of a cupboard and became a doctor.'

Lili turned around and stared at Nate.

Maisie frowned. 'Why?'

Ray began to cry again.

Lili took Maisie's hand and steered William out of the room

too. 'Come on, you two – let's feed Bella.'

Lili closed the bedroom door, giving Nate and his father some privacy to talk. She had a feeling it was long overdue.

'Bella!' Maisie called out as they both ran down the stairs. Lili followed. She found them in the kitchen. Maisie was already opening a tin of dog food. William scooped some biscuits from a large bag in the pantry. Maisie mixed them together in Bella's bowl.

Maisie handed William the dish. 'Wait! Wait!' she told Bella.

Bella sat patiently, licking her chops.

'Good girl,' William said, as he put the bowl on the floor. 'Now – go, go on.'

Bella ran over and started wolfing down her food.

For an old dog, Bella had a good appetite, thought Lili. She smiled at William and Maisie, impressed with the way they were taking care of the dog. Lili's smiled faded. Maisie was going to miss all this – Bella, William, the house, the shop, her painting. She would get no encouragement from her mum to be creative when she returned home.

Thinking of returning to London, she still had something she needed to do first. 'Maisie, sweetheart, do you think you will be okay staying on here a little while longer, just while I pop and visit Joseph at the hospital?'

She nodded her head. 'Yes, I love it here.'

Lili wished she hadn't said that. She would have to remind her this evening that it would be time to return home on Sunday. She had school on Monday. Lili remembered that she needed to text Hannah and let her know where they were. She imagined her plane would be landing soon.

Lili got out her phone and rang for a taxi.

'Are you going to see Joseph's ring?'

Lili looked at her, surprised that she had remembered. 'Yes.' Her eyes darted to William, but he wasn't listening; he was too busy pouring fresh water into the bowl for Bella's bowl. Lili cast her gaze to the ceiling. She could hear Ray and Nate's indistinct voices coming from the floor above. By the sound of things, they were still deep in conversation. Lili shifted her attention to Maisie. 'When Ray and Nate come downstairs, will you let them know I will be back to pick you up as soon as I can?'

Maisie nodded. So did William. He asked, 'Can Maisie stay for a sleepover?'

'Oh, please,' Maisie begged.

Lili reverted to the non-committal phrase, 'We'll see,' meaning *no*. She didn't fancy two children whining at her before she left. Lili had too much on her mind.

As expected, the taxi arrived quickly. She had phoned the same company that Maisie had used the first time they had visited the house, and all the other occasions they visited in the afternoons. They were always quick, sending a car within minutes.

'How's the Hound of the Baskervilles?' the driver asked with a smile as Lili sat in the back.

'Less hound, more …' She thought about it, '… lap dog.' Lili was thinking of how Bella often sat with her head resting on her lap.

'Well, that's quite a transformation. Well done.'

'Oh, I can't take the credit. It was the children.'

'I expect Maisie will want a puppy of her own,' the taxi driver said as they made the brief journey from Thorpeness to the local cottage hospital down the road. 'Will you get her one?'

Lili stared at the driver, wondering why she was asking her that. With other things on her mind, namely the visit to her old school, she had forgotten that everyone still assumed Maisie was her daughter. If it was up to her, she would buy Maisie a puppy. But it wasn't. She couldn't imagine Hannah taking on the responsibility; Hannah was barely responsible for herself. Lili frowned. That wasn't a nice thing to think, but it was true, and poor Maisie always came way down the pecking order after Hannah and whichever new man she had in her life.

Ten minutes later, the taxi arrived at the cottage hospital in Aldeburgh. After paying the fare, Lili stepped out of the car and turned to the entrance. Fingering the ring on her necklace, she walked inside.

11

Lili stood outside the hospital entrance. She was feeling some trepidation about what this visit might throw up after her recent trip to the school. She took a deep breath. She was about to walk inside when her mobile rang, stopping her in her tracks.

'Lili, are you okay?'

'Nate, I'm at the hospital. Did the children tell you I'm visiting Joseph? I will be back as quick as I can. I hope you don't mind …'

'Not at all. William said you took a taxi. I could have given you a lift.'

'I know, but I didn't want to disturb you and your father.' She paused. 'Is everything okay?'

'More than okay. That conversation was long overdue.'

Lili thought so too.

'He wants to see more of Maisie's work.'

'Look, about that …' Lili knew it was time to come clean about Maisie not being her daughter, and her fictitious friendship with Joseph, but she couldn't do it over the phone.

'I asked Dad, and he is going to take on your case.'

'My case?'

'You know, finding the benefactor who paid for your schooling.'

Lili stared at the hospital entrance.

'It's nice of you to visit Joseph. You can tell me how he is when you get back.'

'I will.' Lili walked through the door. She knew her visit wasn't altruistic. She was only there to examine his ring and find out if it had an inscription on the inside of the band, just like hers.

She spotted Joseph's room up ahead. She looked about her, keen to see him before any other visitors turned up. 'Look, I've got to go …'

'Will you stay?' Nate asked.

'Pardon?' Lili didn't understand the question.

'Here, in Aldeburgh. Don't go back to London. Maisie could enrol in the local school …'

They'd had this conversation before. She winced as she said, 'We'll see …'

He went quiet, aware she was fobbing him off. She knew that when she returned to the house, it was time to tell him the truth. Lili sighed. 'I have to go now, Nate.'

'Okay.'

She could tell by the sound of his voice that he was disappointed. 'We'll talk when I get back.'

'Great, I'm looking forward to it,' he said, sounding more cheerful.

Lili switched off her phone. She didn't think he would be very cheerful when he heard what she had to say. She wished she had told everyone from the outset that Maisie wasn't her daughter and Joseph was not a friend. Nothing good ever came from withholding the truth – she knew that. Lili walked up to Joseph's room and hesitated. She was thinking of Ray taking on the case of the mysterious benefactor. Her life wasn't perfect at that moment – far from it. She had enough problems with the breakup of her relationship. Was she ready to open the door to her past? Where would it lead, and who would it lead to?

Lili wavered. In her heart, she had a strong feeling that once she stepped into that room, there was no going back. She could walk away now and tell Ray she did not want his help. Leave the past in the past.

Connie's advice came to mind once again: *only ever look back to see how far you've come.* What was in her past that Connie did not want her to find out? Lili thought of Nate reconciling with his father. She had a feeling he could not move on with his life until they had buried the hatchet. It was what they both needed; to sort out those unresolved issues.

Lili stared at the old man in the hospital bed. She had gone through her life with nobody. She'd had people in her corner – Hannah and Maisie, Alex (before they'd split up, anyway), her close circle of friends back in London, and colleagues at Kew. They were important, of course they were, but she didn't have what she saw with Nate and William, Ray and Sarah. A family of her own; the special bond that only relatives could provide.

She had always thought that when she eventually had children, creating a little brood of her own, it would fill the void – the emptiness she had carried around inside her – and she would be able to move on. However, she knew that Connie was wrong. Her visit to Aldeburgh had made her realise that whatever she found, and wherever it led, it would be worth it to discover who she was and where she was from.

Lili took a deep breath and took the first step towards learning the truth about her past and finding her family. She knew it was time.

❖

'What are you doing?'

Lili flinched. The timing of the nurse walking into the room could not have been worse. She had caught her taking the ring off Joseph's finger. Lili was mortified. It was in her hand. 'It's not what it looks like,' Lili said hastily. 'I wasn't going to steal it – if that's what you're thinking.'

The nurse stared at her.

Lili wanted the ground to swallow her up. When she had walked into the room, she'd seen that Joseph was sleeping and had taken her chance. 'I have a ring just like it.' Lili showed the nurse the ring with the markings on the inside of the band. 'Look.'

The nurse stepped closer and examined Lili's ring.

'That's unusual.'

'I know. It's amber.'

'I'm not talking about the amber. I'm talking about the inside of the band.'

'Oh, you mean the markings. I wanted to see if Joseph's ring is the same.'

'Is it?'

Lili turned the band over in her hand. She knew before she took the ring off his finger that it would have an inscription. She felt it. 'It is,' Lili remarked. 'I just don't know what it means.'

'Let me see.'

Lili handed over his ring.

The nurse got out her glasses from the pocket of her uniform and slipped them on.

'It's Hebrew.'

They both turned around at the sound of a woman's voice. Sarah was standing in the doorway. Lili, startled, got up from her seat next to Joseph's bed, wondering how long Sarah had been standing there. 'I wanted to look at Joseph's ring. I have one just like it.'

'Yes, I heard.' Sarah stepped into the room and held out her hand. The nurse handed over the ring on her way out.

Sarah looked at Lili. 'May I see yours?'

'Oh yes, of course.' Lili put her hands around her neck and unclasped the necklace. She laid the pendant in Sarah's hand. 'Can you tell me why Joseph has an identical ring?' she asked. She stared at Sarah who was scrutinising Joseph's band first.

'He never takes the ring off,' Sarah said. 'The inscription reads, *May our souls be bound everlasting*. She glanced at Lili. 'This is a Hebrew wedding ring.'

'Is mine a Hebrew wedding ring too?'

Sarah picked up Lili's ring. 'Yes, it is.'

Lili nodded. She'd had a feeling it was. 'Like Joseph's, there's an inscription on the inside of the band.'

'Hebrew wedding bands with inscriptions are quite common. You know, you could have gone into a jeweller and they would have shed some light on it for you.'

Lili knew that, but she'd never wanted to look into her past; not until now. 'Can you tell me what it says?' asked Lili, intrigued.

Sarah held up the ring to the light, turning it around in her fingers as she read the engraving.

'Well, what does it say?'

'*May our souls be bound everlasting.*' Sarah lowered the ring and stared at Lili.

Lili looked at her in surprise. Both wedding rings had the same inscription.

'Although these wedding rings are not unusual, each pair of Hebrew wedding rings is unique.'

'Are you saying these are a pair?'

'I believe so – yes.' Sarah stood there examining both rings. 'The question is …' she looked up, studying Lili intently, 'how did you come by my grandmother's wedding ring?'

'Your grandmother's?' Lili didn't understand. She looked at Joseph's ring. 'I thought it belonged to your father?'

Sarah shook her head. 'This was my grandfather's wedding ring. He wore it until he died. The family heirloom passed to my father.'

Lili stared at Sarah. Lili stepped forward, holding out her hand. She wanted it back. It was her most prized possession.

Sarah reluctantly handed it over. 'How did you come by this? Did you find it in a shop?'

Lili shook her head as she threaded the band through the silver chain and hung it around her neck. *Is Sarah a long-lost relative?* she wondered. She was about to tell Sarah about her past when Joseph interrupted, calling out, 'Alena!' He held out his hand to Lili.

Sarah looked at Lili, her brow creasing in a frown. 'Who is Alena?'

Lili turned to her, surprised by the question. 'I was going to ask you the same thing. I thought she was your mother?' Lili knew Joseph's wife had walked out on him and that she had raised Sarah in London.

'My mother's name isn't Alena.'

'Your grandmother …?' Lili ventured.

Sarah shook her head. 'I've never heard him mention that name before.' Sarah perched on one side of Joseph's bed and took her father's hand. 'Dad? Who is Alena?'

12

The nurse popped her head around the door. 'Ah, you're awake.'

Joseph snatched his hand away from Sarah's grasp. 'Who are you?'

'Don't take it personally. He's still suffering from confusion, so this sort of thing isn't unusual.'

Sarah turned to the nurse. 'How long will this go on?'

'I'm afraid it's hard to say. He might be as right as rain tomorrow.'

Lili sighed. Although it had suited her, to begin with, that Joseph was not with it and couldn't contradict her regarding their supposed friendship, she had changed her mind. All she wanted was to ask him about the ring and the woman called Alena.

Joseph turned his head to look at Lili. 'Alena.'

Lili took his hand. 'I'm right here, Joseph.' She glanced across the bed at Sarah, whose expression was one of surprise, until she understood; Lili was playing along to see if he revealed anything about Alena.

'You came back,' he said excitedly. 'I must tell Otto.' Joseph looked about him until his eyes settled on something. 'Otto? Where have you been?'

Lili and Sarah looked at each other. There was no one else in the room apart from the nurse, who was helping Joseph to sit up and arranging his pillows behind his back.

The nurse whispered, 'This sort of thing isn't unusual either, I'm afraid. Sometimes people hallucinate. They see other people, even talk to folk who aren't there.' She paused and looked at her patient. 'Are you comfortable, Joseph?'

He did not respond. They all realised he wasn't in the here and now; he was lost in the past, in a world full of ghosts. 'Otto – where are you going? Don't leave. She's here. She returned, just like she promised.'

The nurse left the room. Sarah resumed her seat, perched on Joseph's bed. Lili stayed seated in the chair at his bedside, holding his hand. 'Joseph, who is Otto?'

Joseph shifted his head to look at Lili. 'Otto loves you. He knew you'd come back.'

Lili fingered the ring. Otto and Alena – were they the couple to whom these rings belonged? She glanced at Sarah.

'I'm afraid I don't know who Otto is,' Sarah said.

Joseph was getting agitated. 'No, Miriam isn't here, Otto.'

Lili exchanged a glance with Sarah, who was miming *Miriam* and shrugging her shoulders as if to say she had not heard that name before either.

Joseph continued, 'I don't know where she is, Otto. They took her. Miriam's gone …' And with that, he cried.

Lili patted his hand, trying to console him.

'I'll call for the nurse,' Sarah said, intending to do just that when a member of the kitchen staff walked in carrying a hot plate of food. 'What's all this, Joseph? We can't have you crying into your dinner, can we?'

Joseph looked at the jolly young woman and smiled.

'Now, that's better. We have roast lamb, mashed potatoes, veggies and gravy.'

Another young woman stepped in with a small table on wheels.

Lili got out of her seat so that the woman could position the table over Joseph's bed. 'I'm in the way. I'd better go.'

'You don't have to go,' the young lady commented.

Lili thought that it would be the best time to leave, while Joseph was busy with his meal, so she didn't upset him.

Sarah followed her to the door. 'You're not a good friend of Joseph's, are you?'

Lili turned around to face Sarah.

Sarah held up the ring. 'You came here for answers.'

'No, I didn't, not to begin with. I honestly did not know that Joseph had the same ring. It was a coincidence that I walked into his shop. The first time I met Joseph, we were just browsing in his shop out of the rain while we waited for Ray's shop to open,' Lili explained. 'Maisie told him we were looking for a holiday rental and he offered us the flat above his showroom. I thought it was a kind gesture from a stranger, but I declined. However, when I couldn't find anywhere else, I came back. That's when he had his fall.'

Lili breathed a sigh, and admitted, 'I don't really know him – not as a friend.'

'Then why—'

'Lie?'

'It's a long story.' Lili did not want to get into how she came to be on an extended holiday in Aldeburgh with someone else's child, not to mention that her partner had dumped her.

'Have you told Nate and Ray this *long story*?'

Lili caught the sarcasm in her voice, the distrust.

'Look, everybody assumed Joseph and I must be good friends if he was letting me stay in the flat.'

'And you let people think that without correcting the misconception?'

Lili said in a small voice, 'I'll tell them when I get back to Thorpeness. I left Maisie with William, Ray, and Nate at The Summerhouse.'

'Ray is at the house?' Sarah said in surprise. 'He never goes there.'

Well, he does now, thought Lili. She changed the subject. 'Nate was surprised you had a date, Sarah,' she said.

Sarah's eyes narrowed. 'I'm not the only one who has been on a date.' She stared at Lili.

'Are you talking about me?' Lili looked at her and shook her head. 'That wasn't a date. Nate just invited me to dinner as a thank you for—'

'Nate?'

'Yes.' Lili saw her confused expression. 'Who did you think I was talking about?'

'Ray.'

'Ray? Whatever gave you the impression that—' Lili stopped mid-flow. 'Oh, the bouquet! It's not what you imagine. I told Ray to stop buying *you* flowers.'

'Oh, you did, did you?'

'There was no ulterior motive, if that's what you're thinking,' Lili added. 'I didn't want Ray for myself – why would I? He's … old.' Lili raised her eyebrows. 'Sorry, that came out wrong.'

Sarah smiled. That was what she had thought; what would a

pretty young woman like Lili want with her husband?

'Look, we met by chance on the beach and ended up having fish and chips together. That's when he asked me, as a woman, for my advice about how to win you back. I stupidly told him to stop smothering you and give you some space. He mentioned that you kept telling him to stop sending you flowers. I thought it was time he listened to what you wanted for a change.'

'So, he sent *you* flowers instead.'

'It was meant as a joke. I think it had become such a habit, so he had flowers delivered to me instead as a thank you for my advice – that's all. Then I realised my proposal had backfired when you told me you'd joined a dating site. You thought he'd moved on.' Lili sighed. 'I can't believe you assumed he was interested in me. I can assure you that is not the case.'

'I overheard him ordering them. When I saw the bouquet in the flat window …'

'You got it all wrong.'

Sarah smiled. 'I can see that now.' She sighed. 'I'm an idiot.'

Lili returned her smile. 'Me too. I'm the last person who should give him relationship advice.' She didn't know how long Ray and Sarah had been apart or the reason they had split up, although she would not be surprised if it had something to do with Nate and their decision to send him away to live with his grandfather. She imagined that decision had festered for years until retirement brought them too much time, which they had spent blaming one another for past mistakes.

'To be honest, my own relationship has broken down. I'm in no position to tell someone else what they should do about their love life. That's how I found myself here, on an extended holiday. My partner doesn't want me back.'

'He just told you not to come home?'

Lili nodded.

'Well, he's an idiot too.'

Lili managed a smile. 'I'm inclined to agree with you.' She glanced at her watch. 'I must go. A taxi is turning up any minute to take me to The Summerhouse to collect Maisie.'

Lili was not looking forward to telling Nate that things weren't all that they seemed. She felt like just skipping town without saying goodbye. It was the thought of seeing his face when she told him that troubled her.

'He's appeared happier this past week,' mused Sarah, thinking about her son. 'At first, I put that down to things going okay at work, to him starting to settle in and find his feet in the local community. Now, I see that those things are not the whole truth of the matter.' Sarah stared at Lili. 'You are the common denominator. You and Maisie.'

Lili shifted from one foot to the other. 'But we are not staying.'

'Why not?'

'It's complicated.'

'How so?'

Before Lili could answer, Sarah continued, 'If it's about the flat, don't worry – I'm sure Joseph will want you to stay as long as you like. And there's the job here too – god knows he could do with help running his shop.'

Sarah glanced back into the room. 'Besides, you can't leave now. You must hang around long enough for my father to get well.' She held up the band. 'We need to find out about this.'

Lili stared at it. Joseph's ring had created more mysteries than it had solved. Why did she have the matching Hebrew wedding ring, and who were these people he talked of, Otto, Alena, and Miriam? Why did his own daughter have no knowledge of them?

Although she wanted Joseph to recover from his fall, she was nervous about what she would discover. Was she related to him, to Sarah? And if she was … Lili didn't want to think about the good-looking doctor with the terrible bedside manner, the young man she couldn't get out of her mind. Might he be a relation?

'Lili?'

'I must go. My taxi …'

'Of course.'

Lili had a question before she left. The way Joseph had spoken about someone called Miriam, the way he had cried … she knew she might be mistaken, but it had reminded Lili of the way a small child, younger than Maisie, would cry. 'Sarah, how old would Joseph have been during the war?' It was an odd question, but Lili was interested to know.

'He was born in the mid-thirties. Why do you ask?'

'What happened to him, to his parents, your grandparents, in the war – do you know?'

'A little. It's not something he talks much about.'

Lili nodded.

While Joseph was eating his dinner, Lili and Sarah took a seat outside in a small waiting area. 'My grandparents were artists,' Sarah explained. 'They enjoyed travelling and would visit their artist friends abroad. They made the mistake of travelling to the Ionian Islands on the eve of the outbreak of war.'

She frowned. 'Although it meant they escaped The Blitz, they were on Corfu during the Italian occupation. Then the Nazi invasion followed. I believe they and their friends made several attempts to escape the island by boat. Eventually, they were rounded up with the rest of the Jews, but my father and grandfather escaped.' Sarah paused. 'Joseph never went into detail about how they escaped or what happened to my grandmother, although I suspect she ended up in one of the, you know …' Sarah trailed off.

Concentration camps. Lili nodded solemnly. Sarah did not have to say it.

'As for my grandfather, he would never speak of it. After the war, they returned to England. The house they rented in London had been reduced to rubble in The Blitz, and their friends and family had perished. My father and grandfather had nobody left but each other, and nothing left but the old summerhouse my family owned where they used to spend the summers before the war. So, they returned to the abandoned summerhouse.'

Lili's mobile phone rang. 'Shit. I forgot to turn it off when I got on the ward.' Lili was about to ignore the call when she saw it was Hannah. 'I'm sorry, I have to take this.'

Lili stood up. 'Look, can I catch up with you about this? My taxi is waiting, and I have to pick up Maisie.'

Sarah nodded. 'Yes, I'd like that. I get the feeling you have some connection to the island of Corfu?'

Lili nodded. She watched Sarah heading back to the ward as she answered her phone. 'Hi Hannah, how was your—' Lili was about to say *flight* when Hannah shouted, 'Where the hell are you?'

Lili held the phone away from her ear for a moment. 'Hannah, what's the matter?'

'I called round to your place to collect Maisie. Alex said you're not there.'

Lili chewed her bottom lip. She hadn't told her the situation yet, that her and Alex had split up and he was packing up the flat to leave for Washington.

'He said you haven't been there all summer.'

Lili forgot to text her and let her know. 'Oh, right. Look, there's no need to get your knickers in a twist,' Lili joked. Hannah didn't laugh as Lili expected.

'Where are you? He said you're in Aldeburgh, in Suffolk.'

Lili frowned as she left the hospital building by the main entrance. Her taxi hadn't arrived yet. 'Yes, I took Maisie on holiday.'

'You took her on holiday without asking me first?'

'Wait – you dumped Maisie on me for a week, then extended your trip. You didn't seem bothered by what I was doing with Maisie. In fact, I recall when I asked you if you wanted to speak to your daughter to hear what she has been doing, you said it could wait until you got back.'

'Well, I'm back now and I want to know why you took her to Aldeburgh – of all places.'

Of all places? Lili wondered what she had meant by that comment. She had thought Hannah would be pleased that she had taken her daughter away to the seaside for the summer. Lili explained, 'We had a hotel room booked for the first week. I think Alex intended it to be a romantic break away. It wasn't going to turn out that way with a kid in tow, so I took her myself and when you said you'd extended your stay, I decided to extend ours.'

'Yeah – I know that already. But where are you now? Alex told me you checked out of the hotel and were renting a holiday flat. He gave me the postcode, but I can't find the place.'

'You're here in Aldeburgh?' Lili said in surprise.

'We drove straight here when I found out.'

'Okay,' She guessed Hannah couldn't wait to see her daughter and tell Maisie all about her holiday. 'Look, I was going to phone you and let you know today. I got a bit confused with the time difference, so I didn't expect you would have landed already.' Lili brightened. 'You'll never guess who I met again.'

'Never mind that,' Hannah cut her off. 'Where are you staying?'

'Well, in a flat over a shop.' Lili wasn't surprised Hannah couldn't locate it. 'There's a little cobbled yard off the main high street.' She paused. *Where was that taxi?* She spotted it pull up at the kerb in front of the hospital. Lili breathed a sigh of relief and waved.

'I want to speak to Maisie.'

Lili got into the taxi. This was awkward. 'She's not with me right now.'

'What?'

'She's fine. You will never guess who I met again. Remember we went to …?'

'Just tell me where she is. I'm picking her up.'

Lili gave her the address in Thorpeness. 'Will you wait for me to arrive? I want to say goodbye to Maisie before you leave.'

Hannah clicked off without responding. Lili looked at her phone in surprise. She leaned forward in her seat. 'Excuse me, but you couldn't put your foot down, could you? I don't want you to break the speed limit, but—'

The driver, who Lili didn't recognise, smiled. 'Don't worry, I know this area like the back of my hand. I'll get you there in double-quick time.'

13

Lili sat back in her seat, worried that Hannah wouldn't let Maisie stay with her again after finding out she'd taken her on holiday without asking first. She'd never had to ask Hannah's permission to do anything with Maisie in the past. Since when had she been interested?

Lili chewed her bottom lip. In hindsight, she shouldn't have left Maisie. But she was okay with Nate, Ray and William looking after her at The Summerhouse. Besides, when Hannah turned up, she would recognise the place. There was nothing to worry about. She'd explain everything to Hannah when she arrived. Lili's smile faded. She knew she'd have to tell Nate as well.

As the taxi turned up the drive, the driver commented, 'I've never driven up to The Summerhouse before.'

Lili nodded. She'd heard that before.

As they approached the house, Lili saw a car already pulling up outside. Lili paid the driver and got out of the taxi. She could see Hannah getting out of the car parked in front.

Lili ran up to her. 'Hannah!' There was no one with her, so she'd obviously decided to make the journey on her own. She looked tanned. Blonde hair scraped back in a ponytail, thick foundation, bright red lipstick, and false eyelashes; she was heavily made up as usual. However, she had dressed down for the flight home in Nike leggings with a strip running down the outside, which matched her black and white trainers. She was also wearing a baggy, oversized Calvin Klein sweatshirt. With a pair of sunglasses balanced on her forehead, she resembled a celebrity failing miserably at going incognito.

Hannah turned around, her eyes wide. 'What the hell – Lili?'

'Look, I'm sorry I left Maisie while I ran an errand, but I know these people, and she was having a good time with her new friend. I was only gone a short while.'

They walked up to the front door together.

'I'm not talking about that – I'm talking about *this!*' Hannah flung her arms wide, indicating the house.

'Oh, yes, well, it's what I was trying to tell you on the phone. Remember we went to that party when we were at school?' Lili was about to mention Nate when the door opened.

'What are you doing here?' Maisie shouted at her mother.

'I've come to pick you up and take you home.'

'I don't want to go home!' Maisie screamed in her face. She ran off into the house to hide.

Her reaction did not surprise Lili.

Hannah followed her inside. 'Why did you bring her here, of all places?'

Lili frowned. There was that phrase again, *of all places*. Then she remembered. This was where—

'Maisie, come back this instant!' Hannah shouted. 'We are leaving *right now*!'

'What's going on?' Nate walked into the hallway and halted when he caught sight of them.

Lili stepped forward. 'Look, I can explain. This is—'

'Hannah.'

Lili looked quite shocked. 'You remember Hannah?'

'Of course he remembers me,' she said under her breath.

Lili heard the comment, although she didn't understand why Nate would remember Hannah. That party years earlier had been packed with teenagers.

William came running down the stairs. 'Why is Maisie crying? She says she wants her mum to go away.' William stared at Lili. Lili was staring at Nate. And Nate was staring at Hannah.

'Maisie, get down here right now! You do not want me to come up and fetch you.'

There was the sound of a toilet flushing. Ray emerged from the downstairs cloakroom to find Nate, Lili, and a stranger standing in the hallway. 'Hello,' he said in the awkward silence. 'I'm Ray, Nate's dad.' Ray waited for an introduction, but none was forthcoming until Lili stepped in. 'This is Hannah.'

Maisie appeared at the top of the stairs. 'I don't want to go home.' She wiped the tears from her eyes as she walked down the stairs.

'I don't want Maisie to go either,' William added, running up to her and holding her hand.

'Can't I stay with Lili just for the weekend – please, Mummy?'

All Lili wanted was for the ground to swallow her up. She could see out of the corner of her eye Nate and Ray turning to look at her.

Ray looked at Hannah. 'You're Maisie's mum?'

'Yes, who did you think I was?'

'Well, er … we thought Lili was …'

'You thought Lili was what?'

Lili chewed her bottom lip as Ray turned to her, his expression one of surprise. This was not how Lili envisaged they'd find out.

Hannah walked over to her daughter. Lili caught her best friend giving Nate a sideways glance as she grabbed Maisie's hand. 'We are leaving. Now!'

Lili looked from Nate to Hannah and back again, still wondering why he should remember her best friend in particular. It didn't make any sense. Lili stared at Maisie. Nate was staring at her too. Lili's eyes went wide. *Of all the places.*

'Let go of the little boy's hand, Maisie.'

'I'm not a little boy. My name's William and I'm six.'

Ray said, 'What about your paintings, Maisie – don't you want to take them home?'

'Mummy, my pictures!' Maisie answered, pulling away from her mother.

'There's no time for that. You can do some more finger-paints, or whatever you've been doing, when you return to school.' Hannah dragged her out of the door.

Lili stared after her, shocked that it was Nate … that Hannah and Nate had … been together at the party. If she'd still had any doubt in her mind, all she would have needed to do was examine one of Maisie's paintings. William hadn't inherited his father's gift, but Nate's daughter had.

'Now, look here …' Ray was about to follow Hannah out of the door when Nate caught hold of his arm, shaking his head. 'I'll deal with it.'

'Why?'

'Because I'm …'

Lili turned to look at him, wide-eyed. He'd guessed the truth, too.

'Just let me speak to her, okay? William, stay here with your grandpa.'

'I don't want Maisie to go. Will you bring her back?'

Nate didn't answer. His eyes locked on Lili for a moment.

Lili tried to say something, but the opportunity was lost.

Nate glared at her and stormed outside. 'Hannah!'

Lili walked to the door and stood in the doorway. She could see Hannah telling Maisie to get inside the car. She slammed the car door shut before turning to Nate.

Lili heard Hannah say, 'I'm not telling you when her birthday is. That's none of your business.'

'What's going on?' Ray asked, standing behind Lili at the door. 'Who is that woman?'

She's my best friend, and she slept with your son, and wouldn't even tell me who the father of her child was, she thought to herself. She bit her lower lip. 'She's Maisie's mother.'

'I realise that.'

'Sorry,' Lili said in a small voice. 'I don't know why I didn't correct that misconception.'

Lili felt a gentle hand on her shoulder. 'Maisie didn't correct that misconception either. I get the impression she loves her Lili very much.'

Lili felt a tear run down her cheek. 'I love my Maisie very much too.'

Ray squeezed her shoulder. 'I know.'

'I'm sorry,' Lili said again.

Ray turned his attention to Nate and Hannah, who were still standing in the driveway, arguing.

'So, Nate knows Maisie's mother?' Ray asked.

Lili sighed. 'We all knew each other as teenagers.' Lili was about to add that they didn't know each other that well, but that wasn't exactly true, considering everything. Instead, she explained, 'We went to the same school. Hannah and Nate met at the party.'

'Ah, the party.'

'You remember that?'

'Yes, I do, if for no other reason than Joseph's rather over-the-top reaction to some kids, presumably drunk, trying to break into the old summerhouse.'

Lili remembered Nate mentioning that. Lili turned around and glanced at William, who was holding Ray's hand. 'It turns out my best friend kept something from Nate …' Lili knew Maisie was Nate's daughter, which meant Ray was—

'Why are they arguing?' Ray asked, looking over her shoulder.

Lili turned around and watched Hannah shaking her head before getting into her car. The car sped off down the driveway, leaving Nate standing there helplessly staring after it. He turned around and stalked back to the house, stopping in front of Lili. 'Did you know?'

'Nate, what's going on?'

He ignored his father's question. 'Did you know?'

Lili shook her head. 'I swear, Nate, I had no idea.'

'How can I believe you when you lied about Maisie being your daughter? What else have you lied about?' Nate stormed off before Lili had a chance to say anything more.

'For god's sake, will someone shut that hound up!' Nate exclaimed.

Lili, Ray and William turned towards the conservatory where

Bella was shut in the room. She was barking behind the door.

Ray looked at his grandson. 'William, please can you let the dog out.'

William ran over to the conservatory and opened the door.

Bella came flying out of the room, nearly knocking William over. She bounded towards Lili and Ray. They stepped aside and watched her run outside and some way down the drive, chasing after the car, barking.

William ran after her, shouting, 'Bella! Maisie's gone.'

Lili saw Bella stop and turn around at the sound of William's voice. He caught up with the dog. They both stood there watching the car disappear before turning back to the house. Lili guessed the dog had been watching through the conservatory window and had spotted Maisie getting into the car.

Lili got out her phone to call a taxi. 'I'd better go.'

Ray heard Nate slamming a door deep in the bowels of the house. He turned to Lili. 'Will someone please tell me what's going on?' Ray furrowed his brow. 'What did Nate mean when he asked you, *did you know*?'

'I swear I didn't, Ray. All these years, she's refused to tell me. I thought the reason was that she didn't know. She was drunk at the party. Everyone was.' *Apart from me*, she thought.

'The party,' Ray repeated, staring at Lili. 'What did she refuse to tell you?'

'Who Maisie's father was.' Lili cast a glance towards the lounge where Nate had stormed off and slammed the door.

Ray followed her gaze.

Lili sighed. It wasn't her place to explain, but he had a right to know. He'd find out, anyway. 'Maisie didn't inherit her artistic abilities, her talent, her gift from her mother.'

His eyebrows shot up as he turned to Lili. 'Are you saying that Maisie is my … my …?'

'Yes, Ray. She's your granddaughter.'

Lili saw the tears in his eyes. She placed her hand on his forearm and smiled. 'I hope you believe in second chances, Ray, because you just got yours.' She opened her handbag and found a pen. She looked at Ray. 'Have you got some paper? I'm going to give you her mother's address in London and her phone number.' Lili had always felt strongly that Maisie had a right to know her grandparents. It was so sad for Maisie that her mother had remained estranged from her own parents, which meant that Maisie was estranged from them too. That didn't have to be the case with Ray and Sarah, though. In fact, Lili would do her best to make sure it wasn't.

Ray stepped into the kitchen and returned with a notepad.

Lili wrote the address and phone number twice. She tore a sheet of paper out of the pad and handed it to Ray. 'I've also jotted the address down for Nate. Will you be sure he gets it?'

'Of course I will.'

'In the meantime, I intend to speak to Hannah.' Lili knew Hannah had been able to cut Maisie's grandparents out of her life, but she couldn't do it to Nate – not anymore. Nate had a right to see his child.

A car turned up the driveway and arrived outside the house. William ran outside again, followed by Bella, hoping Maisie had come back. Lili sighed. It wasn't Hannah and Maisie. It was her taxi. She stepped outside and turned around to take one last look at The Summerhouse. She didn't realise how attached she'd become to this place, these people, all in such a short space of time. She had tears in her eyes at the thought of leaving.

Ray stepped outside too and surprised her by putting his arms round her and giving her a hug. 'I wish … I wish you were Maisie's mother.'

So do I, thought Lili – not just because she loved Maisie so much, but because she was falling in love with Nate, and he'd probably never speak to her again. This would be the last she saw of The Summerhouse or Ray, Sarah, William – and Nate.

Lili pulled back and wiped her face with the sleeve of her blouse. She remembered that she had something to tell Ray before she left, and she'd rather he heard it from her. She took a deep breath. 'Look, there's something I want you to know before you hear it from somebody else. It's about me and Joseph …'

14

She was about to explain, but Ray got there first. 'I know for a fact that Joseph does not have many or indeed *any* friends.'

Lili stared at him. 'You knew, and you didn't mention it?'

'Let's just say I had my suspicions.'

Lili was about to ask why he'd kept quiet about it, but Ray had anticipated the question. 'The reason I've kept it under my hat was for William's sake – and Nate's. My son and grandson were not in a good place, and then you and Maisie walked into their lives. So, I don't need an explanation, Lili.'

Lili felt he deserved one, anyway. She told him all about the argument with Alex over Maisie, and her decision to go to Aldeburgh for a holiday. Then how Alex had ended their relationship in a text, sending her things by FedEx; how, in the meantime, Maisie's mother had decided she'd stay on abroad for an extended break; and how she had come to be in Joseph's flat, meeting all the wonderful people in Cobbler's Yard.

Then Lili went further, telling Ray more than she'd ever told anybody about her past and her fears for Maisie; how she'd always been afraid that someone would take her into care and that she would never see her again.

Lili could feel the tears rolling down her face. 'Sorry.'

'There's no need to apologise, Lili. I quite understand.'

'Nate told me you needed my help. You were found wandering along a beach in Corfu alone when you were three and shipped back to England, where you were put in care until you started boarding school here, paid for by an anonymous benefactor. Is that correct?'

Lili nodded. 'That's all I know so far; that and the fact that my social worker, who I thought was my friend, has deceived me all these years about how my private education was funded.'

'Hmm. Have you spoken to her?'

'Not yet. I can't help thinking that if she's lied all this time, she must have her reasons. Why would she tell me the truth?'

Ray looked thoughtful. 'Yes, you may have a point. So, when they found you, the authorities couldn't trace your immediate family or relatives?'

'Nobody.'

He looked at her askance. 'Everybody has somebody, a friend or a relative … I think it's rather odd.'

Lili mulled it over. Put that way, it made sense. 'If there *was* someone out there, then why didn't they come forward?'

Because, thought Ray, *they had something to hide – some skeleton in their closet.* He sighed.

Lili glanced at Ray. 'Never mind. I know what you're thinking. It's an impossible task.'

'It isn't impossible,' Ray said slowly. 'It's just different. Normally, I find descendants. This time I have a descendant.'

'Me?'

'Yes, you must have some relatives somewhere. I just need to find the house.'

'The house?'

'Ah, what I mean to say is, when I look for heirs to estates, I typically start with a physical place, the estate, someone's home. A property that has been left empty and not bequeathed to anybody in a will, so then I search for that person's descendants. You are somebody's descendant. Everybody has somebody – the trick is to find them.'

But Lili wanted to find living relatives, not dead ones. She told Ray as much.

'Well, you certainly had someone ten years ago, because they were paying for your expensive education. They could still be alive.'

'But in all that time if Connie has never found my relatives …'

'Who is Connie?'

'She's my social worker.'

'The person who you recently discovered had lied to you?'

Lili went quiet.

'Is she the reason you never attempted to search for them yourself?'

'I suppose.' It hadn't been the only reason, though. Lili had been too busy looking to her future, her career, marriage, children, to seek out her past.

'Don't you owe it to yourself to look into this? You could be an heir to their estate. Have you thought about that?'

Lili hadn't. But she had been thinking about Joseph and that ring. Was she a descendant of the artist friends that Joseph and his parents stayed with on the Ionian Islands? Or was she related to Joseph?

Lili was about to tell Ray about her ring when the taxi driver opened his car door and called out, 'Did one of you phone for a cab? I have another fare soon, so I'll have to leave.'

Lili raised her hand, 'Sorry, that was me. I'm coming.' She turned to Ray. 'I have to go.'

'I want to find your relatives, Lili.'

'That's really kind of you, Ray, but I can't ask you to do that. You've got the shop to run and your heir-hunting business. I can't afford your fee.' Right now, she had no job and no home.

As if reading her mind, Ray said, 'Stay. Run the shop. I'll speak to Joseph as soon as I can and persuade him to keep you on – god knows, he could do with the help.'

Lili smiled. 'You know, you're the second person today who's said that to me.'

Ray raised his eyebrows.

Thinking of Sarah, Lili said, 'Before I leave, I want you to know that I gave you some really dumb advice when I told you not to send her any more flowers and just give her some space. Instead, tomorrow buy her flowers, and the next day, and the next. Invite her to dinner. Don't take no for an answer.'

'Invite her to dinner?'

'Oh, yes. And please buy her flowers.'

'I think she was quite shocked that you'd bought them for me.'

Ray slapped his forehead. 'I'm an idiot.'

Lili smiled. 'She said that too.'

'She did?'

Lili smiled. 'Oh, yes.'

'I am going to buy her the biggest, best bunch of—'

The taxi driver honked his horn.

Lili leaned towards him and gave him a peck on the cheek.

'I'll miss you.'

'Don't say that. You'll be back.'

Lili doubted it.

'Quick, give me your mobile number.' Ray handed her the notepad and pen he still had in his hand.

Lili wrote her number down and handed Ray the notepad. 'I'll post the keys to Joseph's shop through your letterbox.'

'I'd rather you didn't.'

'What shall I do with them?'

'What I meant was that I'd rather you didn't leave.'

Lili stared at Ray. She didn't belong here, no matter how attached she had grown to them all. She was just making her way to the taxi when William ran up behind her and threw his arms around her waist. 'Don't go.'

Lili turned around and knelt, wiping tears away from his cheeks. 'I have to, William.'

'Why does everyone always leave?' William cried. He ran off into the house.

Bella stood there whining.

'I'm sorry,' Lili called after him. She looked up at the house and caught Nate at a window.

'I'll call you if I find out anything,' Ray said, approaching the taxi. He opened the car door.

Bella seemed to take that as an invitation. She jumped into the back seat.

The taxi driver turned around and looked at the dog. 'You didn't mention a pet.'

Lili sighed. 'You're not going for a car ride today, Bella.' Lili took two paces back and said, 'Come!'

Bella jumped out of the car.

'Sit!'

Bella sat obediently by Lili's feet. 'Good girl.' Lili knelt and gave her a fuss. 'I'll miss you.' Lili glanced at the house. 'All of you.'

Ray looked at Bella in surprise. 'I didn't know she was so well behaved.'

Lili stood up. 'Maisie and William have been training her. She really is a lovely dog if you just give her a chance.'

Ray kept his distance.

'Stroke her, Ray. She likes a fuss.'

Ray stepped forward and tentatively patted her head.

The taxi driver wound his window down. 'I don't mean to be rude, but I have to leave, now with or without you.'

Ray looked up. 'Stay, Lili. Please. I have a spare bedroom. I can put you up at my place.'

Lili was already shaking her head before he'd finished speaking. 'That's really kind of you, Ray, but I have to return to London.'

She knew it was a fib; she didn't have to return to London. She didn't have to be anywhere. 'Will you water Joseph's plants in the conservatory?' Lili had noticed one of his rare, prized orchids was starting to bloom.

Ray nodded. 'You'll come back, though.'

'Goodbye, Ray.' She opened the car door and apologised to the driver. 'I'm so sorry for holding you up.' Lili had barely put her seatbelt on when the car took off, speeding down the driveway.

Lili turned in her seat and glanced out of the window, taking one more look at the house. She saw Bella running down the drive, trying to catch up with the car. As they turned in to the unmade road that led into Thorpeness and the main road skirting the beach into Aldeburgh, Lili saw Bella stop at the entrance to the property. 'Go home, please,' Lili breathed, hoping Bella didn't continue following them. Bella looked toward the house. Lili guessed Ray was calling her. She stopped and ran back up the driveway, out of sight.

Lili turned in her seat, tears rolling down her face.

'Where to?' the driver asked.

Lili found a tissue in her handbag and looked at the taxi driver. She said under her breath, 'I wish I knew.'

15

The taxi dropped Lili off at the entrance to the yard. She didn't feel like staying the night at the flat. It would be strange not having Maisie there with her. Lili opened the shop and walked straight upstairs. Ten minutes later, she emerged carrying her luggage.

Before turning the lights off, Lili glanced about the shop one last time. There was less stock than when she had taken over running the shop after Joseph's fall, but there was more choice for the tourists, with the rack of amber jewellery – a bestseller, it had turned out – taking pride of place in the window. Lili thought of Joseph. She would have liked to see him again before she left, but that wasn't possible.

She'd looked up the timetable; there was a train leaving for London in thirty minutes. The taxi company said they would get her to the station promptly to catch her train. Lili checked her watch. The taxi would be back any minute. She didn't have time to stand there dawdling, wishing the impossible; that they were her family and this was her home. She switched off the lights and closed the door, locking it behind her.

Reggie in the music shop spotted her closing the shop early.

He noticed her suitcase. He stepped outside his shop. 'Are you leaving?' he said in surprise.

'Yeah, something came up.'

'I, for one, wish you didn't have to go. I'm not looking forward to that grumpy so-and-so coming back.'

For a moment, Lili thought he was talking about Nate. 'Oh, you mean Joseph.'

'When he returns, I'll ask him to have you back.'

Lili thanked him, even though she knew he'd be wasting his time. 'Goodbye, Reggie. I'm going to miss you.'

'And I you.'

Lili glanced at the flower shop. 'I have to go now. I've got a train to catch. Will you say bye to Sarah and Zoe for me?'

'Anything for you, Lili.' Reggie raised his hand, waving her goodbye before stepping back inside and closing the shop door.

Lili nipped across the yard and posted the keys through Ray's letterbox. She could have popped her head into the flower shop and handed them to Sarah or Zoe, but there was a reason she was doing it this way; it would give Ray an excuse to visit The Potting Shed.

Lili stood for a moment in the yard. She hadn't been in Aldeburgh long, but in that time, she'd made friends and found a place that felt like home. But she reminded herself, as she walked through the courtyard to the waiting taxi, that it wasn't – it was just a holiday that had become something more. She wished it hadn't.

❖

As the train left the station, Lili got out her mobile and rang Hannah's number, feeling anxious that she wouldn't answer the phone when she saw who was calling. The train had been delayed, so by the time she boarded and started her journey, she imagined Hannah would have arrived home. Lili glanced at Maisie's little Trunki, which she'd picked up in the flat along with her own suitcase, before she left. She wasn't surprised she'd forgotten to mention Maisie's luggage to Hannah at the house earlier.

Lili breathed a sigh of relief when Hannah answered. 'Hannah, I want to apologise that I took Maisie on holiday to Aldeburgh and—'

Lili was about to mention Nate when Hannah interrupted. 'I'm sorry I flew off the handle like that. It's my fault. I should have told you years ago.'

So why didn't you? Lili wanted to ask.

'We were so young,' Hannah continued. 'I didn't think he'd want anything to do with Maisie. It wasn't something I was proud of. When I saw him at school, after the party, we were both so embarrassed we couldn't look each other in the eye.'

Lili was so relieved she'd patched things up with her best friend. 'I've got something to tell you too. Look, I've split up from Alex.'

'No way! What happened?'

Lili glanced around the carriage. She didn't want to go into it over the phone. 'I'm on the train back to London. I can't return to our flat. Can I stay with you for a few days while I figure out a place to live?' She was about to mention that she had Maisie's suitcase when she noticed Hannah had gone quiet. She furrowed her brow, wondering if she'd lost the signal. 'Hannah – are you still there?'

'I'm sorry, but now isn't a good time, Lili.'

'Pardon?'

'We've hit a bit of a rocky patch too.'

Lili didn't understand. 'But you've just been on holiday together and got engaged. Maisie told me you have moved to a new house.'

'Yes, it was a make-or-break holiday, which went well, beyond well, but we've still got things we need to sort out. Besides, I know he wouldn't like it if I had a friend turn up, you know, out of the blue.'

Lili couldn't believe it. She'd been in the same boat with Alex. How many times, over the years, had Hannah turned up with Maisie in tow? She hadn't turned them away, not once, even though Alex often hadn't wanted them there.

'If it had been any other time … but right now I've got to put my relationship first. You understand, don't you, Lili?'

'I understand,' Lili mumbled. She ended the call, forgetting to mention Maisie's luggage. She didn't feel inclined to phone back. She stared at her phone and then turned to the window so that nobody would see tears rolling down her cheeks. She understood all right. All those years, she had been prepared to drop everything for her best friend. This one time the boot was on the other foot, and she needed help, Hannah wasn't there for her. Alex had been right all along. He had once said, 'I know her type. There will come a time when you need her, and it won't be reciprocated. She'll put herself first and turn her back on you, then you'll find out what sort of friend she really is.'

Lili stared out of the window into the blackness and thought of the other person she could always rely on for help – Connie.

16

'Lili – what are you doing here?'

Lili was standing on Connie's doorstep, intending to ask her the question as soon as she opened the door: *why did you lie to me?* But when Lili saw Connie, she burst into tears. She was thinking of Alex ending their relationship, and then her new friendships in Suffolk – people whom she missed already, especially Nate, William and Bella the dog. 'Oh, Connie!' she said, 'I've made such a mess of things!'

Connie immediately joined her on the doorstep, putting her arm around Lili's shoulders and guiding her into the house. She still lived in the old Edwardian three-storey townhouse she had lived in for decades. It was where she and her late husband had raised their three daughters. She had four grandchildren – all girls too. Photos of her family adorned the walls, and small framed pictures sat on the sideboard by the phone.

The place hadn't changed a bit; the décor was a throwback to the eighties, when Connie and her husband had set about renovating their new home. Lili glanced up the stairs at the stripped wooden banisters, the patterned brown carpet extending from the hall downstairs, and the beige wallpaper with its delicate flower pattern. She remembered the nights she had stayed in this house vividly. Lili had so desperately wanted to be part of Connie's family when she was younger, to live here, and for Connie's girls to be her little sisters. Her first stopover there – or sleepover, as Connie's children had called them – had been when she was four. Connie had been expecting her youngest.

The foster parents that Lili had been with since she had arrived in England from Corfu had thought they couldn't have children of their own. They had been intending to adopt Lili until the woman discovered she was pregnant. Suddenly, they didn't want to adopt anymore. As soon as they found out the good news, they decided that fostering wasn't practical after all and wanted Lili placed elsewhere.

Connie had brought her home to stay a few days with her and her family. After that episode, Lili realised that if she was naughty, or threatened to run away, any foster parents she was staying with would be on the phone to social services, and Connie would have no option but to come and fetch her. Lili recalled that she'd often have her bag packed with the few possessions she had before she caused trouble. Connie would take her to her own home for a night or two until she arranged a new foster home.

There was no shortage of people willing to take care of a little blonde-haired four-year-old – until she misbehaved. This went on for another year; she was in and out of foster homes, in and out of Connie's place. Then everything changed. The last time she packed her bags, ready to move back to Connie's after her latest foster parents had washed their hands of her, she found herself in a small cubby-hole of a room in a new children's home instead. Social services had decided they weren't looking at fostering her anymore. Her plan to get Connie to allow her to stay with her family permanently, if no one else would have her, had gone disastrously wrong.

Then, three years later, an opportunity arose that meant she could leave the children's home. She sat the entrance exam for a posh boarding school on the promise that if she was accepted, she could spend the holidays with Connie and her family.

Everything worked out splendidly to begin with, until Connie's husband was posted abroad with his job, and his family went with him. Although Lili stayed in contact, especially with the three girls, things weren't the same on their return. Lili was older, and she was spending the school breaks with Hannah and her aged grandparents. The visits to Connie's during the holidays stopped.

Lili would never forget the one time she'd heard Connie and her husband arguing. It was the last sleepover she had at this house, when she was in between foster parents, before she ended up in the children's home. She'd heard raised voices, and had crept halfway down the stairs, where she'd found Connie's middle child, who was three years older than Lili, sitting on a stair. She'd whispered in Lili's ear, 'Why are they arguing?'

Even though Lili was a lot younger, she'd put her arm around her foster sister to comfort her, wishing she was her real big sister, and this was her real family. It was why she could never settle down in any of the foster homes. She just felt she belonged here.

Lili would never forget that conversation she'd overheard.

'Why don't we permanently foster her?'

For a moment, Lili had held her breath thinking, *this is it.* It sounded as though Connie's husband, who Lili had thought would be against the idea, wanted her to stay. It turned out that it was Connie who was opposed to the suggestion. 'You know why we can't.'

They said nothing more. Lili assumed it was because Connie was her social worker, and it just wouldn't be the done thing to show favouritism to a child in her care. Even so, she prayed that one day Connie would make an exception. She never did.

Standing in the hall, Lili would rather not revisit that memory. She was wiping her eyes dry when she heard someone call out, 'Mum, who was at the door? You're missing the baby shower!' Connie's middle daughter, heavily pregnant, stepped out of the lounge. 'I didn't know you had company.' She paused. 'Lili?'

The little girl she'd hugged on the stairs all those years earlier was all grown-up and expecting another baby.

'Oh, god, I'm so sorry for interrupting—'

'Don't be silly. Come in, join us.'

Lili could hear other voices in the lounge, her sisters and friends. Lili started to shake her head. This wasn't a social call.

'I'm not staying.'

'Oh, but you are,' Connie insisted. 'The baby shower is winding down. Take yourself up to the spare bedroom. You remember where it is?'

Lili nodded.

Connie steered her daughter back into the lounge saying, 'Lili's had a long day. I'm sure she'll speak to you all in the morning.'

Lili overheard her as she walked up the stairs. Connie's three daughters were all staying the night after the baby shower.

'Lili,' Connie called out before joining the others. 'You can stay for as long as you want, all right?' Lili paused on the stairs and glanced down at Connie. 'All right.' She was too tired to argue, or bring up the other thing – did Connie know who had paid for her schooling? The answer mattered more than ever. She had nobody – apart from Connie. Not even Hannah was going to put herself out to help her. All Lili wanted was to find her family, although the question remained: did they want her to find them? She'd avoided that quandary all her life, but with nothing to lose, she was ready to discover the truth. But not right at this moment. All Lili could do was drag herself, and her suitcase, upstairs and have a lie down. She felt exhausted.

She opened the door to the spare bedroom at the end of the hall and stopped in the doorway. The room hadn't changed one bit, with its old-fashioned chintzy, flowered wallpaper, matching bedspread and pink curtains. Was this how it felt to return to your family home, your childhood bedroom, your childhood bed? Lili didn't really know; all she could do was imagine.

Lili left her suitcase on the floor by the door, still not convinced she was going to stay – there was always a hotel. She lay down, pulling the eiderdown around her. She'd closed her eyes just for a moment – or so she thought – when her mobile phone rang. When she opened her eyes, the room was bathed in soft morning sunshine. Lili hadn't even changed out of her clothes before her head hit the pillow, and she had gone out like a light. She remembered dreaming that Connie had called her for dinner; perhaps that wasn't a dream.

Lili sat up in bed and answered her phone. Her heart had leapt in her chest at the notion that it was Alex, aware her holiday had finished, phoning to see how she was, wanting to patch things up and apologise for his behaviour.

No such luck, thought Lili when she heard Ray's voice. 'Good morning, sweetheart, I hope I didn't wake you.'

'Um, no, not at all,' Lili fibbed, wondering what the time was.

'I have some news.'

'News?' Lili still felt tired and disorientated.

'I've found your secret benefactor.'

It took Lili a moment to grasp what Ray had said. 'Wait – what did you just say?'

'I found the person who paid for you to go through school.'

'That was quick,' Lili replied. She fell silent. Part of her wished she hadn't gone down that rabbit hole; she was afraid of what she might find; that it would lead to her family, but that they wouldn't want to know her. Then she'd be back to square one, where she had always been, all alone – except that this time it would be all the worse for knowing her family were out there.

'Lili?'

She sighed. 'I'm still here.'

'Are you all right? We're all worried about you.'

'You are?' Lili was taken aback. She had assumed that once she'd gone, they'd forget about her. She hadn't expected Ray to get in touch.

'It's true,' Ray said down the phone. 'You know, even Bella has been pining for you.'

'Oh, don't be daft – she's a dog.'

'Exactly, and a German shepherd. They get attached to one person. She's off her food. You know how much she likes her meals. She's missing you.'

Lili knew there was one person who wouldn't be missing her.

As if reading her mind, Ray said, 'Nate too.'

Lili doubted that. Ray was just being kind.

There was a long silence down the phone, heavy with regret on Lili's part for not being honest with them all.

Ray returned to the matter at hand. 'Look, if you'd rather not …'

She knew what he was going to say, but it was too late to back out now. 'Tell me, Ray, who is it?'

'Lili! Breakfast is on the table when you're ready.'

Lili cast a glance towards the door. Connie must have heard her talking on her phone.

'Who is that?' Ray asked.

'That's Connie, my social worker. I'm staying with her at the moment. We've always been really close, like—'

'Family.'

'Yes.' There was a long silence. 'Ray, are you still there?'

'Can we meet?'

Lili was surprised by the question. 'Why?'

'So that we can discuss what I've found out.'

Lili frowned. 'Can't you just tell me on the phone? It's going to take time for us to meet up and I don't think I can stand the suspense.'

'All right,' Ray said slowly. 'Are you sitting down?'

Lili had been pacing the floor. She sat down on the end of the bed. 'I am now.'

She took a deep breath and heard Ray doing the same. 'It's Connie.'

'What's Connie? I don't understand.'

'She was the person who paid your school fees.'

Lili laughed. 'Okay, enough with the jokes, Ray.' She knew he enjoyed a practical joke. 'Now, really, who is it?'

There was a long silence, interrupted by Connie calling up

the stairs again, 'Lili, darling, I've cooked some eggs over easy and streaky bacon just the way you like it. It's on the table.'

Ray sighed. 'I'm sorry, Lili. It's true.'

Lili was pacing again, shaking her head; he'd got it wrong.

Ray continued, 'When I discovered it was your social worker, I looked into the case of the missing English youngster on Corfu that no one came forward to claim. It didn't make any sense. Who would just abandon their child?'

That was the question Lili had asked herself all her life, and the reason she had been reticent about looking for her parents. They didn't want her; that was the conclusion she'd come to.

'I started by going on the assumption that you weren't abandoned.'

'What do you mean?'

'I concluded that something must have happened to your parents, so I looked into newspaper reports. A young couple with British passports, had died on another Ionian Island the day you were found – it was a motorcycle accident.'

Lili shook her head. She got the distinct impression he was grasping at straws. 'I don't see what that has got to do with me.'

'I'm not sure either. Why were they on another island? And if they were your parents, surely someone would have known they had a child – family, friends?'

'So, what's all this got to do with Connie?' Lili asked.

'Well, I started looking into the circumstances of how you were found, police reports, that sort of thing. Digging a little further, I discovered you had been brought home by a newly qualified social worker who was holidaying on the island at the time.'

'Yes, I'm aware of that,' Lili said, getting impatient.

'The thing is, Lili, it was all too convenient, too coincidental. There had to be a connection between the two of you – but what?'

'Did you just say – a connection?'

'Why would she pay your school fees? Out of all the children she's been involved with over the years, what makes you so special? Something happened on that island, Lili – something she's not telling you. It all goes back to Corfu. Call it years of detective intuition – but I'm convinced of it.'

Lili swallowed.

'Are you going to be all right, Lili?'

'Yeah, sure,' she said offhand, not sure how she felt right now. There was just one question going through her mind, and it wasn't something Ray could answer.

'Lili, are you still there?'

'I've got to go.'

'Lili—'

She cut him off, tossing her phone on the bed. She slipped on a jumper. Despite it being the middle of summer, Connie's big old house always felt chilly. She opened the bedroom door and walked down the stairs, slowing when she reached the hallway downstairs. She could hear voices coming from the kitchen. She sidled up to the kitchen and stood in the doorway. The three girls, who'd stayed over, were already at breakfast. They all said, 'Hi,' smiling warmly at Lili. Lili remembered that when she was sent to boarding school, they'd wanted her to live with them instead. Lili shifted her attention to Connie, who smiled and beckoned her to come in and join them for breakfast.

Remaining at the door, Lili looked at Connie. 'Are you my mother?'

Connie dropped her fork; it clanged on the plate.

The three girls stopped eating, sensing a tension between their mother and Lili; surprised faces wondering what was going on.

Connie slowly got up from the table. 'Girls, carry on with your breakfast.' She walked over to Lili.

Her youngest stood up. 'Mum?'

Connie turned to her. 'It's all right, I just need to speak to Lili alone.' Connie motioned to the sitting room next door. 'Lili, let's talk about this in here …'

'Why?' Lili asked.

'It's about your mother.'

17

'You knew her – didn't you?' Lili had sat down on one of the two old leather sofas in the living room. Connie was sitting opposite her, a glass coffee table between them.

'You knew my mother.' Lili's tone was accusatory. She waited for Connie to deny it. If what Connie said was true, and she wasn't Connie's daughter, then that was the only other explanation. As Ray had pointed out, why else would Connie have paid her school fees? Why choose Lili out of all the children she had been involved with over the years? What made Lili so special?

Lili repeated the question.

Connie sat there, looking at her hands.

'You lied to me.' Lili leaned forward in her seat and stared at her. 'I trusted you all these years. How could you!'

Connie sighed. 'It's true. I knew your mother. Not very well. We met on Corfu. She was estranged from her relatives. She said she'd discovered something, a family secret that her mum had kept from her. I don't know what it was, but she talked of returning to England.' Connie couldn't look her in the eye. 'I met both your parents on Corfu.'

Lili swallowed. *Why didn't you tell me years ago?* she wanted to shout. Instead, she asked, 'What were their names?'

Connie was already shaking her head before Lili had finished her question. 'I don't know. We were just kids. We were all teenagers and youngsters in our early twenties, travelling, sleeping under the stars. I guess we were trying to capture some of our parents' – the boomer generation's – free hippy spirits and delaying joining the actual world of work and responsibilities.'

Connie stared off into the distance for a moment before fixing her gaze on Lili. 'I'd just qualified as a social worker. It felt like that was my last summer of freedom before I started my career. That holiday, on the beach in Corfu …' Connie paused. 'You have to understand, people came and went, and a lot of us, your parents included, didn't go by their proper names. We adopted hippy, far-out names like Moon, and River, and Sky…'

'Sky? My surname is Skye. Is there a link?'

'Sky was your mother's chosen first name. I doubt it was her real name,' she added.

'So, it was you who gave me that surname?'

'No, it was you.'

'What do you mean?'

'When they asked your name at the police station in Corfu, you said Lili Skye.'

Lili narrowed her eyes. 'You knew that wasn't correct. I must have been asking for my mother. Ray said it was too convenient, too coincidental that you found me. He believed we were connected somehow.'

Connie had a question. 'Who is Ray?'

'A retired police officer.'

Connie's face went as white as a sheet.

Lili noticed. There was something Connie wasn't telling her. 'In all these years, why didn't you tell me you knew her, or at the very least that you'd met her? Is that why you paid my fees, out of guilt?'

Connie looked up. 'You know about that?'

'Yes. I visited the school, and they told me there are no scholarships at the age of eight.'

Connie sighed. 'That is true.' She shifted in her seat. 'Look, we discussed adopting you, but it just wasn't possible. I'd put myself in an impossible situation. I was your social worker.'

Lili recalled that it was Connie, not her husband, who would not consider adopting her.

'We agreed to do something for you, for your future, and that was to get you out of the care system. I knew the scholarships to private schools for children from underprivileged backgrounds didn't start until children were twelve years old, but I approached the head with an idea. He said that if you sat an exam at eight, and showed promise, then we had an arrangement; the money the council would have paid for looked-after care, topped up with a private donation from ourselves, would support your place at the school for three years. Then you moved on to a scholarship.'

'So, I did get the scholarship at twelve?'

'It wasn't easy getting the council to agree to such an unusual request, but then you, Lili, were always an unusual case.'

Lili stared at her. 'But the current head looked into my records and said I had an anonymous benefactor.'

'Ah, well, you see the council, social services and myself couldn't publicise that we singled out one child to go to private boarding school at the age of eight. Once you moved on to the scholarship, things were more straightforward. I expect the current headteacher looked at the basis on which you started at the school and assumed it had continued throughout your time there. If she'd checked up on when you left the prep, she would have realised you'd crossed to the assisted place scheme.'

'Why didn't you tell me?'

'It never came up. Frankly, I thought it didn't matter. You had what I wanted for you, which was a good education, opportunities.'

'What *you* wanted? What about what I wanted?' said Lili through gritted teeth. 'A home, a family.'

'I couldn't adopt you, Lili, because of my job. I was your—'

'—Social worker, yeah, you told me that already.' Lili eyed her suspiciously. There was still something Connie wasn't telling her – she was sure of it.

'I thought that with an excellent education, you'd move on with your life, have a career, get married, have a family. And your past, well, was your past. Didn't I say to you, only ever look back to see how far you've come? You always liked that advice.'

Lili shook her head from side to side. 'You should have told me you knew my mother.'

Connie sighed heavily. 'I tried to find them, as did the police, but it was impossible …'

'What about grandparents, aunts, uncles? Didn't the authorities post my picture somewhere?' Lili suddenly realised that there had been no social media twenty-four years ago. But wouldn't she have been on the news, in a newspaper, on a milk carton?

Connie guessed what she was thinking. 'It was no use. Nobody came forward.'

They both fell silent, the heavy silence interrupted by Lili's phone. It was Ray. Lili stood up and answered the call as she walked towards the door. She knew she couldn't stay on at Connie's. Not now.

'Hello, Ray.'

'Are you okay?'

Lili glanced back into the room before she stepped into the hall, out of earshot. 'You were right about Connie.' She didn't go into the ins and outs of when and how much Connie had contributed to her private school fees.

'Did she tell you her reasons?'

Lili started walking up the stairs. 'Yes, she knew my mother. Not very well, by the sounds of it. They didn't know each other long.' Lili stepped into the bedroom and glanced at her suitcase, relieved she hadn't bothered unpacking the previous night. 'Before you ask, no, she didn't know my mother's name.'

Lili sighed when Ray asked the reason. 'It's a long story.' She didn't want to go into all that business of using fake names and pretending to be hippy types. It was stupid, and it had cost her any lead she might have regarding who her parents were and where her extended relatives might be. The fact was that she had got excited over nothing. Finding out who her secret benefactor was hadn't led to her family, as she hoped; all it had pointed to was a dead end. 'Look, I have to go.' Lili picked up her coat.

'Wait!'

She stopped. 'What is it, Ray?'

'You said Connie met your mother.'

'That's right, but as I said before, it's a dead end. She didn't know her proper name.'

'But if she'd met her, presumably she'd recognise her if she saw a photo?'

Lili shrugged. 'I guess. But where would you get a photo?'

'Do you remember the young couple who perished in a motorcycle accident on the island of Zakynthos?'

Lili rolled her eyes. Not that again. Didn't Ray get it? It was a simple case of abandonment. They hadn't wanted her anymore. It made sense now. They were free spirits, second-generation hippies travelling, having beach parties, not wanting responsibilities, not wanting her.

'I have a photo of them – the couple who died. I can't take the credit. It was a mate still on the force who found a small, archived obituary from a British newspaper about the couple who died on Zakynthos. It appears that the photo the local police released to journalists was a polaroid someone had taken of them on a beach before they died. The local police had found it amongst the debris of the crash. I'm sending it to your phone now.'

Lili rolled her eyes again, thinking, *if you must*. 'Okay.' Lili heard her phone ping as she finished putting on her coat.

'There, I've sent it.'

'Fine.' Lili picked up her suitcase and Maisie's Trunki.

'You'll show it to Connie, then?'

'Yeah.'

Ray must have caught something in her voice. 'Lili, you will show it to her – won't you? I have been a detective for many years. I have a feeling about this. There's something Connie isn't telling you – I'm convinced of it.'

Lili stopped. That was what she'd thought too.

'Show her the photo, Lili. If it isn't them, then at least we've ruled them out and I can start another line of inquiry.'

Lili smiled. It was just what a police officer would say,

although she couldn't imagine what that other line of inquiry, as he put it, might be. She appreciated his generosity, though.

'You're leaving Connie's, aren't you?'

Lili opened the door and took one last look at the bedroom. She wouldn't be back. 'I have to.'

'I understand. You know there's a spare room here at my place, and the flat is still unoccupied.'

She caught the concern in Ray's voice. Thinking of the flat above the shop, she asked, 'How is Joseph?'

'Oh, you know Joseph – he's a survivor.'

She didn't know Joseph, but she imagined that was a reference to his experiences on Corfu in the war years. Lili touched the ring on the chain around her neck. 'Ray, you mentioned something about other lines of inquiry.'

'Yes, I did,' he said slowly. 'But here's the thing, I've got to be honest. I don't know where to go from here.'

'I do.'

'You do?'

'It's Joseph.'

'Joseph?'

'Yes. This might be nothing, and just a coincidence, but it's about the ring.'

'What are you talking about, Lili?'

Lili told him that she'd discovered she had an identical ring to the one Joseph wore. She recounted bumping into Sarah, on her last hospital visit, and that Sarah had told her the band was one of a pair; Jewish betrothal rings once owned by Joseph's father and mother, Sarah's grandparents. Sarah had never seen the other until Lili showed her the ring.

'I don't know how my parents came by this ring. They may

have just bought it somewhere, but it was my only possession, apart from the clothes I was wearing, when they found me.'

Lili walked down the stairs, still speaking to Ray on the phone, carrying her suitcase in one hand and Maisie's small case balanced awkwardly in the crook of her arm.

'That's incredible. Why didn't you say something before?'

Lili sighed down the phone as she reached the bottom of the stairs. Glancing into the lounge, she saw Connie rising from her seat. 'There's been a lot going on, Ray.'

Connie spotted Lili carrying her coat and suitcase to the door. 'Are you leaving?'

'What does it look like?' Lili replied.

'Pardon?' Ray replied.

Lili shook her head in annoyance. 'I wasn't talking to you, Ray. Look, I've got to go.' Ignoring Connie, Lili was already opening the front door. 'Will you ask Joseph about his ring? Perhaps you could find out about Alena too.'

'Who?'

'Oh, that's the other thing … he kept calling me Alena.'

'Alena?'

'Yes, I get the impression I remind him of someone by that name. Perhaps I look like her?'

'Interesting …' mused Ray.

'I thought she might be his mother, Sarah's grandmother, but she hasn't heard of Alena either.' Lili stepped out of the house. 'Will you ask Joseph when he's … you know … a bit more with it.'

'Of course.'

'Thank you.'

'Is there anything else Joseph said to you?'

'He also mentioned another name – *Miriam*.'

'Miriam?'

'Does that name mean anything to you, Ray?'

'No, I'm afraid not.' Ray changed the subject. 'Where will you go?'

Lili slammed the front door shut behind her. She stood on the doorstep, hoping a taxi would just happen by. 'I'll stay with my best friend for a bit.' At least, that was the plan. As soon as she got off the phone to Ray, Lili was going to call her again.

'Is it Hannah?'

'Yes.'

'Will you send Maisie our love and ask Hannah if … when we can see Maisie again?'

'Of course, I will.' Hannah wouldn't put herself out to let Maisie visit her paternal grandparents, unless … Lili had a thought. 'What about Nate?' Lili ventured, 'does he want to see Maisie?'

'Yes, he does. I passed on the phone number you gave me, so he can get in touch with Hannah.'

'Good.' Lili spied a taxi and held out her hand, hailing the cab. 'I'll speak to Hannah, don't you worry. If she doesn't tell Maisie that you are her grandparents and Nate is her dad, then I will tell her myself. She deserves to know.'

'Thank you, Lili.'

'You don't have to thank me, Ray.'

The taxi came to a stop at the kerb.

'You will show that photo to Connie, won't you?'

Lili frowned as she opened the car door. 'I've got to go.'

18

Lili was about to get in the taxi and phone Hannah when she saw the message from Ray with the photo. She rolled her eyes and said to the driver, 'Do you mind waiting a moment? There's something I need to do first.'

'No problem.'

Lili left the suitcases in the back of the taxi and reluctantly returned to Connie's front door. She rang the doorbell.

When Connie answered the door, the surprised look on her face told Lili she thought she'd changed her mind about leaving.

'I'm not staying. I just want you to look at this photo.' Lili held up her phone. 'Do you recognise them?' She cast a glance back at the taxi. She was eager to leave and call Hannah, otherwise she'd have to check into a hotel, which she couldn't afford.

Lili turned back to find Connie in tears. She said, 'What's wrong?'

'Where did you get that photo?'

Lili told her about Ray and his assumption that she hadn't been abandoned; that he thought something must have happened to her parents. Connie stood there open-mouthed, tears rolling down her face. 'I took that photo on the beach in Benitses.'

Lili swallowed. 'Are they …?'

Connie nodded her head emphatically. 'Yes. It's them. It's your parents.'

'Are you sure?'

'Positive. It's Sky and River.'

Lili stared at the photo. After all these years, she couldn't quite believe that she was looking at the faces of her parents.

Connie burst into tears again.

Lili felt like doing the same, but she held it together just long enough to say, 'What is it you're not telling me, Connie?'

Connie wiped her eyes with a tissue, took a deep breath and admitted, 'They left you in my care.'

Lili frowned. 'What are you talking about?' She was staring at her phone, taking in the young, happy couple smiling back at her. Despite trying to keep her emotions in check, tears rolled down her cheeks.

Regardless of all the hurt, anger, and pain she had been avoiding over the years at the thought that they had abandoned her, she realised she had still wanted to meet them, speak to them, learn their side of the story. Now, she knew that would never happen. Lili took a deep breath. It was a bittersweet moment. There they were, their picture, their names. Her parents were real people, as opposed to the fictional characters she'd always imagined, but they were as gone from her life as they'd ever been.

'They were going on a trip. I assumed it was somewhere on Corfu, but they did say they would be staying overnight. It never occurred to me that they were visiting another island.'

Lili looked up. 'Are you saying that you were looking after me when strangers found me wandering alone on the beach?'

'Yes … I … I left you in one of the beach huts we were living in. I wanted to go to a party that evening. I thought you were asleep.'

'You left a three-year-old on their own?'

She nodded. 'I am so sorry. When I discovered you were missing, I went to the police, and…'

'Somebody had already found me, a tourist, and taken me to the police station.'

'Yes,' Connie mumbled.

Lili wiped her eyes dry and stared at her. All along, Connie had claimed she had been holidaying in the area when she'd heard about an English child wandering along the shore alone. So as a qualified social worker, she'd offered her services, accompanying Lili back to England when they couldn't find her parents. But that wasn't the whole truth.

'You didn't tell the police that I had been in your care.'

'Look, I didn't want to get your parents into trouble for leaving you with a virtual stranger. I was a social worker, so I knew where that sort of thing could lead.'

'You mean, *you* didn't want to get into trouble.'

'I'm sorry,' she said again in a small voice. Connie couldn't look her in the eye. 'I was a newly qualified social worker.'

'I know that!' Lili snapped.

Connie raised her eyes and faced her. 'Don't you see? I had a child in my care and I … they would have classed it as neglect, leaving you on your own like that.'

'You'd have lost your licence to practise, and your career would have been over before it even started.'

Connie looked at the floor. 'Yes.'

'That's why you got me into that private school and

contributed towards the costs of the prep. Guilt money.'

Connie didn't deny it.

Lili's mind was racing, 'So, you didn't tell the police that you knew my parents – Sky and River.'

'It wouldn't have mattered, don't you see? That wasn't their actual names.'

'But you were aware they were going on a trip. Ray found the local police report. They assumed my parents had drowned during a beach party on Corfu the night before or had flown back to England, abandoning their child. They didn't look at other possibilities.'

Lili glanced at her phone, at the photo of her deceased parents. 'Do you know what this means, Connie?' Tears were streaming down Lili's face again. Twenty-four years had passed since she was discovered on that beach. If Connie had told the authorities the truth, they might have made the connection with the couple who had died in Zakynthos the day Lili was found. What if they'd then traced her extended family, her grandparents? She wouldn't have grown up in care or been sent to a boarding school.

'I know what you're thinking, Lili. The authorities might have connected the dots with …' She glanced at the photo. 'Your mother mentioned she was estranged from her parents. I told you that she'd discovered a family secret, and that she'd travelled to Corfu to search for something.' She shook her head. 'I don't know why there was a rift with her family, but perhaps growing up with your biological family wouldn't have been the best thing for you.'

Lili scowled at her. 'That wasn't your decision to make!' She put her phone in her pocket and turned on her heel.

'Where are you going, Lili?'

As far away from you as possible, thought Lili, although she wouldn't dignify the question with a response. Why did Connie care?

When she returned to the taxi, Lili gave the driver Hannah's address. As the car sped away, she glanced out of the rear window and saw Connie return to the house and close the door. She expected that Connie was glad to see the back of her. All these years she'd been harbouring that guilty secret, and finally she was shot of it – and of Lili.

Lili turned around in her seat. She was about to phone Hannah, and was not looking forward to another awkward conversation, when it rang. Lili imagined that was Connie phoning to try to apologise again and persuade her to stay.

Lili looked at her mobile, surprised and relieved it wasn't her. 'Hannah – hello.'

Lili was about to launch into another apology over Maisie and the holiday in Suffolk she hadn't told Hannah about when her friend beat her to it. 'I am so sorry, Lili. All those times I've crashed at yours, just turning up with Maisie. You never turned me away – not once. You're a loyal friend – my best friend. I can't believe the one time you asked for my help …'

Lili heard her sniff down the phone.

'I've had such a terrible night over it. I want you to stay with me, Lili. Will you come? Please say yes.'

Lili smiled. 'I'm on my way …' It was a figure of speech, although on this occasion it was literally true.

'Great.'

'Oh, Hannah, I can't wait to see you. I've got some incredible news. I've found out who my parents are.'

'You are joking.'

'No joke.' Lili glanced at the taxi driver eyeing her in the rear-view mirror. She didn't want to go into the details over the phone, to discuss the fact that her father and mother had been dead all these years, or to tell her best friend about her crap morning at Connie's. She would wait until she arrived.

When Lili ended the call to Hannah, she knew she had to ring Connie. There was a question still bugging her that she hadn't asked.

'Connie, it's me. I have a question. Why a boarding school in Suffolk?' Lili felt stupid for asking. There was probably no significance apart from that it was cheaper and more convenient to send her out of London.

'Ah, I forgot about that. Yes, there was a reason I sent you there, and no, it wasn't because I wanted you as far away as possible – if that's what you're thinking.'

Lili stared out of the taxi window. Connie was quite correct; that's just what she had been thinking.

'If I'd wanted to do that,' Connie said, 'I would have packed you off to Scotland – not just a couple of hours down the road by train.'

'So, why did you send me to a school near Aldeburgh on the Suffolk Coast?'

'When I was choosing your school, I remembered your mother had talked about a place in Suffolk, a town she'd once visited with you on the trail of some family history. I thought that if I sent you there, then you would be in an area with some connection to your past, however tenuous …'

Lili thought of Joseph and the Hebrew betrothal rings. Did she have a connection with Joseph and his family?

Connie continued, 'I hoped if she resurfaced and returned to England …' Connie trailed off.

'… that she might find me.' Lili thought of the photos on her phone.

'But it was not to be,' Connie sighed heavily. 'I'm really sorry. I shouldn't have lied to the police in Corfu. Instead, I should have told them that I knew your parents. It is unforgivable.'

'It is,' Lili confirmed.

'I know. If you tell me their names, I can make inquiries…'

'Isn't it a bit late for that?' Lili scoffed. Did Connie really think she could make amends now? It had been twenty-four years. What did she imagine she was going to find?

Lili thought of Ray. If anyone could discover her long-lost relatives, a retired police officer, and a good friend, was her best bet. Besides, she trusted Ray to tell her the truth.

'I've got to go.' Lili hung up and immediately made another call. Ray answered his mobile phone on the second ring. Lili thought of the young couple in the photo who he thought might be her parents. 'It's Lili. You'll never guess what …'

19

Lili stood on the pavement outside the house, wondering if she had the correct address. The taxi driver had dropped her off in a small crescent of detached properties in the leafy, well-to-do area of London called Muswell Hill. Hannah's house was the third property along. Looking up at the gorgeous residence, Lili's first impression was that her best friend had fallen on her feet.

As Lili stepped forward, the front door opened. It wasn't Hannah, but Maisie. She came running out, flinging her arms around Lili's waist, stopping her in her tracks. 'Mummy told me you were coming to stay,' she said excitedly. 'I've missed you!'

Lili smiled. 'Me too. Look what I've got!'

'My Trunki!' Maisie took the case, cradling it in her arms.

Lili looked up at the house. There was no sign of Hannah. 'Where's your mum?'

'Oh, they're all in the garden.'

Lili caught the frown on Maisie's face. She frowned too, wondering if this was a bad time. 'Has your mum got company?'

'She's always got company,' Maisie said as they walked up the steps and through the door into the spacious entrance hallway of the Edwardian home. Lili could hear music and the chatter of conversation. It sounded like a party. Lili looked at Maisie. 'Is your mum having a party?'

'Yes, it's an engagement party. Mummy has lots of friends.'

Lili felt offended that she hadn't been invited. Looking around the interior of the property, she guessed an unemployed, single horticulturist of no fixed abode wouldn't have much in common with Hannah's new crowd. She imagined some of them were her neighbours who lived in her posh street of large, expensive houses.

Lili heard children's laughter coming from the garden. She looked at Maisie, wondering why she wasn't playing with the other children. 'Have you made some new friends like Mummy?'

Maisie shook her head. 'They don't like me. They call me silly names behind the grown-ups' backs.'

Lili was about to ask what sort of names when Maisie said, 'I don't want to talk about it.'

'Okay.'

'Do you want to see my room?'

Lili nodded.

Maisie left her suitcase in the hallway. 'Let's get some snacks first.'

Lili left her case by the front door and followed her into a spacious modern kitchen with shiny white cupboards, expensive oak worktops and a huge American-style fridge. There were platters of food laid out on the kitchen table. It surprised Lili to see catering staff preparing the fare and taking it out into a marquee in the garden.

Lili spotted Hannah as she walked towards the patio doors.

Hannah popped her head inside. 'Lili, I'm so glad you're here.'

Lili cast her gaze over Hannah's shoulder at her new friends in the marquee; the women were adorned in designer gowns. Standing there in her jeans, sweatshirt, and white trainers, Lili felt not only under-dressed, but intimidated by Hannah's new friends. Perhaps that was how Maisie felt too.

'Maisie wants to show me her room.'

'Okay. Come outside and join us afterwards, won't you?'

Lili nodded, although she doubted she would. 'Your house is …' Lili searched for the right word.

'Ridiculous,' said Hannah, smiling.

Lili looked at her. That wasn't quite the word she would have used, although it seemed apt; the house was ostentatious for three people. Perhaps that was what Hannah had meant.

'Is your fiancé a footballer?'

Hannah hesitated. 'Er, no. Now, don't be long, I can't wait to introduce you to my friends.'

One of the catering staff interrupted their conversation, checking where Hannah wanted the drinks laid out in the marquee.

Maisie tugged on Lili's sleeve. 'Come on!' She had piled two paper plates full of party food. 'Here.'

Lili took the plate and cast a glance back at Hannah, who was having words with the staff, complaining that they hadn't prepared enough food.

Lili looked at her platter as she followed Maisie up the stairs. Her mouth was watering at the sight of the canapés. After the eventful morning – and skipping breakfast – Lili was starving.

Maisie opened the door to a small room on the first floor, just at the top of the stairs. 'I chose this bedroom because it's cosy. All the others are too big.'

Lili looked around at the room. She smiled at the colourful posters that brightened up the bland magnolia walls. They were pictures of her favourite superheroes from *The Avengers* – the movies that Maisie was into watching at the moment. Casting her gaze further, Lili spotted a crib in the corner. She walked over to the crib, half-expecting there to be a baby inside.

'That's for my new brother or sister.'

'Your mum's having a baby?' Lili blurted.

Maisie shook her head. 'Not yet, but she said she's getting everything prepared for one after they are married. I have to get used to the idea.'

'Don't you want a little brother or sister?' As Lili said it, she was thinking of William. Maisie already had a little brother. She didn't know if Hannah had told her, though.

Maisie shook her head. 'I don't like babies. They don't do anything.'

'Babies quickly grow into …' Lili paused, 'well, sisters or brothers like William.'

Maisie brightened. 'I like William. I wish he was my brother.'

Lili stared at her. So, Hannah had whisked her away and not told her the truth. Lili frowned. She had a right to know about William, her half-brother, about her father, Nate, and about her grandparents.

'Shall we make a den and then we can have a picnic?' Maisie said.

Lili smiled. Using a white sheet from the bed, together they made a makeshift tent with pillows and cushions to sit on.

The afternoon of playing games with Maisie drifted into the evening. Lili didn't feel any inclination to join the party. At some point, Maisie took another trip downstairs for more food and a large glass of milk. Eventually, she changed into her pyjamas, and Lili read her a bedtime story, sitting with her on her bed. 'Are you sure you don't want me to fetch Mummy to give you a goodnight kiss?'

Maisie shook her head.

Lili gave her a goodnight kiss instead.

'I enjoy having a story. Mummy's new fiancé, Kyle, says I'm too old for that sort of thing. Anyway, I go to bed when I like, but I always take up a glass of milk and read to myself before I go to sleep.'

Lili wasn't pleased to hear that Kyle sounded like a jerk, and that Maisie went to bed when she wanted. Children needed routines and boundaries. Maisie seemed to have sorted out her own bedtime routine, though.

'Can you take me on holiday to Aldeburgh again?'

Lili smiled. 'We had a good time, didn't we?'

Maisie nodded. 'Oh, yes.'

'What were your favourite things?'

As Maisie drifted off to sleep, she recounted their time spent hunting for amber, her paintings, the yummy fish and chips they'd eaten on the beach with William and Ray, and their stay in the flat above Joseph's shop. She liked the flat and told Lili their new house was too big. She carried on talking about the things she'd enjoyed about their trip until she fell asleep.

Sitting on the bed, propped up by a pillow, Lili was also thinking about what she'd enjoyed about their holiday. One person kept coming to mind – Nate. Had she fallen for the doctor with the crappy bedside manner? Lili tried to think of anything else but Nate. It wasn't working. Watching Maisie sleeping, Lili's eyes grew heavy.

20

Surprised she'd fallen asleep sitting up on Maisie's bed, Lili woke to the sound of raised voices. She looked at Maisie, but she hadn't stirred.

Lili stood up and stretched. She went over to the window. Maisie's bedroom was at the back of the house. Down below, the garden was empty. During her catnap, the party had wound down and everyone had gone home. Lili felt relieved. She strolled over to the bedroom door and opened it. She was about to walk out of the room when she overheard Hannah and Kyle on the stairs.

Lili heard Hannah exclaim, 'You said *buy whatever you want*, so I bought a Mercedes. It didn't bother you at the time.'

A Mercedes? Lili mouthed. So, that was what the car Hannah had turned up in to collect Maisie was. She had thought it quite flashy at the time, but she wasn't very au fait with cars. She could see they were rolling in money, though.

'I know I didn't say anything. Quite frankly, I've had a lot going on, but I didn't think you'd go out and buy a car. What were you thinking? I meant lingerie or something.'

'So, I spend fifty grand,' Hannah said. 'There's more where that came from – isn't there? You said so yourself.'

Lili slowly closed the door and sucked in a breath. *Fifty thousand pounds on a car? Just what did Kyle do for a living?*

A peculiar thought crossed Lili's mind; Hannah always seemed to fall in with the wrong crowd. Lili had assumed that this time was different, and that Hannah had fallen on her feet. She had imagined that her friend's new partner was a city slicker – a trader, or a lawyer like Alex. But something was telling her that he might not be on the up and up. She closed the bedroom door quietly, hoping Hannah didn't glimpse her and realise she had overheard their lover's tiff.

She checked again that Maisie was still asleep and thought of their earlier conversation about the holiday. Then, something dawned on her; she'd left an important item behind in the flat. 'Oh, god!' she whispered under her breath. She had put the box Alex had sent by FedEx – the one containing most of her possessions – in a cupboard, and when she'd hastily packed her suitcase to leave, she'd forgotten all about it. She didn't care about her clothes, her small DVD collection of favourite movies, the few ornaments she'd collected over the years or even her precious books on horticulture; what really mattered to Lili was her file – the one she'd been given when she officially left care at eighteen.

There wasn't much in it. There were some childhood photos that had been taken by different foster carers, as well as Connie, over the years. But it was the single sheet of lined paper with the details of where she'd been found on Corfu, what she was wearing, and the police report that she was most concerned about; that was the only connection she had with her past.

Lili listened carefully at the door. She couldn't hear Hannah and her partner arguing anymore. It was her chance to slip away.

She felt bad for leaving, but she had no choice if she wanted to retrieve the file.

Lili had just stepped out of the bedroom when she almost walked into Hannah, who was striding along the hall.

'Oh, Lili. There you are. I'm sorry the party went on for a bit. Why don't you come downstairs and have a glass of wine? I sure as hell could do with one.'

Lili shook her head, but her expression gave her away.

'Ah, you heard us arguing.'

Lili didn't deny it. 'I didn't mean to, but you were—'

'Loud – I know! Sorry about that.'

Lili said nothing more, but she got the impression Kyle was having money issues. 'Look, I'd better go.'

'Oh, Lili, please don't.'

'I have to.' Lili told her about the file she'd left behind in Aldeburgh as they walked downstairs.

Hannah turned to her. 'I'll go.'

'What?'

'I need to get out of here. I'll drive to Suffolk and collect your box if you don't mind baby-sitting Maisie for me.'

'What about …' Lili stepped into the hall. There was no sign of Kyle.

Hannah rolled her eyes. 'He's probably in the movie theatre watching a film.'

'You've got your own cinema?'

'It's in the basement, but it's tiny, there's two rows and only eight seats, but yeah – crazy, huh?'

'So, what does Kyle do for a living?'

'Oh, you know, a little of this, and a little of that. He's in business.'

Lili stared at her. If that wasn't a euphemism for something shady, she didn't know what was.

'So, how about it, Lili? I'll get your stuff, you stay here, watch TV. There's our lounge through there. Grab a bite to eat. There are plenty of leftovers from the party.'

Lili thought about it. It beat going to the station and trying to catch a train and then a bus at the other end. Lili knew she'd also have to book in somewhere and stay the night, only to have to do the return journey the following day. With a car, Hannah would be there and back in no time.

'Okay, but as long as you're sure.'

Hannah grinned. 'I'm sure. It's an excuse to get out of the house for a couple of hours.'

Although Lili had posted the flat latchkeys in the letter box of Ray's shop, she'd found a spare key that she'd taken off her the keyring and put in her purse just in case. She'd forgotten all about it. 'Here,' she said, handing over the key. 'If you walk through the shop, there's a door at the end on the right with stairs that lead up to the flat above. I left the box in the cupboard over the stairs.'

Hannah took the key. 'Was there anything else?'

Lili thought of the amber necklaces hanging in the window to sell. Although Maisie had created them, the fact that they were in the shop made her feel uneasy about asking Hannah to take them. Lili shook her head. 'No, nothing else.'

'What about a little keepsake?' Hannah asked.

'What do you mean?'

'You worked there and weren't paid a bean. From what Masie told me, it sounds as though you kept the place going successfully in the owner's absence.'

Lili looked at her blankly. She still didn't know what Hannah was getting at.

'Oh, don't worry. Look, the sooner I get going, the sooner you'll have your file.'

'You're a good friend, Hannah.'

'Don't thank me. You've given me an excuse to get out of the house.' Hannah leaned in and gave Lili a hug. 'See you later.'

'You don't mind if I make myself a cup of tea – do you?'

'Don't be silly. Of course not. Remember to help yourself to the leftover party food.'

Lili smiled at Hannah, then made her way to the kitchen and closed the door just as Kyle emerged from another room. He spotted Hannah reaching for her coat and looked at her in surprise. 'Are you going out?'

'Shh, let's not start arguing again, please.' Hannah glanced down the hall. She heard Lili in the kitchen putting the kettle on. 'I've got company.'

'What?'

'Remember, I told you my best friend is staying for a few days.'

'So, where are you off to?'

'I'm just going for a drive. Don't worry, Lili will keep an eye on Maisie.'

'Where are you going – exactly?'

Hannah rolled her eyes. 'I said, just for a drive.'

'Where?'

Hannah sighed. She could feel this was quickly building into another argument. She grabbed a jacket off the coat rack and stepped outside, beckoning him to step out of the house with her, out of earshot of Lili. 'Look, my friend has left something behind at the place she was staying in Aldeburgh, so I'm doing her a favour and returning to pick it up.'

'What place?'

'It was a holiday rental above some shop.'

'A shop? What sort of shop?'

Hannah remembered Maisie saying something. 'Antiques – I think.'

'Antiques?'

Hannah narrowed her eyes. She wagged a finger at him. 'Don't get any ideas.'

'What do you mean?'

'You know very well. And before you ask, I'm not telling you where the antique shop is.'

He shrugged. 'You don't have to, but if you want to keep your expensive wheels, you better bring me back a souvenir from your trip to Suffolk.' He smirked.

Hannah shook her head, eyes wide. She knew what he was asking. 'I can't.'

'Why not? It's not like she's there anymore. What would she care? I suggest you break a window or force the back door. Make it look like a rob—'

'Shh, keep your voice down! She's in the kitchen.' Hannah closed the front door. 'No, I won't do it.'

Kyle stopped smiling. 'Where do you think all this comes from?'

By all this, he was referring to the house, the clothes, the parties – the car. Hannah glared at him. 'I'm not stupid.' She knew very well where it came from.

'I know this is what you've always wanted.'

Hannah bit her lower lip and looked at him sheepishly. She'd *thought* it was. She'd always aspired to be a WAG, but the funny thing was that she finally had what she'd craved, but she wasn't sure it was all it was cracked up to be.

The party hadn't been much fun. Her new friends were boring, the food was expensive, the house was all show; the only thing she really liked was her shiny new car, and even that was coming at a price – in fact, it all was. She'd rather have spent the afternoon with Lili and Maisie upstairs.

Hannah started walking towards her car.

'I think I'll come with you.'

She paused and turned around. 'I want some time on my own.' That was the whole point of the trip.

'Okay, have it your way – but you'd better bring me something back.'

Hannah rolled her eyes. 'Fine – whatever.' If the shop was brimming full of stuff, surely there would be a small item she could take that the owner wouldn't miss. Then she had a better idea; she could stop at a cash machine on the way and withdraw some money, then pay for an item. That way, nothing would go missing. She didn't want to get Lili in trouble.

'It had better be worth something.'

Hannah shrugged. 'What do I know about antiques? It's probably a load of old junk, anyway.'

'Well then, bring back a selection, so at least it will increase your chances.'

'You said *one* thing.'

'Well, I changed my mind.'

Hannah threw him a cold, hard stare. She was quickly changing her mind too – about him. She was aware, though, that for the first time, she didn't have Lili to fall back on; she couldn't crash on Lili's sofa or in her spare room if she decided one day that she wanted to walk out. She *was* well and truly stuck. Then it occurred to her that if she had a job, she wouldn't have to depend on a man.

'What a silly thought,' she said to herself under her breath. It was easier to have a partner, a husband to support her and Maisie – wasn't it? She frowned. Not if her partner made her do things she didn't want to do – like steal from a shop. What a way to pay her best friend back for all the times she'd helped her out. Hannah didn't want to think about that. This was an absolute one-off. She had no intention of making a habit of joining Kyle's business. However, she was considering taking his advice; if she made it look like a break-in, no one would be any the wiser.

On the other hand, thought Hannah as she sped off down the street, if she didn't do that, perhaps whatever she took wouldn't be missed? Then the police wouldn't get involved. From what Lili had told her, the owner of the shop who was in hospital was old and confused; he might not remember a couple of missing items.

By the time Hannah was well on her way, she'd decided that she wouldn't break a window. Pulling the car to a stop at a red light, Hannah was just slipping the key into the pocket of the jacket she'd flung on the passenger seat, when she noticed she had grabbed the wrong coat – it was Lili's. Hannah rolled her eyes. At least it had a hood; it was raining.

The traffic lights changed. Lili patted the coat pocket before setting off again. At least she didn't have to break in. Nobody would even know she had been there.

21

Reggie was just closing his shop when he thought he saw Lili in the courtyard. She'd been in the antique shop. It surprised him to see Joseph's prize orchid in her hands. Was she intending to visit him? He'd understood from Ray that the plan was to leave the orchid in the shop as a surprise for Joseph when he was discharged from hospital the next evening. Ray knew that the curmudgeonly old man would insist on visiting the shop on his way home to check everything. He would not expect one of his prize orchids to be in the shop and in bloom. Reggie didn't know the first thing about plants, but Ray had told him it had flowered; apparently, it was quite the rare event. Reggie had heard that Joseph wasn't being discharged as soon as they'd anticipated. Perhaps there had been a change of plan and that was the reason Lili had returned to collect the orchid.

'Lili?' he called out. Although he didn't see her face, he did recognise her distinctive raincoat as she hurried towards High Street. 'Lili!' he shouted again, hurrying after her. He saw her close the boot of her car and get into the driver's seat. He called one more time as she sped away, disappointed she hadn't heard him.

❖

Hannah pulled the hood on the jacket down and glanced in the rear-view mirror. The old man from the shop across the courtyard was too slow to catch up with her.

She had smiled when she'd found the antique shop was in a small, cobbled yard off the main thoroughfare, out of the way of prying eyes and passing motorists. By the time she'd arrived, it was early in the evening; the traffic out of London had been worse than she'd expected.

She'd assumed all the shops in the courtyard would be closed, and she hadn't expected to see anyone. When she'd heard someone call Lili's name, she'd felt bad for not turning around to tell the old man that she wasn't Lili.

He'd only caught her walking out of the shop with the flower – not all the other items. The plant was for Lili. *Why not get my best friend a souvenir from her time working here?* she'd thought. *And something for Maisie too.* There was a painting Maisie had talked fondly of. It had been hanging upstairs in the flat – until Hannah took it down. She'd brought it back for her daughter. She had also taken all the amber necklaces from the display case in the window. She'd heard all about the jewellery her daughter had made to sell in the shop. As far as she was concerned, they belonged to Maisie.

Hannah looked at the plant in her hand. She didn't know what sort it was, but Lili would. It was unusual, ghostly white, and delicate. It wasn't the prettiest flower in the world, but Hannah told herself that it was the thought that counted. She placed it on the passenger seat next to Lili's box. She set off.

Hannah answered her mobile phone while she was driving.

She didn't want to pull the car over; she wanted to get home as soon as possible. It was already getting dark. She was taking a chance, so she kept her eyes peeled for any police cars around; she couldn't afford to be pulled over with a load of stolen goods onboard.

'Did you find it?'

'Yes, it's on the front seat as we speak. I'll be with you shortly.' Hannah ended the call to Lili and glanced at the box. Thinking of Alex, she mumbled, 'What a bastard.' She was glad she'd picked up the plant. It had only been an afterthought; she'd caught sight of it in the window on her way out of the door. She smiled, hoping it would cheer Lili up when she saw it.

Her thoughts drifted to Kyle. Her smile faded when she thought of the car loaded with stuff from the shop. She shook her head. She'd got a bit carried away. Undecided over what was worth taking, she'd chosen as much as would fit in the boot. There was no shortage of antiques. At least when he saw the amount that she'd brought back with her, he would have nothing to complain about.

❖

'This is all a pile of junk!'

They were standing on the driveway with the boot open. Hannah's smile vanished. 'When you told me to bring some antiques back, didn't I say it was probably a load of junk?' She wished she'd hadn't taken quite so much. Hannah shut the boot and opened the passenger door. 'Here, help me with this box.' She put the box in his arms and reached inside for the potted plant. When she turned around, closing the car door with her foot, Kyle said, 'What's that?'

'Oh, this? I saw it in the shop. It's kind of pretty, so I brought it back for her.'

'Let me see.'

She watched him put the box down on the driveway and get out his phone. He pointed at the flower. 'That's an orchid.'

Hannah looked at the plant. 'So?' She glanced at him. 'What do you know about flowers?' She was being sarcastic.

'Oh, you'd be surprised. If they are rare – and valuable.' He took a photo of the plant.

'What are you doing?'

'Just sending the picture to a mate.'

'Well, don't think you're having this. I brought it back for Lili.' Hannah started walking towards the house.

He got to the front door first, barring her way.

Hannah looked at him. 'I need you to fetch the box.' She couldn't manage it and the plant too.

'I'll bring in the box. You can give it to Lili. After all, that's what she asked you to fetch for her – didn't she?'

Hannah nodded.

'You can keep all the crap in the boot.' He held out his hand. 'But I want the flower.'

'Why?'

'You don't know what you've got there – do you?'

'It's an orchid, like you said.'

'Yes, and orchids are valuable. But that plant is one of the rarest of them all. And it's bloomed.'

Hannah stared at the plant. 'So it has.' It looked nothing special.

'It's a ghost orchid, Hannah. They are rare because they only bloom at night.'

'Ah. That is unusual. So, you're saying this is worth a bit of money?'

Kyle grinned. She knew that look. It was the same expression he had whenever he scored big. Hannah smiled to herself when she realised he hadn't spotted the painting she'd brought back for Maisie, although she reckoned that it was just as worthless as the crap in the boot.

'It's worth six figures.'

She looked at the wimpy little plant in the flowerpot. 'Six figures – for this? You must be joking. Are you saying you'd get a hundred grand?'

'Probably more than that.' His expression turned earnest. 'Look, I'm in a bit of trouble. This is going to dig us out of a hole – big time. We can keep the house …'

Hannah wasn't sure she wanted the house.

'Your car too.'

Hannah threw a glance over his shoulder at the beautiful, shiny red, soft-top Mercedes – her dream ride. She reluctantly handed over the plant.

'Did you do like I said and stage a robbery?'

Hannah bit her lower lip.

'You are joking me!'

'I didn't think it was a great idea. The police would get called straight away. If no one knew things had been taken, at least not right away, it would give you a chance to fence the stuff.'

'Okay, yeah, that's a good plan, especially as we're not talking about crap antiques now.' He glanced at the flower in his hand.

So did Hannah. 'The thing is … it didn't go according to plan.'

He looked up sharply. 'Don't tell me you were seen!'

Hannah nodded her head.

'For god's sake, Hannah.'

'Yes, but not like you think. I went and grabbed Lili's coat by mistake, so that's what I was wearing when …' She trailed off.

He got the picture. 'Someone thought you were Lili?'

'Yes.'

'Well, that's fortunate, isn't it?'

'No, it's not. She'll get into trouble when they discover things are missing from the shop.'

His expression darkened. 'No, Hannah, *we* are going to get into trouble if the police trace her here. Who knows how many people she's told about coming to stay with you? You've got to get rid of her.'

'I can't do that. Lili has split up from her partner. She has nowhere to go.' Hannah caught sight of the box sitting on the driveway.

He followed her gaze. 'What is it?'

'Lili mentioned something on the phone before she turned up about finding her parents.'

'So what?'

'It's a long story, but they found Lili wandering alone on a beach in Corfu when she was a child.'

'Corfu?'

Hannah nodded.

'Does it sound as though a return trip is in order?' he mused.

'I think it does, yes.'

'Could you persuade her to go, Hannah – like immediately?'

They stood staring at the flower, both aware it would solve all their problems.

'But what happens when she returns?' Hannah asked.

He shrugged. 'Not our problem. We'll be long gone.'

'What do you mean?'

'I'll sort out renting our house and we'll take an extended trip, maybe to Thailand, definitely the Far East.'

Hannah wasn't talking about that. 'I didn't mean us, I meant what about Lili?'

'What about her?'

'Won't she be in trouble when she returns?'

'Like I said before – not our problem?'

'But if she gets arrested, it will be our fault. She's my friend. I don't want her to get into trouble.'

He threw her a sly grin, glancing at the car. 'I'm afraid it's too late. That horse has already bolted.'

Hannah's bottom lip quivered. 'What have I done?'

'Oh, get a grip, for god's sake. Think about yourself and your daughter. You don't want to end up in prison – do you?'

Hannah stared at him.

'So, we stick to the plan. Persuade Lili to go to Corfu. If she hasn't got the money, we will pay for her plane ticket because she can't stay here. Then we'll pack our bags and jet off to a nice island somewhere. We could get married on a beach – you've always wanted to do that, remember?'

Hannah swallowed. He was right. 'What about Maisie? She should be returning to school soon for the start of the new term.'

He frowned. 'I don't know. She'll have to tag along, do some home-schooling, I guess.' He thought for a moment. 'I've got a better idea. What about boarding school? We'll have the money.'

Hannah's eyes went wide. 'No way!' She knew she hadn't been the best mother over the years, but she wasn't about to send

Maisie away, like her own parents had done to her. She looked at the flower, wishing she'd never set eyes on the damn thing. Her thoughts returned to Lili. 'I don't want her to go to prison.'

'It might not come to that if she stays in Corfu. You said yourself she's searching for her family. Perhaps she'll find them there.'

Something in Lili's voice when she'd mentioned her parents over the phone had told Hannah it would not be as simple as that.

Kyle put a hand on her shoulder. 'Look, right now we should think about the immediate situation. Here …' He handed Hannah the plant. 'Take that back to the car and leave it on the front seat. I will go and grab the box.'

Hannah wavered on the doorstep. If only Lili would open the front door and surprise them, then she'd have to give her the orchid, and his plan to sell it would have to be ditched. However much she didn't want to get her best friend in trouble, Hannah didn't have the nerve to walk in and hand it to Lili. She turned around and took it back to the car. She got the impression Kyle owed some not very nice people money. This would get him out of whatever fix he was in, and then they could move on.

As she put the plant back in the car, she hoped he was right, and that Lili would stay in Corfu. She had no reason to return, given that Alex was out of the picture.

Hannah shut the car door and locked it, managing a smile for Kyle when she caught up with him in the hallway. Hannah knew she wasn't strong like Lili. Not the type to be on her own, she needed a man to look after her and Maisie. *Pity I always choose the bad boys,* thought Hannah, wishing she and Nate hadn't been so young when they'd fallen into bed together at that party. Things might have turned out differently if they had been madly in love with each other. But they were just two drunk kids wallowing in self-pity, drawn to each other because they'd both been cast aside by their parents. That was the reason she hadn't told him about her pregnancy, and why she'd refused to let on to her best friend that she knew who Maisie's father was.

It had been an embarrassing episode that she would much rather forget, although there had been times when Hannah had wondered how her life might have turned out if she'd told Nate about the baby and forced him to stand up to his responsibilities. Perhaps he would have married her, and they would have been together all these years.

There's no good wishing, her grandmother used to say. Besides, she doubted it would have lasted. They hadn't loved each other.

She'd Googled Nate after she'd returned home from collecting Maisie and had found his profile on LinkedIn. She'd discovered he'd gone to medical school and become a doctor. Judging by the age of his son, who wasn't that much younger than Maisie, he must have met someone at university and had his second child during his degree.

Hannah frowned. She didn't mind that Lili had taken Maisie on holiday; it was where she'd taken her that was the problem. Hannah had been afraid that this would happen, and that after all these years, Nate would discover the truth. Her stomach churned at the thought of where that might lead.

She knew she hadn't been the most responsible parent in the world – by any stretch. Sometimes she looked at her young daughter and felt that Maisie was more grown-up than she was. Why hadn't she seen that until now? At the party, some of her new friends had asked where Maisie was. Hannah had told them she'd probably made herself a glass of warm milk, found a story book and taken herself off to bed. They'd thought she was joking.

Hannah sighed. In the past, despite her behaviour – the many failed relationships, jetting off on foreign holidays at a moment's notice and leaving Maisie in the care of her friend, sofa-surfing on Lili's couch more times than she cared to remember – she knew Lili had made sure social services would never have reason to step in and take Maisie away. But Lili couldn't protect her from Maisie's father – or her grandfather. She'd Googled him too. He was a retired police officer. And what was she? A thief. Hannah swallowed. That thought sent shivers down her spine.

Carrying the box, she followed Kyle down the hall, thinking she must do her part, protect herself, and persuade Lili to go to Corfu as soon as possible. The flower was in the car, along with the many other items she'd stolen from the shop. There was no good wishing she hadn't done it. He was right; that horse had already bolted. And they were bolting too, to a nice island somewhere in the Far East – and Maisie was *not* going to be packed off to a boarding school.

22

'Oh, you're back,' exclaimed Lili. She was sitting in their kitchen, watching the ten o'clock news on a large wall-mounted TV screen and eating some leftover smoked salmon sandwiches, when Kyle walked in carrying her box. He set it down on the table for her.

'Thank you.'

He threw her a disarming smile. 'You're most welcome.'

Lili caught Hannah throwing him a look she couldn't quite fathom.

He passed Hannah, touched her arm, and leaned in to kiss her on the cheek. Lili could have sworn he had whispered something in her ear too. She was envious; she wondered what it felt like to be so much in love. Surprisingly, Alex didn't come to mind – but Nate did.

Lili swiftly brushed that thought aside. After leading him on and allowing him to believe Maisie was her daughter, she couldn't imagine he'd ever want to see her again.

Thinking of Maisie, she glanced at her best friend. She was dying to ask her about Nate and what she was going to do about letting him see Maisie.

Lili noticed that Hannah was preoccupied and not her usual chatty self. Recalling the argument she had overheard on the stairs, she sensed something was troubling her friend; perhaps that something was Nate. Lili looked at her box and decided that it wasn't the right time to bring up the subject of Maisie's father. Besides, she had enough issues of her own.

'Aren't you going to open it?' Hannah asked.

Lili said, 'I hope the most precious thing is in this box.'

'Whatever do you mean?' Hannah blurted.

Lili looked up, wondering why she sounded so defensive. 'I'm talking about this,' Lili said in relief when she found the file.

'What is it?' Hannah asked.

'It's the file they gave me after I officially left care when I turned eighteen.' Lili didn't add that it was the time when she had intended to go straight to university, but circumstances – namely, her pregnant best friend who needed her support – had meant her plans changed.

Lili didn't begrudge having put things on hold. She had still achieved her degree. If she had moved away from London to study, she wouldn't have gained the work experience at Kew.

She had no regrets about the lovely bond she had built up with Maisie either; something she would not have had if she hadn't been around. But Lili was still upset about Alex. She didn't blame Hannah for the fact they had split up. Yes, she had put on her over the years, perhaps a little too much, and it meant there were times her relationship with Alex had been strained with a mother and toddler crashing at theirs; it wasn't ideal for a young couple in love. But Maisie was eight. They'd got through the worst of it. Why had he decided to call it a day now?

At the back of her mind, Lili knew the answer to that: Hannah turning up with Maisie again had been the final straw. She supposed he had been envisaging what their future lives would look like. What would happen if they had children and, as time went by, there was also a sulky teenager, who wasn't his own, crashing on their sofa? Lili guessed he had been looking into the future and had decided that enough was enough.

Lili gave her best friend a sideways glance. She had always felt she owed Hannah. If it hadn't been for her, boarding school wouldn't have been quite so much fun. Especially the holidays. Lili felt fortunate to have spent them with Hannah at her grandparents' cottage. When Connie and her family had moved abroad with her husband's job for a time, without Hannah she would have remained at school alone, or back in a room in London in care.

Thinking of Connie, Lili opened the file. Inside was a single sheet of paper. There was a passport-sized photo attached to one corner with a paperclip.

'What is it?' Hannah asked.

'It's everything I know about my background before I came to England.' It wasn't much, but it was all she had.

'May I see?'

Lili removed the clip and handed her the picture of a small child.

'You were so cute with those ringlets.' She looked up. 'You still are.'

'Thank you.'

They exchanged a smile.

'It was so good of you to drive all that way to get it. I know this doesn't look like much, but it means a lot to me.' Lili reached over and squeezed her hand, feeling grateful she had such a wonderful friend who would do that for her. She didn't think she would have been able to face going back to the shop or bumping into Sarah or Ray or any of the lovely people in the courtyard who had taken her under their wing. She felt she had let them all down.

Hannah glanced at the file. 'Have you considered returning to Flower Island?'

Lili looked at her best friend, perplexed. 'Where?'

'Don't you remember? You used to talk about it all the time when you first started the boarding school. It's where they found you? It must be in your file.'

'No, the place they found me was Corfu.'

'Yes, I know that now, but for some reason you called it Flower Island.'

Lili hadn't thought about that in years. She raised an eyebrow.

'See, you do remember. I wonder why you called it that?' Hannah Googled it on her phone. 'Sometimes it's nicknamed Flower Island because of the abundance of wildflowers and especially the rare—' Hannah stopped. She didn't want to bring up the subject of orchids.

'Rare …?'

'Oh, er, it doesn't matter.' Hannah took a deep breath. 'Look, I think it would be a great idea for you to go. In fact, as you are in between jobs …' *and relationships*, thought Hannah, 'why don't you go now?'

'Are you trying to get rid of me?' Lili said, pretending the question was asked in jest. She could tell by Hannah's voice there was something going on.

'No, not at all. I could lend you the money – if that's the issue.'

Lili frowned. 'Now I'm definitely getting the impression you're trying to get rid of me.' Since when did Hannah offer to lend her money? Normally, it was the other way round. Hannah and Kyle didn't seem short of money, but Lili knew that appearances could be deceptive.

Hannah sighed.

Lili looked at her. 'There's something going on, isn't there?'

'I don't know what you mean.'

'I'm your best friend. We've known each other for years. I know when something is bothering you.'

Hannah went quiet.

'Are you in some kind of trouble, Hannah?'

'No, er, just relationship problems.'

Lili smiled. 'Oh, I can relate to that.'

'Sorry to hear about you and Alex. I thought—'

'Yeah, so did I.'

'Look, I want you to stay, but now isn't—'

'A great time,' said Lili, guessing what she was going to say.

Hannah shifted in her seat, avoiding Lili's gaze.

Lili was convinced there was more that Hannah wasn't telling her, but whatever was going on, Hannah didn't want to talk about it.

'Don't you want to go to Corfu, Lili?'

'Money isn't the issue. It doesn't cost much to fly to Corfu and stay on the island for a bit.'

'Then what is it?'

Lili started scrolling through her phone. 'I want to show you something, Hannah.' Lili held up her mobile and showed her the photo of a young couple who appeared to be in their twenties.

Lili handed over the phone for Hannah to take a closer look.

Her eyes went wide. 'That woman looks like you.' She glanced at Lili. 'Are they …?'

'They're my parents.'

Lili told her about the discovery that Connie had got her a place at the private boarding school when she was eight, that she'd done it out of guilt, and that she had known Lili's father and mother. Lili explained that her parents had left her in Connie's care while they were away on a trip, but Connie never divulged that fact. What Connie didn't know, and why she could not explain why they failed to return for her, was that they'd visited another island and had been killed in a motorcycle accident.

'I don't get it,' Hannah interrupted. 'Why didn't your relatives come forward after your parents died?'

'Well, that's the thing; Connie didn't know a lot about my parents, but apparently my mother told Connie that she was estranged from her family. It appears they are not aware of my existence.'

'And your father?'

'The same, I guess. Sounded as though they were bumming around the world. And then I came along …' It sounded to Lili as though her mum had been a bit like Hannah, although she didn't voice her thoughts.

'So, your grandparents didn't know they had a grandchild – a little girl who'd been left behind on Corfu.'

'Precisely.'

Hannah scratched her head. 'That's really sad,' she said, 'and all because your mum had fallen out with her parents …' She went very quiet.

Lili stared at her. She had meant to say to Hannah that she

should patch things up with her parents; Maisie deserved to know her maternal and paternal grandparents.

'Well, now you know their names, you can find your relatives.'

'I already have somebody working on that.' Lili didn't want to mention Ray, although she knew she'd promised him she would speak to Hannah about seeing his grandchild.

'What do you think the significance of the rings is?' Hannah asked when Lili told her all about the discovery that the ring she'd always worn on a chain around her neck was one of a pair of Hebrew wedding bands. The other had belonged to Joseph's father, Maisie's great-great-grandfather.

Hannah stared at her. 'Wait – are you saying you might be related to Maisie's father's side of the family?'

'I don't know. Right now, all I've got to go on is the photo on my phone and this ring.' Lili held up the band on the end of the silver chain around her neck.

'Well, you know where to start – don't you? You must return to—'

'Corfu. Yes, I knew you'd say that!' Lili fell silent.

Hannah bounced out of her seat. 'Great. Now, let me fetch my laptop and we can book your flight.'

'Okay,' she said slowly. Since when had Hannah taken such a keen interest in her life? Her best friend was usually so self-absorbed.

Hannah returned with her laptop. 'Ah, there's a flight first thing tomorrow morning.'

'Tomorrow?'

'And there's seat availability,' Hannah remarked.

Lili stared at the screen displaying the EasyJet flight to Corfu.

She wasn't sure what she would find there. Her parents were long gone. It would be a better idea for her to go back to Aldeburgh and speak with Joseph. But although she wanted to find out about the significance of her ring, she couldn't imagine showing her face in Cobbler's Yard.

'Corfu it is, then,' Lili said with a wisp of a smile. She handed over her passport and her bank card. Hannah booked her flight while Lili picked up the photo of herself as a toddler. If nothing else, she could at least visit the beach where she'd been found.

The article about the young couple who had died on another island that Ray had discovered had stated their funeral arrangements. It sounded as though her father's body had been repatriated to England to be buried. However, her mother had been laid to rest on Corfu in the British Cemetery. That was where Lili intended to go to pay her respects. Although it had all happened a long time ago, she was hoping she might find someone on the island who known her mum.

Lili was aware she was clutching at straws; Ray was far more likely to unearth her relatives through going down the genealogy route to build her family tree, with a bit of help from the local police in Zakynthos where her parents had perished. Perhaps one of her parents had links to the island; she imagined that was what Ray was trying to find out. What were they doing there? Lili would like to know whether there was any significance to their visit to the island.

She already had an idea. Connie had mentioned Lili's mother's estrangement from her family because of some secret she had uncovered. Lili was convinced that their trip to the other Greek island had had something to do with that.

She glanced at Hannah, who was busy filling in her passport

details. Lili imagined that without Hannah pushing her to go, she would find plenty of excuses to delay the trip. For a start, there were her relationship issues. During her taxi-ride, Alex had surprised her by texting to apologise about how thoughtless he'd been to box up all her possessions and send them by courier. He'd said his behaviour over the past month had been inexcusable and had asked whether she could she ever forgive him.

Lili hadn't known how to reply. It wasn't just about the box. It still upset her that he hadn't discussed his promotion with her and the move to Washington. She had a life in the UK.

Or did she? She'd not attended her interview at Kew, and the flat she'd shared with Alex wasn't a permanent home. There were her London friends, of course, but they could easily keep in touch on social media. It was Maisie and Hannah that she would find hard to leave behind – especially Maisie.

However, Alex had been right when he'd said she had her own life to lead; she still wanted children and a family of her own. The problem was that youngsters changed at an alarming rate in just a short space of time, and she knew that if she moved with Alex to Washington, she would lose touch with Maisie all too quickly. Lili didn't know if she was ready for that, or if she ever would be.

Lili cast a glance at Hannah, who was returning from the study with her plane tickets printed out. She didn't know if she was ready for her trip to Corfu either. There would never be a right time to take the journey. She just had to make the effort and go. Perhaps then, whatever she discovered – or didn't discover – she would be able to lay the ghosts of the past to rest and move on with her life.

'Here are your plane tickets to Flower Island.' Hannah placed the boarding passes on the kitchen table in front of Lili. She picked them up, wishing Hannah would stop calling the island by that name. It just reminded her of the job in Kew she hadn't attended the interview for.

Right now, she had nowhere else to go. Whatever was going on between Hannah and Kyle, it was obvious she couldn't stay there for long. If nothing else, at least she would have a cheap holiday in the sunshine.

Alex had asked her to meet him, but she'd been in two minds. Hannah had actually done her a huge favour and made up her mind for her; she was definitely going to Corfu on the trail of a family secret.

23

Lili glanced over her shoulder at Maisie, who was asleep on the back seat, as Hannah pulled the car into a parking space at the airport terminal drop-off zone. Lili's flight was at six in the morning, which meant she'd had to get up early to make it to the airport two hours before departure. Before they'd left the house, Lili had gone upstairs to kiss Maisie goodbye and had woken her up. She'd had to tell her she was leaving, and Maisie had insisted on joining them. Still in her pyjamas, she'd pulled on her dressing gown and slippers and got into the car. Lili smiled at her. Despite wanting to see Lili off, Maisie had fallen asleep on the way. Lili didn't want to wake her. She glanced at Hannah, who looked troubled. Lili was convinced there was something her friend wasn't telling her. 'Hannah …' she began in a hushed voice.

Hannah switched off the car engine and turned to her, avoiding her gaze. 'Look, things are not what they seem. Kyle isn't exactly on the up and up, and I've done something I shouldn't have.'

Lili looked at her in surprise. Hannah had fallen on her feet – hadn't she? 'What's going on, Hannah? You can tell me. I'm your best friend.'

'Are you?'

'What's that supposed to mean?'

'You've got your London friends.'

That was true, but Lili said, 'So, why am I here with you and not them?'

Hannah fell silent.

'Whatever it is—'

Hannah interrupted her. 'Look, just promise me that if …'

Lili noticed she was choosing her words carefully.

'If something happens, then you'll take care of Maisie.'

'Nothing's going to happen, Hannah. Whatever is going on, we can figure it out.'

Hannah took Lili's hands in hers. 'Just promise me, Lili. She can't end up in care. Whatever you think of me, please don't let that happen.'

Lili heard Maisie shift in her seat behind them. They both glanced at the back seat. Maisie was still asleep.

Lili turned to face Hannah and realised she would not tell her what was going on. Lili sighed. 'I wouldn't let anybody take her away – you know that. Whatever happens, Hannah, you can count on me.'

Tears rolled down Hannah's face. 'Now, I wish you didn't have to go.' She looked at her watch.

So did Lili. Time was getting on and she had to move it if she didn't want to miss her flight. Lili was about to get out of the car. 'Do you want me to stay?'

Hannah hesitated before she replied. 'No, go to Corfu. You need to find your family. It's what you've always wanted.'

Lili looked at her. 'That's not true.'

Hannah managed a smile. 'Like you said, we've known each

other a long time. You're always on at me about patching things up with my parents.'

'Sorry about that.'

'Don't be. I know why, though. You might have kidded yourself over the years, saying the past doesn't matter, quoting that silly mantra – *only ever look back to see how far you've come* – but you didn't fool me. And now you can't fool yourself. It's important to know where you're from, Lili, and find your long-lost relations. I bet there are some grandparents out there somewhere who would love to get to meet their amazing granddaughter – if only they had the chance.'

'Oh, I don't know about that.' Lili was thinking about what Connie had told her. Apparently, Lili's mother had been estranged from her parents.

'I do,' quipped Hannah. 'I know all about it. You've reminded me countless times. I saw the way Ray looked at Maisie when he found out she was his granddaughter – it was love, pure and simple.'

'I remember how much your grandparents idolised you, Hannah.'

Hannah had tears in her eyes at the mention of her beloved grandparents.

Lili said quietly, 'A child deserves to know their grandparents – *both* sides – otherwise they miss out on so much.'

'I know.'

Lili hoped that meant what she thought it meant; Hannah would not only let Ray and Sarah into Maisie's life, but she would start thinking about building bridges with her mum and dad. She knew Hannah's parents had done a bad thing, sending her away into care when she was in her teens, but perhaps they'd felt it was the right thing to do at the time. She thought of Ray; she knew it didn't mean they had no regrets. She'd be prepared to bet they lived with those regrets every single day. For Maisie's sake, and for her own, it was worth the conversation to find out.

It made her wonder about her mother and what had led to her estrangement from her family. The only thing she had to go on was the small titbit of information Connie had gleaned that hinted at a secret she had uncovered.

Lili hugged her best friend. Hannah was right: she wanted to find her relatives – she always had. She wanted to find her grandparents and discover what had caused the family rift.

Aware that time was getting on, Lili drew back and said, 'I'd better go.'

'I know.'

Hannah grabbed her hand. 'Remember your promise.'

Lili glanced at Maisie. 'I will. But Hannah, believe me, nothing bad is going to happen.'

The look on Hannah's face told Lili she wasn't convinced.

'I'll be back before you know it,' Lili said as she opened the car door. She noticed that her words didn't seem to cheer Hannah up.

Lili expected the rush of cold air to wake Maisie, but she was sound asleep. Although Lili was disappointed that she couldn't give her a hug and kiss goodbye, she said to Hannah, 'Tell Maisie I will be back soon, okay?'

'Okay.'

Lili lingered for a moment, still unsure after the odd conversation with Hannah that she should leave.

Hannah noticed her hesitating. 'Please go, Lili. I'll be fine.'

Lili didn't believe her. Even so, now her flight was booked, and she was at the airport, Lili was surprised at how she was feeling; nervous but excited at the prospect of tracing her relatives. She was ready to return to Corfu and be in the place where her parents were last alive, and where she had lived with them for a time.

As Lili made her way to the airport terminal, she tried not the think of the enormity of the point in her life that she had reached. In one horrible day, when Hannah turned up at The Summerhouse, her life had disintegrated; she'd had to leave Aldeburgh and then, to cap it all, Connie had turned out not to be the trusted friend Lili had thought she was. On top of all that, Alex had texted again; he was leaving for Washington soon – he still wanted to meet up before he left. It was her choice to go to Corfu instead. She wondered if she was having regrets. What if he wanted to get back together? Now, she would never know.

All she had brought with her was her dwindling savings, what she owned in a small suitcase and a plane ticket to an island she barely remembered. The box from FedEx with the remainder of her possessions was now stored on Ray's boat. She stopped in front of the check-in desk. She found she was having second thoughts; not just about this trip, but about letting Ray dig into her past. Despite Hannah being upbeat about the prospect of her finding her family, a part of Lili wondered if Connie was right. Maybe the past should be left in the past. For the first time, Lili was feeling apprehensive about what she might discover.

She recalled the conversation with Connie when she'd asked the reason for sending her to that boarding school in Suffolk. That was when Connie had said that Lili's mum had talked about an area in Suffolk, a town she'd once visited on the trail of her family history. Lili recalled what she'd told her: *When I was choosing your school, I remembered your mother had talked about a place in Suffolk, a town she'd once visited with you on the trail of some family history. I thought that if I sent you there, then you would be in an area with some connection to your past, however tenuous … I hoped if she resurfaced and returned to England …* Connie had trailed off.

… *that she might find me.* Lili remembered replying.

That would never happen now; her mother was long dead. But she had found Joseph, eventually. Lili had a feeling that she was connected somehow to his family, and whatever secret she might uncover would not be to anyone's liking.

Despite all that, she handed over her passport and checked in her bag. If nothing else, at least she could visit her mother's grave and pay her respects. After this trip, Lili doubted she'd go back.

24

Lili arrived at the beautiful Bella Venezia, a small boutique hotel in a thriving quarter of Corfu Old Town. A five-storey former gentleman's residence, it was in a quiet street close to the harbour. She was looking forward to exploring the area. The taxi she had taken to the hotel had driven through the town and given her a glimpse of what was in store. But for her first day in Corfu, she had other plans.

On arrival, Lili received a glass of cool kumquat juice – the oval orange citrus fruit that Corfu was famous for. It didn't take long to check-in. She was pleased her flight had been so early; it meant she had arrived in time for breakfast outside on the terrace. Tables were laid out in the shade of orange and lemon trees.

She had been lucky to get a room at short notice. She had booked the hotel online when she was in the departure lounge, waiting to board her flight. There were very few vacancies in Corfu Old Town for seven nights. It had cost her more money than she had intended to pay. There was a range of much cheaper accommodation in the beach resorts along the coast – but she had her reasons for staying at this one.

After breakfast, she freshened up in her small but modern and comfortable room and then approached the reception desk in the foyer to hand over her key before she set out.

Dimitris, the concierge, greeted her by name. 'Ah, Miss Skye! Your guide is waiting for you in the lounge.'

Lili smiled. The staff had been so helpful on her arrival. They'd asked what her plans were and suggested a guide to show her the sights. At first, Lili had been reticent. Her reason for staying there was to visit the British Cemetery in the town, and she didn't need a guide to show her the way. She would be able to find it herself; it was marked on the Old Town street map and was walkable from the hotel. However, someone who could speak the language and tell her the history of the island might come in handy, so Lili had accepted.

The guide only asked for a small donation at the end of the tour, so she could hand over as much, or as little, as she wanted. Lili had looked up the going rate for a tour guide. She didn't want to take advantage, especially as the guide had been recommended by the lovely staff at the Bella Venezia.

Lili stepped into the comfortable lounge area to find a slim older man in his sixties, wearing a cream suit and a Panama hat. According to the concierge, he was a retired professor who enjoyed showing foreigners around his native Corfu.

He came forward as Lili approached. 'You must be Lili.' He shook her hand as he offered a friendly smile. 'I'm Spiros.'

He spoke with only a wisp of a Mediterranean accent. Lili felt guilty for not attempting to look up some basic words and phrases in Greek. Despite spending her early years there, she felt like a typical tourist who was too lazy or inept to find out about any of the local customs or learn a little of the language or culture. Although, to be fair, it had been a spur-of-the-moment decision to travel there, so there just hadn't been the time.

Lili had the small pocket guidebook she'd picked up at the airport to hand. 'Would you mind if we started at the British Cemetery?'

'Of course. Right this way.' He extended his arm toward the entrance.

Lili followed him out of the door and down the concrete steps to the street. It surprised her when he stopped in front of a silver BMW parked outside by the kerb. He opened the passenger door. She had assumed it would a walking tour of Corfu Old Town.

Spiros caught her expression. 'Ah – you thought it was a walking tour.'

Lili nodded. 'I don't mind, though,' she blurted, not wanting to offend the nice Greek man. 'It is rather hot out.'

He smiled. 'My sentiments exactly. But I didn't bring the car because it is, as you say, rather hot.'

Lili noticed he hadn't broken out in a sweat, and he was wearing a suit. Lili in her sleeveless polka dot dress and sandals, hair tied back in a ponytail, could feel the perspiration running down her face just making her way down the steps to the car.

'My friend, Dimitris, the concierge, mentioned that you wanted to go to the British Cemetery. That's why I brought the vehicle – otherwise it's a bit of a walk.'

Lili didn't mind walking, but maybe not in this heat – and it was only mid-morning. She wasn't sorry he'd driven. 'Thank you.' Lili smiled at Spiros and got into the car.

He shut the door behind her and climbed into the driver's seat, turning on the engine and ramping up the air-conditioning.

Lili felt a cool breeze on her face and was thankful that the old BMW had air con. She turned to her guide. 'I want to visit the British Cemetery, but as we're going by car, would you mind taking me to the beach first?'

'Shall I wait while you return to the hotel to collect your bathing suit and towel? I can suggest a quiet, most beautiful cove in—'

'Oh, er no, I'm not intending to go swimming or sunbathe.' Lili hadn't meant to interrupt him, but she already had somewhere in mind. She couldn't pronounce it, so she showed the old gentleman her precious sheet of paper from social services and pointed at the Greek name. 'Do you know it?'

'Of course.'

'I'd like to go there first, please.' Lili had fancied stopping off at the beach on her way in the taxi from the airport that morning, but she'd wanted to check into her hotel and have breakfast first.

Lili caught his expression. 'What is it?'

'There are pretty coves on the island to see. That is just one long stretch of waterfront. I'm afraid you may be disappointed.'

Lili shook her head. 'I can assure you I won't be.'

He didn't look convinced.

As they set off, Lili told him why that shoreline had a special significance.

He took his eyes off the road for a moment to look at her, dark bushy eyebrows rising as he listened to her story. 'You're her! The little English girl they found wandering the beach alone.'

'You remember that … me?'

'Yes, it was all over the local news. It's not something you forget in a hurry. It was a very unusual case. It is not uncommon to hear of children getting lost, but to find a child wandering alone and the parents missing …'

He took his eyes off the road to glance at her once more. 'Strange,' he said, shaking his head.

'I wanted to see the beach where I was found.'

'I get the impression you have not been back to Corfu since?'

'That's right – I haven't.' Lili stared out of the car window. She didn't expect to recognise anything; she had been too young the last time she was there.

She watched the honey-coloured facades of the grand detached residences flashing by along the beautiful waterfront. She was looking forward to exploring this part of Corfu Old Town too and walking its long, wide boulevards overlooking the crystal-clear waters of the Mediterranean Sea.

Lili recalled what she'd read about Corfu during her flight. According to the guidebook, things had changed since the package holiday heydays of the seventies, eighties, and nineties. Back then, certain areas of Corfu enticed young backpackers who just wanted to party, giving some of the beach resorts a bad name. Connie and her own parents came to mind. Now it seemed that Corfu attracted more discerning travellers; those who sought peace and tranquillity, beautiful beaches, and day trips to see the sights.

The guidebook intimated that the nightlife in the Old Town comprised of couples and families with children going out in the cool evenings to walk along the promenade and sit outside little restaurants for dinner. They passed many such restaurants in the car, and Lili could see the staff setting up tables. The town was still relatively quiet, apart from a few tourists, but it sounded as though it really came alive at night. Lili was looking forward to a meal alfresco and walking the streets straight from her hotel door.

As they left the beautiful Old Town behind them, Lili promised herself a boat trip around the island. Her guidebook suggested this was not to be missed.

Lili noticed that the long stretch of highway leading to the resort of Benitses was full of shops, some displaying billboards. There were potholes in the road and lots of moped riders darting in and out of the traffic, honking at the cars in their path. It made her head spin. Looking out of the window at the rather ugly shopping strip on either side of the main road, Lili wondered if she would rather visit one of those pretty coves her guide had mentioned about after all.

'How far is the beach?' Lili asked.

'It's about twenty minutes to Benitses. So, are you here looking for your parents?'

Lili shook her head. 'No, I found them.'

'You did? Well, that's fantastic news. I always wondered what became of them.'

Lili said nothing more. She left him to his misconception that they had turned up alive and well to claim her and that they were all living happily ever after. If only that were true.

Spiros turned left at a set of traffic lights. A sharp bend opened out on to a pleasant stretch of road with a lot fewer cars and no shops. Lili looked out of the side window and discovered they were on a winding, scenic coast road. Her spirits lifted. She was feeling that perhaps the resort of Benitses would be worth the trip after all.

25

'This is it.' Spiros pulled into a parking space on the street that ran parallel to the beach. Across the road was the small town of Benitses with its small stretch of souvenir shops, two grocery stores, a bakery shop and some restaurants and bars.

Behind the town centre, narrow lanes wound their way up the hillside. Its cobbled streets, with their villas, cottages and two-storey flats, were now home to locals and more mature tourists, giving it a relaxed atmosphere.

Lili liked the place. Benitses also had a harbour, which she had spotted before they parked at the beach. There were yachts and boats moored, bobbing on the calm water.

Lili got out of the car. Wooden planked walkways ran from the promenade down the sandy beach. Lili had never seen these before and imagined they were so people could walk down to the waterfront, avoiding the hot sand. Dotted about were seats and low tables with parasols.

Lili walked alone down to the water's edge, carrying her sandals by their straps in one hand. She tried to picture the beach as it might have been twenty-four years ago, without the wooden walkways or the chairs and small tables. There were people sitting at the tables, sunning themselves and eating their takeaway food from the local delis and eateries across the road. She tried to imagine a young couple with their child, paddling right there at the water's edge.

'If only you hadn't gone to Zakynthos,' she whispered, staring at the horizon. She felt a lump in her throat at the thought that if they hadn't, they might be there with her, taking a trip down memory lane together. But such a thing could never be.

Lili's eyes dropped to the sand between her toes. She was beginning to wish she hadn't made the trip. What had she hoped to gain from going back there, apart from sad thoughts of what might have been?

Lili slipped her sandals back on and returned along the planked walkway to the promenade. Across the road, she spotted Spiros sitting at a table outside a restaurant. He waved.

Lili returned his wave and made her way across the road to join him. The attentive restaurant staff appeared as soon as she sat down. She ordered a cup of English tea and sat staring at the beach.

They finished their drinks in silence.

Lili was feeling sorry for herself, and wasn't interested in conversation or exploring the town, with its quaint streets and friendly atmosphere, as she had intended.

Spiros, sensing she wanted to leave, said, 'Would you like to return to Corfu Old Town and visit the British Cemetery next?'

Not really, thought Lili, but it was on her to-do list, to see her mother's grave. She nodded. 'Do you think we can stop on the way to purchase some flowers?'

❖

After stopping off along the main road to buy a bunch of flowers from a street vendor, they returned along the coast road to Corfu Old Town. On the outskirts of the town, they pulled into a long residential street with houses on one side and a six-foot-high wall running the length of the road on the other. Lili guessed that behind the wall was the cemetery.

After finding a parking space, Lili followed Spiros to a cast iron gate set in the wall. The gate creaked on its hinges as they stepped inside the cemetery.

He gave her a potted history of the place, but Lili wasn't listening. The first thing she noticed, apart from the size, was the sudden quiet from the cacophony of noises outside in the town beyond. She couldn't hear cars or people. The only sounds were crickets and birds.

Lili found the cemetery quite different from the ones at home, with their neat rows of gravestones. Here, it was as though she'd stepped inside *The Secret Garden.* There were winding paths in various directions through a canopy of mature trees, which provided respite from the midday sun. There was an abundance of flowers along with some potted plants and old stone garden ornaments dotted about the place.

She caught Spiros saying the cemetery was a haven for wildlife. Apart from the two of them, there didn't appear to be another soul around.

It was much larger than she had expected. Lili looked at the bunch of flowers she had in her hands. She'd thought it would be straightforward to find her mother's grave, but the graves appeared to be in no discernible order; it was as though someone had just randomly picked each spot under a tree or over by the boundary wall.

Spiros stopped talking and looked at the flowers. 'You've come here to visit a grave, haven't you?'

Lili nodded. 'My mother.' She stared about her. 'I have no idea where it is.'

'Wait here. I will find the caretaker. He is a good friend and has worked here all his life. I'm sure he will know.'

They returned down a path to the entrance, where there was an old-fashioned cast iron bench next to a wooden trestle table. On the table was a visitors' book. Lili didn't fancy writing her name and a message inside. Instead, she took a seat and watched Spiros walk over to a small single-storey building. He knocked on the door.

Lili stood up when an old man appeared at the door. He stepped outside the house. She heard Spiros speaking to him in Greek. She'd started to approach them when the old man spotted her.

'Alena?'

Spiros turned around and looked at Lili. The old man, his eyes wide, was still talking in Greek.

His reaction when he saw her reminded Lili of Joseph when he first set eyes on her. 'What is he saying?' Lili asked.

'He says you're a ghost.'

26

Lili placed the flowers on her mother's grave. A part of her wished the news article had got it wrong, and that it was another couple who had perished. She stared at the little inscription on the gravestone of a young woman, her mother, who had died when she was younger than Lili was now. The question she kept asking herself was why her mother hadn't been repatriated to England to be buried there – why had she been buried in Corfu?

Lili returned to the path where her guide and the old caretaker were standing waiting for her. The caretaker appeared older than Joseph. Spiros told her that his family had looked after the Corfu British Cemetery for generations.

She noticed the caretaker still shied away as though he was afraid of her. 'I'm not a ghost,' Lili said again. She had so many questions. Before she asked a single one, he started talking in Greek. Spiros translated. 'He says he is sorry that he thought you were a ghost. He believes they come back.'

'I don't understand. Does he think he sees the ghosts of people here?' Lili cast her gaze towards her mother's grave. She didn't believe in that sort of thing. although she wasn't surprised that he thought he saw things, given that he lived in a cemetery.

'No, he's not talking about the souls resting here.' They walked together through the graveyard as Spiros told Lili about what happened on Corfu during the war.

Lili came to an abrupt halt. 'Did you just say *death boats*?'

He nodded solemnly. 'Very few people know about what took place when the Nazis occupied the Ionian Islands during World War Two. Most people have heard of the trains taking Jews to Auschwitz, but very few are aware of the death boats transporting them from the islands to meet their fate.'

Lili fell silent. She glanced at the caretaker. 'I remind him of somebody he knew from the past, don't I?' Lili looked at Spiros as he repeated in Greek what she'd just said.

The caretaker nodded. 'Alena.'

'Who was she?' Lili asked, wondering if it was the same woman that Joseph had confused her with. It seemed too much of a coincidence not to be. *If I bear such a striking resemblance to her, was it possible that I am related to Alena?* thought Lili.

'Was she taken on a death boat?' She waited for Spiros to repeat the question, holding her breath to see what he said. Lili listened as he recounted the old man's story. 'He was just a small child, but he remembered the young woman and her parents being taken away. The wealthiest family on the island, they owned a vineyard. Alena's parents often had artists and writers staying with them, and hosted parties for their foreign friends.'

He continued translating, 'Everyone assumed the family would get away, leave Corfu to find a safe haven abroad, but it was not to be.'

Lili looked at Spiros. 'Was Alena married? Did she have children who might have survived?'

'You're wondering if you are related to her.'

Lili did a quick mental calculation; if Alena had been a young woman when she was sent on the death boats to Auschwitz, then she might be …

'Your great-grandmother.' Spiros read her mind.

Lili confessed. 'I don't know anything about my parents' backgrounds. I've only just found out about them.' Lili gave an abridged version of what had happened. 'A friend discovered they had an accident around the time I was found, but it sounds as though my mother was estranged from her family. I haven't met my father's relatives either. I think my grandparents didn't know I existed.'

'That explains a lot, and why no one came forward for you.'

She turned to the caretaker and asked again, 'Did Alena have children?' She looked to Spiros to translate for her once again.

The caretaker who until that point had had no shortage of things to say, fell silent.

Lili stared at him. 'Did they take children on the death boat?'

'They rounded up everyone they could find – including children. Non-Jewish families on the island tried to hide their neighbours, especially the children, by taking them in and pretending they were their own. Some were smuggled by boat to neighbouring islands.'

'Neighbouring islands?' repeated Lili. 'Like Zakynthos, by any chance?'

'Possibly.'

Lili turned to the caretaker, repeating her question yet again regarding whether Alena had had children, feeling irritated that he seemed to evade the question. She caught the caretaker looking at Spiros. She saw something pass between them. 'What is it?'

'There were rumours, stories passed down about the family – a scandal some believe they tried to cover up.'

'Do you know what it was?'

'Alena wasn't married, but it was rumoured that she fell in love and had a secret liaison with a young artist from abroad who used to stay at her parents' house when he was visiting the island.'

'So, she might have had a child out of wedlock? Is that what you're saying?'

He nodded.

They both turned to the caretaker when he started speaking. Lili waited for Spiros to translate, taking in his words.

'The caretaker's mother used to work as a cleaner at the wealthy family's villa. Alena went to stay with family friends in England for many months, supposedly to better her English. No one was fooled when she returned to the island with those friends who already had a son and now had a new-born child – a girl.'

Spiros listened to the caretaker for a while again and then continued to recount the old man's story.

'The English family visited the island often. The cleaner would take her own little boy, the old man standing before us, with her. He remembered the day the Germans invaded. He was playing with two children – a boy around his age and the girl, who must have been around three – when the German soldiers came to the house. They confiscated all the art hanging on the walls and their antique furniture. A few days later, they returned and took the family too, along with their Jewish friends. Nobody had expected they would invade the Ionian Islands, let alone round up all the Jews.

'What happened to the children?' Lili asked.

'They were never heard from again.'

Lili stared at the old man. *So, the Nazis took them.* Lili couldn't hide her shock. They had all perished in a concentration camp, which meant her resemblance to the young woman from the wealthy Greek family, Alena, was just a coincidence, and her theory that Alena's illegitimate child was her grandmother was not true.

'But,' Spiros continued, translating something further, 'his mother told him the children were safe.'

'Safe? How was that possible?' Lili wondered if that was what a mother would tell her child to spare him the horror of what would have happened to his friends. All the same, Lili could feel her heart racing. What if it were true? 'Was it Zakynthos? Were they taken there?'

She saw the caretaker looking at her in surprise. He nodded.

Spiros was surprised too. 'How could you possibly know that?'

Lili glanced across the cemetery toward her mother's grave. They had meandered back through the gardens, making their way towards the entrance. Lili stopped by the table with the visitors' book. She turned to look at her two companions. 'Apparently, my mother had discovered a family secret. It sounds as though she had been seeking the truth about her family's past, and whatever she had learned, it led her to the island of Zakynthos.' Lili stared at the old man. 'What would have happened to the children if they made it to that island?'

Spiros asked the caretaker and nodded at the answer. 'He says that a family on the island would have taken them in.'

Lili frowned. Even if it were true, she knew she was grasping at straws. Her mother's trip to Zakynthos and her own resemblance to a young woman from decades earlier may just be a coincidence – especially if Alena's little girl had grown up in Greece. Lili's mother was English. It didn't make sense. Lili voiced her thoughts.

'If Alena's child was your grandmother, and she grew up in Greece, she might have met and married an Englishman and moved to England,' Spiros said, before translating his answer for the caretaker.

Lili nodded. That was plausible. Out of the corner of her eye, she saw the caretaker shaking his head. She turned to him. 'What is it?'

She watched him turn toward her mother's grave. His gaze shifted back to Lili as he spoke, this time in broken English. But she understood well enough. He told her he had been there when her mother was laid to rest.

'You remember her funeral?'

He nodded, telling her that there had been many, many people at the funeral.

Lili swallowed. 'Are you saying she had a big family?'

He smiled. 'Many, many people.'

'From England?'

'No, no, not England. Israel.'

Lili stared at him. '*Israel?* I don't understand.'

Spiros spoke to him in Greek. Lili couldn't wait to hear what he said in response. When he stopped, Lili turned to him. 'What is it – what did he say?'

'He says he is sorry. He didn't realise that you were looking for your family. At the funeral, he spoke with the mother of the young woman who had died.'

'He talked to my grandmother?'

'Yes. It sounds as though they talked at some length. That's how he knew they came from Israel for her funeral.'

Lili recalled Connie saying something about her parents meeting on a kibbutz in Israel. This was all making sense now. Even so, Lili frowned. There was something she didn't understand: if her mother had been from Israel, why had she been buried in the British Cemetery?

She looked at Spiros to repeat the question in Greek. Afterwards, he listened to the caretaker and nodded before turning to Lili. 'He remembers a tall, thin man with a moustache. He was her father, your grandfather, and he was English.'

'He was English?'

The caretaker nodded.

A tall thin man with a moustache, thought Lili. Oh, how she'd love to meet her grandparents. She wouldn't get her hopes up, though. It had been so many years since the funeral, and she didn't know whether they were still alive or even know their names. She knew Ray was working behind the scenes to find them, though. She imagined he had requested a copy of her parents' birth certificates to discover the names of their parents – Lili's grandparents – in order to build her family tree and start searching for them.

The tour guide had a suggestion. 'Perhaps your mother was born in England, and then they moved to Israel?'

Lili thought that it was a possibility, and that it might also explain why her mother had been laid to rest in the British Cemetery – but it still left one big unanswered question. Why hadn't she been repatriated to England or Israel? It wasn't as though she had died on the island.

'So, why was she buried here, in Corfu?' she asked.

'Ah,' the caretaker appeared to understand Lili's question.

Lili waited for an answer, but none was forthcoming. She looked at Spiros, who shrugged his shoulders. Lili turned her attention to the old man. He held his hands up in a gesture that said *I don't have a clue.*

But Lili did. It was all making sense now. Lili thought of her mother's trip to Zakynthos. Lili believed her mother had been on the trail of her own grandmother and what happened to her after the German invasion. If her trip had been about Alena and the discovery that she'd had an illegitimate child – *my own grandmother*, thought Lili – was that the secret she'd uncovered that had led to the family rift? There was a reason it didn't always pay to delve into the past. It might uncover a secret someone was trying to protect.

However, if her grandmother was Alena's illegitimate child, it still didn't explain why she had buried her daughter on an Ionian Island she would barely remember, unless …

There was only one explanation. Her grandmother knew all about her past, her illegitimacy, her biological mother Alena, and her once-prominent family who lived on Corfu. That's why she'd laid her daughter to rest on the island from where her family originated.

Lili took a breath. Of course, all that was conjecture, but she asked, 'What do you think happened to the children who escaped to Zakynthos?'

That the caretaker knew, or at least had some idea about. So did her tour guide. 'After the war, many fled to a place of refuge. A place where, although they missed their homeland, Greece, they could start new lives without fear of religious persecution.'

'Israel.'

The coincidences were mounting up, but it still didn't mean Alena was her great-grandmother, or the little girl who had escaped the death boats was her grandmother. Until she thought of Joseph.

It couldn't just be a coincidence that Joseph remembered a young woman called Alena who Lili resembled. Lili recalled what Sarah had told her; she knew little about her father's experiences as a child caught up in the Nazi invasion of the Ionian Islands, but what she did know was that his parents often visited friends on the island of Corfu.

He must have known Alena. They might have all stayed with the wealthy Greek family who hosted get-togethers for their artist friends from abroad. She guessed they were all there – Alena's illegitimate child too – when the island was invaded.

The caretaker had mentioned that the children had been smuggled off the island and placed in the care of Greek families. She guessed Joseph and his father had been reunited and then returned to England. She believed Alena's child had fled with a Greek family from Zakynthos to Israel after the war, and that they had brought her up there.

Was it true – was Alena's love-child also her grandmother? Lili looked at the caretaker. She was thinking of something Joseph had said, another name Sarah had never heard pass her father's lips before. *Miriam.*

27

Lili turned to the old man with one more question before she left the cemetery. 'Do you remember the names of my grandmother and grandfather, who you met at the funeral?'

He shook his head. Lili sighed. Of course he didn't remember. It had been too long ago. She would need to have some patience and leave it to Ray to look into her ancestry and her family tree. At least she could tell him one thing: he'd been looking in the wrong place. He needed to turn his sights from England to Israel.

The caretaker started talking and gesturing towards his house. Lili didn't fancy stopping for tea or coffee, although she wasn't surprised that he was offering; during the little time she'd spent so far on the island, she'd found that the people were friendly and generous to a fault. However, she would have to decline his kind offer. She was intent on getting in touch with Ray and telling him all about her trip to the British Cemetery.

Spiros said to Lili, 'He has kept records over the years. Come with me if you want to know their names.'

'Are you serious?'

'You would not believe the red tape. We must keep records

as long as your arm. Officialdom is officially a royal pain in the arse over here.'

Lili laughed at the English turn of phrase as she followed the caretaker into his little single-storey stone-built home. She wasn't laughing when she stepped outside.

'Are you all right, Lili?'

She turned to Spiros. The caretaker had accompanied them outside too.

Lili swallowed. 'Yes, I think so.'

'It must be quite overwhelming, hearing your grandmother's name for the first time.'

But that was just the thing – it wasn't the first time Lili had heard that name. Miriam. She couldn't wait to return to England and speak to Joseph. Perhaps he could tell her why her mother had been estranged from her family when she died. Lili couldn't help but think it must have been more than discovering her own mother had been born out of wedlock. There must be something else. Lili's thoughts turned to Alena's secret lover, the father of her love-child; that was probably something she would never find out. But on the other hand, she thought.

Her eyebrows shot up. Right now, Joseph was her only living link to her past. He'd known her great-grandmother, Alena, and her grandmother, Miriam. He'd been smuggled to the island of Zakynthos with Miriam – she was sure of it. What could he tell her about Alena? Would he have known Alena's sweetheart, Miriam's father? Lili thought of the Hebrew wedding ring in his possession that Sarah knew nothing about. Was it possible that Miriam's father had given it to him for safekeeping?

All those questions were running through her mind as she walked with the two men back toward the entrance to the British

Cemetery. She glanced to her right through the trees and spotted a headstone. That wasn't unusual. They were dotted about, some quite inconspicuous, partially hidden under the dense foliage. What had caught her attention was an inscription she thought she saw on the slab.

She approached the headstone and read the engraving. 'That's weird.'

Spiros caught up. 'What is it?'

'I know of someone back in England who has the same name.' Lili was thinking of Joseph's father.

'Perhaps he was buried here,' he commented.

Lili shook her head. 'That's not possible.' Lili stared at the gravestone. 'This person died in nineteen forty-three.'

'I see. Then it's just a coincidence.'

Lili was about to agree, when she caught sight of a little headstone next to the deceased young man. It appeared to be his son, a boy – Joseph. They had the same surname. Lili could accept one coincidence – but two? The father and son buried there were around the same age that Joseph and his father would have been when they escaped the island while these two perished. Lili went cold.

The caretaker caught up with them.

'Is something wrong?' he asked in broken English.

Spiros, who was staring at Lili, replied, 'I'm not sure.'

Lili barely registered their presence. According to Sarah, her grandfather, George – the same name on the memorial – was a Jew from Vienna, and he'd travelled to England after the war to bring up his son, Joseph. Lili's eyes flickered to the second headstone of a little boy aged five called Joseph. George and Joseph.

Lili stared at the simple markers. She was there to uncover the truth about her family and find her grandparents – if they were still alive. She had not travelled all this way to unravel a new mystery. Why had Joseph's father stolen the identities of this man and his son? And why had they both lived in England for decades under assumed names?

28

'So, what are your plans for the rest of the week?' Spiros asked.

They were in his car, heading back to the hotel, even though Lili had assured him he didn't have to make the return journey; she could have walked it from the cemetery, and it would have given her a chance to see some of the town. She had told him that as they drove along the coast road.

'In the afternoon heat, with everything closed?' He had looked at her and smiled. 'Mad dogs and Englishmen.'

She had glanced his way and returned his smile.

'Look,' he had said, 'I'll take you to your hotel, but relax, have a siesta, and then when it's cool, go out and explore the Old Town. I can assure you that you won't be disappointed. Everything comes alive later in the evening.'

Lili looked at the passing scenery as they made their way to Corfu Town. She thought about returning to Benitses. It had been quite an emotional experience to walk along the beach where she had last been with her parents. Now she regretted leaving. The guide had suggested she spend some time exploring the village, but she had another reason for going back too. Although it was unlikely, there was a possibility that she'd run into a local who remembered her family, or even remembered her as the toddler found wandering along the shore alone.

Spiros turned into Zampeli Street and parked the car. It was mid-afternoon, and Lili was feeling the effects of her early morning flight. She thought she just might take his advice and have a siesta.

As her guide turned off the engine, Lili reached into her purse to pay him for the trip. Spiros wouldn't take her money. Shaking his head at the wad of notes, he said, 'I'm just delighted to help a young woman searching for her family.'

Lili put the euros back in her purse.

'I can show you some more of the sights during your stay,' he offered, smiling at the English lady whose company he had enjoyed over the last few hours. He had liked learning about her life since she had left Corfu, but he just wished the story of her childhood hadn't had such a sad ending, with her parents dying the way they had. He hoped she could find her extended family – the grandparents whom the cemetery caretaker had met at her mother's funeral.

Lili glanced out of the window at the hotel before turning to Spiros. 'I wish you'd let me pay for the tour.'

He shook his head, still smiling. 'You've already given me something.'

'I have?'

'Your company for a few hours and letting me join you on part of your quest to find what you're looking for. It has been quite … intriguing.'

Lili thought that was one way of putting it. She found it in turns emotionally draining and frustrating. She wasn't sure how much closer she was to finding out the truth about her past. And now she had another mystery; the gravestones with the names of two people who were very much alive.

Lili frowned at Spiros. 'Well, in that case, I'm afraid you might find taking me on any further tours a bit, well … conventional.'

Spiros grinned. 'Conventional is good. I can take you on a trip around the island, or may I suggest a boat tour or a visit to a vineyard along with some wine-tasting?'

'Thank you for the suggestions, Spiros. I haven't decided what to do with the rest of my break.' She caught his brow crease in disappointment. 'But if I need a guide, Spiros, I will call on you, I promise.'

He nodded, smiling again as he got out of the car and walking round to open the passenger door for her.

Lili skipped up the steps to the hotel entrance and turned around to wave. Spiros was already in his car. He tipped his Panama hat before setting off.

Lili entered the cool interior of the building. The concierge greeted her and asked if she had enjoyed the tour. She imagined he thought she'd been doing a normal island excursion, not visiting a cemetery or walking in the footsteps of her late parents in Benitses. All the same, Lili smiled. 'He was the best. I'm sure I will call on him again in the course of my stay.'

Lili took her key and was about to return to her room to freshen up when she had a thought. 'Would you have any information on the Old Town?' Lili wanted to do a self-guided tour. However, she was going to take Spiros' advice and venture out later when it was cooler.

The concierge said, 'Just a moment.' He left the reception desk and walked into a small office.

Lili didn't have to wait long. He returned with a comprehensive street map that contained a suggested walking tour of the Old Town, along with a helpful appendix with brief descriptions of places of interest to see on the way. He had also included some leaflets highlighting other areas that might be worth visiting on the island.

Lili headed back to her bedroom and made the mistake of lying down for a siesta. A couple of hours later, she emerged from her room. It was late afternoon. She realised she had underestimated how drained she was from the events of the last few days. It didn't seem possible that she hadn't long left Aldeburgh, landed at Connie's, and then headed to Hannah's before flying here. It was enough to make anybody's head spin.

She closed her hotel room door behind her. As much as she wanted to stick with the plan and head out to explore the Old Town this evening, and eat alfresco at a restaurant, she accepted she'd get more out of her self-guided tour if she left it to the morning.

At the bar, she ordered some food – a sandwich and salad were all she fancied in this heat – and sat outside on a cushioned wicker chair at a table in a shady spot. There were other guests enjoying drinks and meals in the cool, shady patio at the back of the hotel. She smiled at two children playing a game of chess with giant plastic chessman on a large chess board.

Lili looked in her bag. She had brought the pamphlets and map with her. When she'd eaten, she intended to sit and plan out the rest of her holiday.

29

Wearing a light cotton dress and comfortable sandals, Lili walked through the restaurant and straight outside. It felt like déjà vu. She'd only been sitting out there on the patio the evening before with all the pamphlets and the street map of Corfu Old Town. This morning, she had brought just the map.

She was one of the first down to breakfast, and the staff were still setting up the tables. There was a reason she wanted to get an early start; she intended to set off on the walking tour before the mercury rose towards midday and the heat became stifling.

Lili chose a table under an arbour formed by some wisteria trees, whose sweet perfume hung in the air. She appreciated the shady spot, even in the morning sunshine. She ordered a pot of tea from a waiter and then went to choose some items from the buffet inside the restaurant. Returning to the table with some fresh fruit, cereal and a pastry, she spread out the street map to get her bearings. The hotel was situated just a couple of minutes' stroll into the Old Town.

After breakfast, Lili left the shade of the garden, picked up her sun hat and a bottle of water from her room, then handed her key to the concierge on reception. She already had a plan for how she would spend her day. She decided to visit the Old Venetian Fortress in the morning before it became too crowded. Spiros had told her how the population of the small Old Town swelled every time a cruise ship came into port. There was one docked that day.

Lili made her way down the stone steps of the hotel and turned right. She followed the street map, heading for the Spianada, a large square in front of the old fortress. As Lili entered the square, she slowed and took in the views. It reminded her of a leafy London park, with huge trees and statues and monuments pointing to Corfu's illustrious past. Lili smiled when she saw the garden benches, well-positioned in shady spots for people to rest out of the heat. It would be the perfect place to take a break later in the day, after her visit to the fortress.

She had read in her guide that the area dated from around 1628. It was surrounded by some fine old buildings and fronted by the sea, and Lili thought it was charming.

Making her way through the park, she crossed the bridge over the artificial moat and reached the entrance to the fortress. Small fishing boats nestled in the water below. Lili stopped and took a picture on her phone. She hadn't intended for the trip to be a holiday, but once she was there, the opportunity to see some of the sights on the beautiful island was too good to miss.

Inside, the citadel was just as impressive. She made her way up the winding paths to the top, which afforded glorious views of Garitsa Bay. Pausing to take more photos, Lili spotted a small cafeteria, the perfect spot for a break from sightseeing. Taking a seat on the veranda, she ordered a Greek iced tea and admired the spectacular views. With the blue waters of the bay below and the rooftops of the Old Town glistening in the sunlight, it did not surprise Lili that the fortress attracted so many visitors.

She opened her map again. Sipping her ice-cold drink, she read about some of the highlights she had to look forward to. She had planned to devote the cooler part of the morning to wandering the streets of the Old Town and then visit a museum in the afternoon. The trouble was that the views were breathtaking; if she wasn't careful, she would spend the rest of the day in the military stronghold.

Gathering her sunhat and shoulder bag, Lili left some euros, including a tip, in a little tray for the waiter. She retraced her steps and exited the fortress. Turning right, she skirted the Bosketto Durrell, a quaint garden with statues dedicated to writers and artists who had once lived on the island.

Lili heard children's laughter coming from the playground. It reminded her that she wanted to buy souvenirs for Maisie and William. Passing a beautiful colonnaded building housing the Museum of Asian Art, she continued her walk around the bay past the St Nicholas Gate, one of the four original gates into the old town. Looking down from the fortification wall, she noticed sunbathers already stretched out on the rocky shore below. She thought it looked a delightful spot to catch the sun or take a cool dip in the sea.

She made her way along one of the little side streets. She looked up at the tall Venetian buildings and shuttered windows and noticed a red bell tower in the distance. Continuing along the cobbled street, with its myriad of souvenir shops and more upmarket individual boutiques, Lili glanced at her map and discovered she was heading toward Saint Spyridon Church. *Little wonder I spied the bell tower*, thought Lili. According to the informative appendix at the back of the map, it was the highest in the Ionian Islands.

The streets were now buzzing with locals and many tourists. Following the walking tour, she came across the entrance to a small church in a square. Before entering its calm interior, she covered her shoulders with a light rainproof jacket from her bag and put on a headscarf. Inside the church, paintings decorated the ceiling. She paused to examine the wonderful silver incense burners that were dotted about.

Lili turned over her map and read the description. Built in the 1580s, it was a Greek Orthodox church. She was about to continue reading when she heard an infant crying. She looked up and noticed a small gathering at the front of the church. A baptism was taking place. Unsure whether she should stay, Lili hovered by a stone pillar, reflecting on the loss of her parents and the details of her early years; had she been christened or baptised? Watching the ceremony, it struck her that she might never know.

Leaving the church, she retraced her steps and walked toward the Liston Arcade. With its impressive colonnaded arches, it was an ideal spot for Lili to stop for lunch, as it faced the Spianada and the old fortress. She wasn't surprised that it was very touristy, with many bars and restaurants, but it was in a beautiful setting.

Taking a seat at a table outside a restaurant, Lili ordered a simple Greek salad and some sparkling water and sat reflecting on what to do with the rest of her day. She had intended to visit a museum in the afternoon, but with the influx of tourists from the cruise ship, she imagined long queues for tickets. Lili thought she might leave that for another time.

Instead, after lunch, she headed back into the Old Town to browse the shops and pick up some souvenirs. She wanted to buy some postcards too and send one to Maisie and Hannah. She smiled to herself, thinking that she must thank Hannah for encouraging her to make the trip. It was something she had been meaning to do but had always put it off. Finally, she was there, and she wished she'd visited years ago.

After wandering a myriad of alleyways and cobbled lanes, and discovering hidden squares with fountains and monuments, Lili found she had fallen in love with Corfu Old Town. By the time she'd strolled up and down the streets with far too many souvenir shops, she felt laden down with purchases.

She'd bought gift boxes of Kumquat, a traditional sweet that looked like small oranges and lemons, along with a colourful bracelet for Maisie with beads that spelled out the name of Corfu's capital in Greek. There was a matching necklace that Lili just had to buy for her too. She'd also found something for William – a hand-carved yo-yo – not that she felt she would see him any time soon after the way she and Nate had parted. Lili tried to brush that thought from her mind as she retraced her steps to the hotel.

Leaving the presents in her room, Lili walked through reception and out into the garden with a postcard and pen. She sat down and wrote one to Maisie and Hannah, telling them all about her day exploring Corfu Old Town.

Lili wandered back inside to ask the concierge at the desk if she could post them from the hotel. The young man nodded and smiled, asking Lili if there was anything else he could help her with.

'Yes, as it happens, there is.'

Lili returned to the garden with a bus timetable. She had planned what she would do the next day. She wanted to return to Benitses.

30

Lili spotted the booth where she could purchase the ticket for the bus before departure. She had arrived in good time, thanks to the helpful young man at the hotel reception who had given her the directions to San Rocco Square. It was from there that she could catch the number six bus to Benitses. She was aiming for the first one that left before nine in the morning.

Lili fumbled in her purse for change for the machine. She wasn't pleased to discover that she was ten cents short of the correct fare and only had notes. She glanced over at the terminal, aware that the blue bus had already arrived and that people were boarding. Lili had been wondering if she'd get a seat. Now it looked as though she wouldn't be catching the bus at all.

She looked about her to see if anyone could change a ten euro note. Lili rolled her eyes. How stupid not to think of this the day before. She could have got some coins when shopping for souvenirs.

An old gentleman in the queue saw her holding up her ten euro note. He tapped her on the shoulder and said something in Greek. Lili looked at him apologetically. 'I'm sorry, I don't understand.'

The old man switched to broken English. 'If you need change, there's a shop around the corner.'

Lili glanced at the bus. 'Thank you. I wanted to get the first bus, but I'm ten cents short.' *Why does it have to be one euro and ten cents?* Lil thought. *Why not just one euro?* 'Can you change a ten euro note?' she asked.

He shook his head but started searching through the pockets of his coat, anyway. His eyes brightened. 'Look, I have ten cents. Give me your euro.'

Lili handed it over, thinking it wasn't a very fair exchange. Then the old man made off with both coins. 'Hey!' Lili called after him. He was heading for the booth. *Did I just pay for his bus ticket?* she wondered.

When he returned a moment later, he handed her a ticket.

'Oh.' Lili's face turned crimson. 'Thank you, so much.'

He stepped aside to let her climb aboard the bus. Lili took a seat and smiled at him as he passed by, walking to the back of the vehicle to join some other passengers. She could hear them conversing in Greek.

His generosity and friendliness overwhelmed Lili. She knew it was only ten cents, but if she'd been in a similar position in London, she'd have needed to forget about the kindness of strangers. *If you'd lost your purse there, you'd better be prepared to walk home*, she thought.

As the bus moved off, Lili thought of Joseph. His neighbours felt he was unfriendly, a recluse, but he hadn't appeared like that when she'd met him. However, she knew his reputation; Lili recalled the little gravestone bearing his name. Perhaps there was a reason he kept himself to himself. Did he have something to hide?

The bus full of passengers set off from the terminal. Lili sat back to enjoy the thirty-minute drive to Benitses. She recognised some of the route that Spiros had taken when he had driven to the British Cemetery. After a short time, they left the town behind and travelled along the coast road. Lili opened the small guidebook that one of the reception staff had found for her. She was looking out for the Kaiser Bridge, designed and built for Kaiser Wilhelm II. Apparently, he had been fond of Corfu and had had the bridge built so he could walk closer to the water. According to the guidebook, he had also purchased Achillion Palace. Lili had already decided to visit the palace later in the week.

The road took a sharp bend. Lili spotted the bridge on the left. Soon afterwards, with beautiful views of the coast, they arrived at the centre of Benitses. When Lili stepped off the bus, her first thought was of what a lovely little town Benitses was. The main street across the road from the beach comprised some small restaurants with outside seating and views of the sea, two grocery shops, and a bakery. Behind the main boulevard were narrow, cobbled streets and pathways rising gently up the hillside.

When she had first gone there with Spiros, her mood had clouded her view of the area; it was the place she associated with being abandoned by her parents. But this time, she had returned intending to explore the town and enjoy her time there.

Lili's first impression as she walked along the pavement toward the little parade of shops and tavernas was that it was a thriving village with a more traditional Greek feel. She'd read that planning laws prohibited buildings above two storeys in this area, which meant there were no large tourist resort hotels. There were small bed-and-breakfasts and villas to rent, but she got the impression there were more local people living here. There were day-trippers like herself, but the town wasn't overrun with tourists.

Lili had been reading about Benitses during the car journey. It had been a notorious clubbing nightspot years ago. Now it had a calmer, more genteel atmosphere.

As she stood on the pavement, deciding what to do first, she smiled at some local children as they passed by, each with a large backpack on their back. She guessed they were walking to school.

She wandered through the town. Up a cobbled side street, between the shops, she discovered a little café; its colourful assortment of chairs and tables lined the pavement. She hadn't walked very far, but the smell of freshly brewed coffee enticed her to take a seat at a table. The café owner came out with the menu.

She ordered a cappuccino and a pastry and then opened her guidebook while she waited. The description of Benitses was only brief, so she shut the book and looked around. Although it was early, several locals were already sitting at the tables chatting animatedly. Lili imagined her parents sitting there, enjoying the warmth of the morning sunshine and the friendly, relaxed atmosphere.

Lili took her time drinking her cappuccino before setting off again to wander the back lanes. She continued walking the small, cobbled lane which wound its way up the hillside. A young Greek woman who was sweeping the front step outside her villa greeted Lili warmly as she walked by.

The old village had retained its character with a maze of long, narrow streets and alleys to explore. Lili found steps that led from one street to another, and she even discovered a small square dominated by a church. Lili took a breather on the bench in the square under the shade of an olive tree. The peaceful setting enchanted her. If she returned to Corfu in the future, which she had every intention of doing, she'd already decided this was where she would stay, in Benitses.

She set off again. She loved that many of the alleyways were lined with terracotta pots full of flowers. Vines with a purple-coloured flower covered the walls of some villas.

After an hour, she made her way back down the maze of cobbled streets and crossed the main coast road, where the bus had dropped her off. She strolled along the promenade towards the colourful marina she remembered from her last visit, where yachts were moored in the harbour.

After a circuit of the marina, Lili bought a filled roll and some sparkling water from a grocery shop nearby. She had packed a book to read while she waited for the bus to return to Corfu Town. The hotel had a library of sorts; other tourists who had stayed had left books they had finished so they could be enjoyed by others.

She returned along the promenade to the beach. Walking down a wooden boardwalk, she found there were lots of seats on the waterfront to choose from. She wanted to sit near the water's edge. Although it wasn't a sandy beach, that didn't deter sunbathers. Some people were swimming, and she could see children playing games and stacking pebbles further up the shore.

Lili opened her book and tried to concentrate, but her thoughts kept returning to that event years ago, when her mother had left her with Connie to make the journey to Zakynthos. Hearing children's voices made her wonder how her parents could have left her with a virtual stranger. She realised those were different times, though; she couldn't imagine anyone doing that now.

She finished her lunch, put the novel down and opened the guidebook instead. There were many places to explore on the island, but without a car she was dependent upon the buses to get around. She didn't mind. Taking the bus, she felt like a local. Looking in her travel guide, Lili made plans for the following day. Apparently, the Achillion Palace was a must-see place. Even better, there was a bus that took her straight there. Lili snapped the book shut and smiled, satisfied that the next day would turn out to be another memorable day.

Lili put the guidebook back in her handbag, along with the novel, and took out a small bottle of sun cream she'd bought in the shop along with her lunch. She rubbed some on her arms and legs. Adjusting the wide-brimmed straw sunhat she'd also purchased, she lifted her sunglasses and sat staring at the sparkling green water lapping on the shore just inches from her bare feet.

As she unwrapped the filled roll, she glanced around and saw tourists, mainly couples, drifting down to sit on the beach with street food they'd bought in the town. Seeing couples together brought Nate to mind. Lili reached into her handbag for her phone, surprised that Nate was at the forefront of her mind rather than Alex. After what had happened, she didn't expect Nate to text her, but she was debating whether to get in touch with him. Lili changed her mind and put her phone back in the bag. She doubted he would be interested in an apology from her. However, she knew there was one person who would love to hear from her.

Lili smiled when she thought of Spiros. He had said he would take her on a tour of the island. She was thinking of taking him up on that offer later in the week.

As she gazed out over the water, Alena came to mind, and the hundreds of others who had been forcibly removed from Corfu by boat, never to return. While she was here, she wanted to find out more about the wealthy family who had once owned a vineyard and about the daughter, Alena, who just might have been her great-grandmother.

31

Lili sat in the lounge area of the Bella Venezia Hotel, scrolling through the photos on her phone. She hadn't long returned from her trip to the Achillion Palace, which had been built for the Austrian Empress Elisabeth of Austria as a refuge to help her cope with the tragic loss of her only son. Perched on a hillside, the palace had breath-taking views of Corfu Old Town and the surrounding countryside and coast.

She had enjoyed her day exploring the majestic building and gardens, collecting many photos to show Hannah and Maisie when she returned from the trip. The most impressive was that of the Dying Achilles, which was the centrepiece of the terraces. Lili recalled that she had been taking a photo when a tourist asked if she would like to stand by the statue and he would take her picture. Posing by the figure, she looked tiny by comparison. Lili smiled at the photo before putting her phone away.

She had changed into a pair of navy chinos, a cotton blouse and a light waist-length jacket. She checked her watch. She was going into the town for an evening meal – the concierge had made a reservation for her at a restaurant he'd recommended. She knew it was time to set off, but something was playing on her mind; despite numerous calls, she hadn't got through to Ray or Hannah.

She stood up and walked through to the reception. She wanted to try to contact them using the hotel's phone. The receptionist guided her to a small booth in the corner by the stairs where she could make a private call. Lili would have preferred to take it in her room, but the phones provided were only for internal calls to contact reception or the concierge for room service.

Lili started dialling Ray's number first, longing to tell him what she had discovered in the British Cemetery. His number rang and rang and then went to answerphone. Lili left a brief message and asked if he could call her back when he had a chance. Lili frowned when she had no luck with getting through to Hannah.

Disappointed that she hadn't been able to speak to either of them, Lili still headed out to the town for a meal. Crossing the road straight in front of the hotel, she made her way down Guilford Street, which was full of restaurants, cafés and shops. Lili hadn't seen it so busy before; the last time she had ventured into the town, it had been early in the morning. This was her first visit in the evening.

The area was buzzing with many people seated outside, choosing to eat alfresco. Lili stopped at a small venue with tables under a colourful awning. She said in Greek, 'I have a reservation,' even though she knew the waiter probably spoke English. She had asked the reception staff who had booked her the table to teach her the phrase. The waiter smiled and offered her a menu. He beckoned her to a dinner table for two, set back slightly from the street.

The waiter left her to browse the menu, returning with a bottle of sparkling water and a breadbasket. Lili already knew what she wanted; she ordered a moussaka and a small side salad, which arrived more quickly than expected. Lili followed the delicious meal with a coffee and sat people-watching as tourists and locals passed by the restaurant. She was enjoying the balmy evening; it was so different from evenings at home, which were chilly even at the height of summer. The atmosphere enthralled her. Spiros had been right – the town came alive at night. There weren't just young couples out and about; among the crowds were entire families – young and old – enjoying the beautiful town together.

Her thoughts turned to Alex and the reason for the breakup of their relationship. Surely, the years they had spent together meant more to him than a promotion. But then Lili thought she was as much to blame, not jumping at the chance to go to Washington. Instead, she'd put her relationship with Maisie and Hannah first.

Lili wasn't sorry when the waiter interrupted her thoughts. She paid the bill and left a generous tip, deciding to join the throng of people heading further into the town. She strolled along the street and reached a large square named after the imposing Venetian Town Hall. She read the little plaque with interest; it was built to house nobles and officers of the Venetian navy.

Making her way down an alleyway adjacent to the square, she noticed a shop selling beachwear. She hadn't bought a swimming costume with her, as she hadn't been expecting to make a holiday out of her impromptu trip to Corfu. Entering the shop, she browsed the racks of dainty two-piece bikinis, pulling a face. There was no way she would fit into those. She turned to the rack of swimsuits instead, choosing a simple black swimsuit and then a dark grey sarong. Lili liked the pretty pink flowers along the hem of the sarong.

Her intention had been to take a short bus trip to a sandy cove for a swim the next day, but a young lady in the street handing out leaflets about boat tours around the island gave her a better idea. The boat trips not only included a scenic route, taking in the coastline around Corfu Old Town, which sounded a spectacular sight to see, but lunch was included. Even better, she would be able to take a dip in one of the beautiful, calm, emerald-green bays. Lili felt encouraged to give it a try.

She booked an excursion there and then, paying for it in cash. The young woman handed over her ticket. The price included being picked up by minibus from her hotel and taken to the port where the boats departed. They would also drop her back at the hotel after the trip. Lili thought that it seemed good value for money. She didn't have any plans for the following day, so the boat trip was a brilliant idea.

Lili had already spoken to Spiros about the tour of the island that he had suggested. She'd also mentioned visiting some vineyards in the area if there was time – not that she expected to find the actual one where Alena had lived. At least it would give her an idea of what a Corfiot vineyard might look like and an insight into the families who lived and worked there.

❖

Lili waited in the hotel foyer for the minivan to arrive, thinking of her conversation with Spiros. He was delighted that she had got back in touch. He was busy, but he had managed to fit her in the day after the boat trip. That suited Lili. Spiros had arranged to collect her and take her on what he said would be an unforgettable trip around the beautiful interior of the island. Lili was looking forward to the tour and seeing her lovely guide again.

She heard her name being called and looked up to see that a young woman with a clipboard had arrived at the hotel reception. Lili put her phone away. She'd been checking for any messages, but still no one had got back to her.

'Hello – are you Lili Skye?'

Lili nodded at the young woman.

'I am Maria, and I will take you to join the boat tour.' She glanced at her clipboard. 'You are the last person I needed to collect, as your hotel is quite close to the port.'

Lili followed Maria outside and climbed into the waiting minivan. There were already eight other people inside. They all greeted her with a friendly smile and a good morning. She guessed they were all tourists, like herself, mostly English, although two sisters and their mother sounded Irish. Like the others in the minivan, Lili had a bag with a large towel, a swim hat and sun cream. The hotel had thoughtfully provided a beach towel.

Arriving at the boat, Lili was pleasantly surprised at the mixture of people already on board. After buying her ticket on impulse the previous night, Lili had regretted it. She had assumed there would be young couples on the boat. The fact that there were families with children, older couples, sisters with their mum, and even other solo travellers put her at ease. The last thing Lili wanted was to appear the odd one out. She didn't want to feel uncomfortable, and lonely, for the entire day, because she was no longer part of a couple. After seeing the people she would be spending the day with, she began looking forward to the trip.

The tour would take in the north coast, with a stop for a swim and lunch before they returned later in the evening. The excursion also included a stop at a small bay to try some snorkelling. It all sounded great fun. Lili had never done anything similar before – at least, she had never done so and enjoyed it.

Once, when she had gone abroad with Alex, they had arranged something similar – a small boat trip off the coast of Turkey. Unfortunately, Alex was not a boat person. She had thought at the time that it would have been a good idea if he'd told her that before they'd booked. He'd spent the entire trip alternating between being sick over the side of the boat and lying on a bench, wiping his brow and groaning. Lili had never been so embarrassed. The captain had eventually decided that enough was enough and had asked them if they would disembark. They'd had to get a taxi back to their hotel.

Lili was going to enjoy every minute of this excursion. In fact, recalling that episode, she realised there were advantages to travelling alone; she could do as she pleased with the guarantee that nobody would spoil her day. She slipped on her sunhat and sunglasses. She hoped that it would turn out to be an unforgettable trip – for all the right reasons this time.

❖

Lili returned to the hotel later that day. She waved at Maria, who had dropped her back in the minivan from the port, and smiled as she skipped up the steps. The boat trip had been a great success, just as she expected. They had sailed into caves and swum in crystal blue waters. The views of the coastline – especially around Corfu Old Town, and further up the coast towards Albania – were, for Lili, the highlights of the trip.

The simple lunch, a seafood salad, had been delicious. There was also wine, freshly squeezed orange juice, lemonade and plenty of coffee. Everyone on board had clearly had a wonderful time, and Lili had noticed a real camaraderie among the passengers. She thought that it had been down to the jolly captain and crew – with their interesting seafaring tales and entertaining singsongs, they'd had everybody in hysterics.

By the end of the trip, as they returned to the harbour, she had sensed that she wasn't the only person who was feeling a little deflated. It had all been over too soon, and they'd known they would be parting ways. It had been one of those amazing experiences that Lili knew she would look back on and treasure for years to come.

'Did you have a wonderful trip?'

Lili stood at the desk as the concierge handed her the room key, and replied, 'Oh, yes – I had the most amazing time.' She didn't want to dampen her mood, but she had to ask, 'Were there any messages for me?' Mobile reception could be patchy, so when she'd phoned them on the hotel phone, she'd left both Ray and Hannah a message to contact her at the hotel.

The receptionist smiled. 'Ah, yes – you have a message.'

Lili grinned. Thank goodness. She'd been starting to worry.

The receptionist handed her a note.

Lili retreated to her room. Unfolding the note, she sat down on her bed to read it. 'Oh.' It wasn't a message from Hannah or Ray. It was from Spiros and contained details of the island tour the next day.

32

Lili had enjoyed a leisurely breakfast. She'd returned to her room to gather her bag, hat, and a cold bottle of sparkling water from the fridge that the cleaning staff replenished each day. She waited in the hotel lounge for Spiros to arrive. She was looking forward to the tour around the island, but she couldn't believe the last day of her trip to Corfu had arrived already. She was determined to make the most of it. With her life at home feeling in complete disarray, she didn't know when she'd be back.

She could see the reception area from where she was seated. As Spiros walked through the door, she went up to greet him. 'Kalimera.'

Spiros smiled, doffed his Panama hat and bowed as he too wished her a good morning in Greek. They walked down the steps of the hotel together and along the road to where he had parked his car. Lili chatted about her fantastic boat trip as they set off through the town.

'It sounds as though you had a wonderful day, Lili. I hope what I have planned for you today meets with your approval.'

Lili caught the playful glint in his eye. He knew full well it would. She smiled at him. She was looking forward to it. The trip was going to be perfect. When Lili had phoned Spiros to ask him to be her guide for the day, she had told him she would like to visit a vineyard. She wanted to get a feel for what Joseph had experienced as a child in Corfu, staying with Alena's family – but she certainly hadn't expected him to find the actual place Alena's parents had owned. It was now a thriving vineyard and winery, well-known for its tours and wine-tasting.

Lili was so excited. She couldn't quite believe she was on her way to see the place where Alena had once lived and that Joseph had visited as a child.

Spiros turned on the radio, and with some traditional Greek folk music playing in the background, they headed toward the Ropa Valley. The scenery was rather flat. Catching the look of disappointment on her face, Spiros told her that it had once been a lake. It had been drained over time and was now an important habitat for a variety of wildlife.

Traversing an area of pine trees, they passed the village of Giannades. Spiros turned off the road at a sign for a vineyard, starting up a long drive that Lili guessed led to the house. 'Oh, my god, is this it?' Lili was getting excited.

Spiros glanced at Lili and smiled. 'Yes, this is the vineyard.'

All around, and stretching into the distance, Lili could see a plethora of pine trees, olive groves and vineyards. Spiros had booked Lili on a tour of the winery.

At the end of the drive, Lili's heart leapt at the sight of the house. It was just as she had imagined it would be. As they got out of the car, Lili spotted a young lady standing in front of the property, surrounded by a small group of people who had already arrived for the tour. She came forward to greet them.

Spiros said good morning to the guide and then left the

group. He walked over to the café and gift shop where, Lili imagined, he'd sit whiling away the morning with a cup of coffee and the newspaper she noticed he'd brought with him.

Lili joined the other tourists who were waiting to be shown around the vineyard. Spiros had told her there would be a tour of the house too; some rooms were open to the public. Lili couldn't believe her luck. She was standing outside the sprawling vine-covered three-storey honey-coloured villa where Alena and her parents had once lived, and where Joseph and his family had stayed.

Lili got out her phone to take some photos. She was looking forward to speaking to Ray and telling him all about the tour. She realised that she'd love to show Joseph the pictures and see if he remembered the place – but she doubted she'd be seeing Joseph again. Or Nate. Lili tried not to let that thought spoil her last day on the island.

'This way.' The young tour guide started up the steps to the house. Lili couldn't stop smiling. She imagined Alena skipping down these very steps with the little English boy who was her cover for her liaisons with an artist friend of the family.

Touring the villa, Lili could tell they had staged it to show how a well-off Corfiot landowner and his family might have lived in a bygone era, years before Alena's parents settled there. Lili didn't enjoy the tour any less for it – she was just so excited to have the opportunity to go into the villa.

Inside, dark oak furniture contrasted with colourful curtains and painted vases with figures from Greek mythology. There were handwoven rugs throughout, which covered many of the flagstone floors. The thick, whitewashed walls made the interior feel cool. Lili had brought a light cardigan with her, which she'd draped around her shoulders. She took it off and slipped it on properly to keep the chill off her arms as they moved from room to room.

As they walked into an impressive dining room with an oak table that could seat at least ten people, the guide said, 'This table survived the plunder of the Nazi invasion of the Ionian Islands in the Second World War.'

The members of the tour party, including Lili, who had been ambling around the room and taking in the fine views of the vineyard from the windows, gathered around as the guide continued. 'They took away not only the Jews from the island but looted their valuable art and antiques. This table survived because of the sheer size and weight of it. Everything they took had to be loaded onto boats and shipped back to Germany.'

'Along with the Jews,' Lili added, her face growing crimson when she realised everyone had heard what she said.

The tour guide turned to Lili. 'That is true.'

'Where were they taken?' asked one of the group. Lili saw the woman's partner rolling his eyes at the question.

The guide answered anyway. 'To the camps.' What had happened afterwards, everyone knew. It needed no explanation.

'The family who lived here before the war,' Lili ventured, wondering how much the guide knew about them. 'They didn't survive, then?'

The guide shook her head. 'They were all taken. The Nazis tried to burn this place down, but they didn't succeed. For many years, it lay abandoned, the villa falling into disrepair. The once-thriving vineyards and olive groves succumbed to pests and nature, as nobody had been there to look after the place. Decades later, back in the sixties, two brothers on a trip from the

Greek mainland ventured into this part of Corfu and came across the ruins of the villa and the abandoned, overgrown plantation. In twenty years, no descendants of the family who had lived there before the war had come forward to claim the property or the land. The brothers worked the land and repaired the villa, making it habitable. The plantation has since passed to their children's children and, thanks to the family, they have not only restored the villa to its former glory, but the vineyard and winery is one of the most successful on the Ionian Islands.'

'So, are you saying that the Germans took the entire family?' one member of the party asked. Lili glanced at her. It was obvious that the people in the tour group were still interested in the family who had once lived there.

'Yes.'

'Were there children?'

'I believe so, yes.'

'Were they taken too?'

Lili thought of Alena. Sadly, she already knew the answer to that question.

'There was a rumour …' the guide began.

Lili had been staring at the table, imagining Alena and her family and friends seated around it, enjoying their meal, oblivious to the events that would soon unfold and change all their lives in ways they could never imagine.

Lili looked up when she heard the guide mention a rumour.

The young woman said, 'There was talk of a German who rescued some children from the island.'

'Are you saying,' the English lady in the tour group continued, 'that one of them, a member of the family, might have survived?'

She shrugged. 'It's possible. Anything is possible. But I'm afraid we'll probably never know. They would have been smuggled out of Corfu and taken in by a family on another Greek island. Many Jews then fled to start new lives in the newly created state of Israel after the war, never to return.'

Lili stared at the woman who was asking the questions.

'You'll have to excuse my wife,' said the woman's husband. 'She loves history – especially family history and genealogy.'

The woman glanced at her husband. 'I'm so sorry,' she said to the guide. 'I'm holding up the tour with all my questions.'

'There's nothing to apologise for. I'm just sorry I can't tell you more about the family.'

Lili was sorry too, although she had enjoyed the tour of the house nonetheless.

The wine-tasting afterwards was a novel experience for Lili. The guide was knowledgeable, and Lili found it fascinating to see the wine-making process at first-hand. She browsed the small museum and the gift shop next door, buying a small gift box of wine, even though she had no one to give it to. Hannah wasn't into red wine. Lili thought that perhaps she'd keep this one for herself. It was significant to her that the grapes had come from the very trees that had been used to produce wine in Alena's day.

Lili carried the gift box, wrapped in crepe paper inside a plastic bag with the name of the vineyard emblazoned on it, and rejoined Spiros, who was waiting by the car.

'That was a wonderful tour. Thank you, Spiros.'

He grinned. 'I thought you'd enjoy it. Getting inside the house was a bonus – eh?'

Lili returned his smile. 'I'll say.'

Before Lili got back into the car, she watched the small tour group disperse, leaving the garden in front of the villa quiet, save for the sounds of birdsong. Lili closed her eyes for a moment and imagined Joseph as a small boy, enjoying his lunch outside, seated at a long trestle table in the sunshine with his parents and their Greek friends, the vineyards stretching into the distance as far as the eye could see.

Lili opened her eyes at the sound of a clunk from the car door as Spiros settled into the driver's seat. After one last look at the villa, Lili got in beside him and they set off.

After a brief stop at the quaint village of Pelekas, where Lili got out once again and strolled around to enjoy the views, Spiros headed toward the Ambelonas winery, where he'd made a reservation for lunch.

The menu was extensive. Lili didn't know what to choose. She opted for a chicken risotto and a side salad with a lemon tart to follow. Spiros thought Lili had made an excellent choice and ordered the same. Later, he introduced Lili to their host, and she learned more about the two oldest Corfiot grape varieties grown in the area.

Spiros took a circuitous route back to Corfu Old Town so that Lili could get a glimpse of the wonderful scenery and take in the views of the coastline. He stopped the car outside the hotel and walked around to open the passenger door for her to alight. Lili reached for her purse, anticipating that he would refuse any payment for the tour. Spiros was already shaking his head at the sight of her purse. Reluctantly, Lili put it away.

'It has been my pleasure, Lili, to show you my beautiful island. I hope you take back some fond memories of your time spent here when you return to England.'

Lili stood on the pavement as Spiros added, 'I wish you all

the best with the search for your relatives. You have my card – please get in touch. I would love to hear how your story ends.'

Lili had tears in her eyes as he leaned forward and kissed her on both cheeks. 'Until next time.'

Lili watched him get back into his car and drive down the street until the car swung around the corner and disappeared.

'Until next time,' said Lili, sad to see him go. She turned for the hotel, aware that this was it. Her holiday was over. The next day, she was catching her flight home.

33

Lili walked into her hotel room after speaking to the concierge. She had also checked her mobile phone for messages yet again. She sat down on her bed and sighed heavily. Despite leaving numerous messages and sending texts during the week, she hadn't received a single call or text back from either Hannah or Ray.

Before she packed for her flight the next day, she decided to make one last call. She resorted to phoning Nate. He picked up straight away.

'You've got some nerve getting in touch after what you did.'

Lili swallowed. This was just what she had expected. Ray had been wrong; all was not forgiven. Lili wished she'd told him about Maisie before Hannah turned up unexpectedly, but there was nothing she could do about it now. 'Look, I need to speak to Joseph.'

'Where are you?'

'I'm in Corfu, but I'm coming home tomorrow.'

'What's your flight number?'

Lili thought it an odd question, unless he was planning to meet her at the airport. She smiled, convinced that was it. 'Hold on, I'll give it to you.' Sitting on her bed in the hotel room, Lili reached for her bag and found the return ticket. She reeled off the number. 'Are you going to pick me up?'

There was a pause. 'I'm sending a welcoming committee.'

Lili was about to ask what he'd meant by that, although she guessed he had a shift at work and wouldn't be able to make it himself. She didn't get a chance to find out if Ray would meet her instead, because Nate abruptly rang off. Or was she cut off? She tried calling him back, but it went straight to voicemail. Lili didn't bother leaving a message and started packing.

❖

Lili stayed in her seat, waiting for the seatbelt sign to switch off. They had mentioned the weather in England as they came in to land. Lili glanced out of the window. It was raining, and she didn't have an umbrella. She was just thinking that she'd have to make a dash for it to the airport terminal when the captain told everyone to remain seated. There were murmurs of disapproval amongst the passengers, who were being forced to wait longer than usual before disembarking. Lili switched on her phone and see if she had any messages. Nothing.

When she looked up, she spotted two uniformed police officers making their way down the cabin. A middle-aged woman seated next to Lili turned to her and whispered, 'I wonder what's going on?'

Lili's first thought was that there was a terrorist on board. She didn't tell the woman sitting next to her what she was thinking. Like everybody else who had spotted the officers boarding the plane, she was waiting to see which passenger they were there for.

The police passed Lili's seat. They appeared to be looking at the seat numbers. 'Seat number 23,' she heard one say. 'We've passed it.' They turned around.

Lili stared at them as they approached. That was her number.

One officer said, 'Lili Rose Skye?'

The woman sitting next to Lili looked at her wide-eyed and then got out of her seat so quickly that she dropped her handbag. The other officer picked it up for her and helped her into the aisle.

Lili nodded. 'Yes, that's me.'

'Can you come with us, please?'

Lili stood up, gathering her coat and bag. She didn't know what this was about, but she understood the police officer wasn't asking. 'Yes, of course.'

As Lili moved down the aisle, there was a hushed silence in the cabin. She glanced around, not surprised that the other passengers were staring at her. 'Let me take those.' The officer took her coat and bag.

'I don't understand … what's going on?' She hadn't broken any rules on the flight. She'd stowed her bag under the seat and not been drunk or rude to the other passengers.

Lili felt something cold envelope her wrists. She looked down to find an officer had handcuffed her. Lili stared at the handcuffs in shock. 'Am I being arrested?'

One officer led the way and the other brought up the rear as Lili moved down the narrow cabin aisle towards the exit.

Lili could feel her face glowing red in embarrassment. 'I don't understand …' she repeated as she walked down the flight of stairs to the runway to a police car was waiting.

Lili stopped in front of the car. She turned to the officers.

'There has been some mistake. A *big* mistake.' Lili recalled the last phone conversation with Nate, when he made that that odd comment about sending a welcoming committee. Lili looked at the police car, which was surrounded by officers. *Is this what he meant?* she thought. *Was this her welcoming committee?* His dad had been a cop, and probably had friends in high places. Lili grimaced. She'd thought she was on good terms with Ray.

'Look, this is ridiculous. Tell Nate I'm sorry about Maisie, truly I am.' He was doing this to get back at her, embarrass her. 'If I can just have my mobile phone to call Nate or Ray. Actually, I'll speak to Ray, he'd be the best person to clear all this up.' Lili looked at the officer standing in front of her. 'Do you know Ray?'

'Gawd, can someone shut her up!' the officer blurted.

Another police officer stepped forward.

'Miss Lili Skye, I am arresting you on suspicion of the theft of antiques.'

Lili stared at him, open-mouthed. 'I beg your pardon?'

'Along with a prize orchid from George and Son Antiques.'

'A prize orchid? Joseph doesn't keep orchids in his shop.' She looked at the officer who was reading her rights as though he was off his rocker. 'There's been some mistake. This is just ridiculous!'

Fifteen minutes later, Lili was shown the inside of a prison cell in the local police station. She sat staring at its four walls as the truth sunk in; she really had been arrested and charged.

'I want my phone call,' she yelled. Lili had a silly thought: at least if she went to prison, she wouldn't have to concern herself about being homeless.

'Perhaps my day just got better.'

Lili knew she wasn't in her right mind to have thoughts like that. Sitting on the bed, something occurred to her. Why had they gone to all the trouble of boarding the plane to arrest her? Why such a fanfare over the theft of a few mediocre antiques from a small independent shop in a quaint seaside town in Suffolk? It's not like they were worth much. Anyone would think she was some sort of master criminal who had intended to go on the run. It made little sense. Did they know she was just a horticulturist from Kew? If someone had broken into Joseph's shop, why did they assume she was the guilty party?

'You will get your phone call in due course,' a male voice said from behind her door.

'Good!'

Lili had to wait an excruciating hour before she was allowed her call. She dialled Ray's number. She grasped the receiver so hard her knuckles went white. 'Please, please answer.' Someone had made a big mistake. She hadn't stolen anything. She'd been in Corfu, for god's sake – Ray knew that. Lili didn't believe he was involved with her arrest.

'Ray? Ray – is that you?' Lili breathed an enormous sigh when she heard him reply, 'Yes, it's me.'

'I'm in a spot of bother, Ray.'

'I know.'

Lili hoped that his answer didn't mean he had something to do with her arrest. 'I'd never steal from Joseph.'

'I know that too. I've already spoken with the desk sergeant. They know that you had nothing to do with it, Lili. You should be free within the hour.'

'Oh, thank god!' Lili exhaled in relief. 'Look, I don't know what's going on—'

Before she said anymore, Ray filled her in. 'It happened just before you left for Corfu.'

'Oh.'

'I'm afraid, on paper, it all pointed to you. Reggie thought he saw you, Lili. Then the police discovered you'd booked a plane ticket, last minute, just hours after the theft. It wasn't looking good. That's why they arrested you.'

'But it wasn't me.'

'I know, but Reggie swore he spotted you, going back and forward from the shop, loading stuff up in a car. He said he recognised your distinctive coat.'

'But I don't even own a—' Lili stopped abruptly.

'—car. Precisely!' There was a pause. 'They thought you were an accessory.'

'An accessory?'

At first Lili didn't understand until a police officer passed her in the corridor while she was still on the phone to Ray. The officer was escorting someone else to her cell. Lili's eyes went wide when she saw who it was.

34

'I'm afraid it was Maisie's mother who robbed the shop,' Ray said down the phone. 'You were on the evening news. When Hannah saw that you'd been arrested, she called me and said she was turning herself in.'

'I wasn't an accessory,' Lili said, as Hannah caught sight of her and mouthed, 'I'm sorry,' as they led her away.

'Yes, Hannah told the police you had nothing to do with it. But she had a key, Lili. That's why Reggie didn't report it, as there wasn't any sign of a break-in. It was only when Sarah visited the shop the next day and noticed things missing, along with the orchid, that the alarm was raised.'

'What orchid?'

'Joseph's ghost orchid. It had bloomed. Joseph had his hip operation and was due home. He wanted to stop by the shop, so we thought it would be a delightful surprise if his prize orchid was there in the window.'

Lili frowned. 'Well, that was dumb.'

'Yes, in hindsight it was, but how were we to know the place would be robbed?'

Lili shook her head. 'I sent her there to collect some of my belongings that I'd forgotten to take with me when I left – that was all.' Now Lili had an idea why she had been arrested at the airport; Joseph's prized orchid was worth six figures. 'I don't understand why she'd do such a thing. And believe me, she would have no idea how much the plant was worth.' Lili guessed Hannah had seen the flower in the window and thought she'd give it to her best friend.

Lili frowned. That did not explain why Hannah had stolen Joseph's antiques. Then she recalled the row she'd overheard between Hannah and Kyle; she was certain that they were having financial troubles.

She couldn't believe what Hannah had done, taking advantage of her as she had. Had that been why she'd offered to collect Lili's stuff in the first place? Maybe it hadn't just been a chance to get out of the house. Had her plan all along been to steal from the shop?

Lili recalled how keen Hannah had been for her to take the next flight to Corfu. Now she understood; it was so she was as far away as possible when the theft was discovered, otherwise the police might trace her to their home.

Lili couldn't believe that after all she had done for Hannah over the years, this was how she had repaid her. Something one of her friends had once said to her came to mind: *Hannah needs to grow up and take responsibility for her own life, and that of her child. You're not responsible for her. The day will come when you won't be around to bail her out of trouble.*

Thinking of Hannah being led away to a prison cell, Lili guessed that day had arrived.

Her heart suddenly sank. *Maisie*! 'What about Maisie?!' Lili exclaimed down the phone.

'It's okay, Lili, she's with me. Well, she's with her father at the moment.'

Lili thought she heard children's voices in the background. She would bet that William was delighted to have his big half-sister back.

Ray added, 'I'm up at the house too.'

Lili caught the police officer standing off to one side, pointing at the clock on the wall. Lili nodded in his direction. 'Ray, I have to end the call soon.' She paused before she added, 'Nate does know it wasn't me who stole from Joseph, doesn't he?' Now Lili understood why Ray hadn't answered her texts or messages, and why Nate had seemed so angry with her over the phone when she'd called his number. It hadn't been to do with Maisie; it had been over this. Until Hannah had come forward and confessed, they'd assumed it was her.

Ray replied, 'Don't worry, I've filled Nate in.'

'Thank you, Ray.' Not that Lili thought it would do any good. He'd still be mad at her.

'What are your plans for after they release you?'

Lili thought of her friends who lived in London, her closest friends. She knew they would put her up while she figured things out. In hindsight, Lili wished she'd gone to them first instead of Hannah.

'I know what you're thinking, Lili,' Ray said. 'Listen to me. None of this is your fault. She would have screwed up whether you'd handed her the key to Joseph's shop or not. If it wasn't stealing from the antique shop, something else would have happened. It was on the cards.'

That was what her other friends had said.

'You're not responsible for Hannah – or Maisie.'

Lili sighed. That was what her friends had said, too.

'You must think about yourself, Lili. By the way, how did your trip to Corfu go?'

Lili didn't have time to get into that; not over the phone while standing in a police station. After what she'd discovered about his father-in-law, it was quite possible that Joseph and George had lived a lie since they'd returned to England after the war, taking the assumed names of two dead people. That was illegal.

Lili glanced at the officer watching her and said to Ray, 'Can we meet? I need to see Joseph.'

'Of course, Lili. I have a spare cabin on the boat. Come back and stay as long as you like.'

'You are too kind,' Lili replied, although she wasn't sure how much he would appreciate her visit when she told him what she'd discovered.

There was something else she wanted to say before her time was up. 'Look, Hannah isn't this sort of person. She just made a mistake. Do you think you can get the charges dropped?' She had already guessed what his response would be.

'I'm afraid that is out of my hands. Talk to Joseph. He has had his hip operation. He is due to be discharged. I would imagine Sarah is on her way to The Summerhouse with him as we speak.'

Lili noticed her suitcase and coat on the reception desk, ready for her to leave. 'I might try to catch the next train to Suffolk today.'

'That's fine by me,' said Ray. 'I'll look forward to seeing you.'

Lili had meant to ask about Nate, but she didn't. What she asked before she got off the phone, because it was still bugging her, was, 'Did you have something to do with my arrest? Do you know they escorted me from the plane?'

'They arrested you at the airport?' Ray said in surprise. 'I assumed you'd returned to Hannah's house.'

'Yes, as soon as the aircraft landed. They made me feel like a terrorist. I know the orchid is worth a bit of money, Ray, but I still don't understand all the commotion over a few antiques that were not worth all that much – pardon me for saying.'

'Neither do I,' Ray said slowly.

The officer walked over. 'It's time to leave.'

Lili nodded. 'Right, I've got to go, Ray. I'll let you know if I catch a train today.' She rang off.

Lili was just picking up her suitcase and coat when the desk sergeant said, 'We have a few questions.'

Lili frowned. 'Questions? I thought I was free to go?'

'Yes, you are, but it would help with our investigation if you cooperated.'

Lili shrugged. Although she was keen to leave, this might give her an opportunity to defend her friend. Hannah wasn't a criminal. She hadn't planned this. She'd just made a bad, spur-of-the-moment decision. At least, that was what Lili wanted to believe.

She left her belongings where they were and followed the police officer into a small room with a desk and three chairs. Lili took the single seat in front of two plain-clothes officers. She felt absurdly nervous, as though if she said the wrong thing, they might arrest her again.

Lili folded one hand on top of the other on her lap. She was wondering what they were going to ask. She anticipated there would be questions about her best friend.

The older of the two officers opened a file and slid a photograph along the table towards Lili. 'Do you recognise this?'

Lili stared at the photo and nodded. 'I think so.' She looked up and caught the two officers exchange a glance. The older officer, about Ray's age, took the photo back. 'What can you tell me about it?'

'Was that stolen too?' Lili asked. That made sense – not that any of this regarding Hannah's behaviour really made sense; she wasn't a thief. But she had been upstairs to the flat in order to retrieve the box, so she must have seen the painting. Lili stared at the photo across the desk. 'Was that stolen too?' she asked again.

Lili shifted nervously in her seat when they didn't answer her question. 'Maisie, my best friend's daughter, liked the painting. It was a shame it was hidden under a dust sheet, so I hung it on the wall in the flat above the shop. I didn't steal it, if that's what you're implying.' Although she guessed Hannah had.

'We gather it didn't come from the shop, though. We didn't see it listed in the inventory,' said the young officer in the seat next to his colleague.

Lili shook her head. 'No.' She didn't want to get into trouble, but there was no good hiding the truth. 'Look, I probably shouldn't have …' She was going to use the word *taken*, instead she said, 'shifted it, but …'

Lili didn't want to blame it on the dog, but she did. 'It was Bella's fault that curiosity got the better of me.' It had also been Maisie's fault, although Lili didn't mention that she'd wanted another painting to go with the one they'd already found in the flat.

'Bella?'

Lili turned to the younger officer who had spoken, his pen

poised over a notepad. 'Yes. Bella is Joseph's guard dog, but she is a big softie at heart. Anyway, I was curious as to why Joseph had a guard dog. I thought it might be something to do with the basement—' On one of her visits to the house to water Joseph's plants, she'd nosed around the house, discovering the basement and another painting under a dust sheet. She shouldn't have taken it back to the flat and hung it on the wall, but she did.

'There's a basement in the shop?'

Lili shook her head. 'No, no. I'm talking about the basement in Joseph's house.' She knew what they were going to ask her: what was she doing at his house?

'So, let me get this straight. You discovered the painting at the antique shop owner's property?'

Lili nodded again. 'It's a long story. I have a key and I've been feeding Joseph's dog and watering his plants. It all started when I found some pet food—'

Lili had just started her explanation about the very first time she'd visited The Summerhouse with Maisie, after discovering some pet food in Joseph's groceries that had been delivered to the shop by mistake, but the officers were already out of their seats. They grabbed their jackets from the backs of their chairs and rushed out of the room.

Lili stared after them thinking, *was it something I said?* She turned her head to look at the officer who had escorted her to the room; he was still standing by the wall in the corner. He too was staring after his colleagues.

Lili coughed into her hand. 'Ahem. Excuse me – does this mean I'm free to go?' She hoped so. She'd felt she was under interrogation and had been starting to feel quite intimidated while answering their questions.

The uniformed officer stepped out into the corridor. He reappeared a moment later. 'I guess so.'

Lili shrugged, thinking *how odd* that the interview had ended so abruptly. She wasn't sorry.

On the way out of the police station, she collected her luggage, her coat, and her phone. Lili stood outside and looked up the train times to the south coast. 'Crumbs!' If she got a move on, she would make the next train.

Lili walked down the street and hailed a cab. 'Liverpool Street Station, please,' she said as she sat down in the back of the taxi. The prospect of seeing Joseph was at the forefront of her mind, but her first stop had to be The Summerhouse. She wanted to see Maisie first and check she was okay. *Goodness knows how she feels about her mother being arrested*, Lili thought. She knew she had to set her own feelings about Nate to one side; she guessed he wouldn't be pleased to see her. At least Ray had put him in the picture regarding Joseph's shop; he knew she had nothing to do with the robbery.

Lili made it to the station in time to catch the next train. She still had the phone number of the taxi company she'd used before. She called them as soon as she was seated and arranged a taxi to take her straight from the station to The Summerhouse. After a quick pit stop to see Maisie and tell Ray what she'd discovered in the British Cemetery in Corfu – not just about her relations, but about Joseph – she would set off to the hospital to meet him. If he was already at the house, all the better.

35

Lili leaned forward in her seat as the car turned up the drive. 'What on earth …?'

The taxi driver stopped the car. She was the same driver who had driven Lili back and forward countless times when she was looking after Bella and watering Joseph's plants. She had seen the flashing blue lights too. She glanced at her passenger. 'It looks as though something has happened up at the house. Do you want me to turn around?'

Lili stared out of the window; she was afraid somebody had had an accident. What if it was Maisie? Lili swallowed as she shifted her gaze to the driver. 'No, please drive on up to the house.' She needed to know what was going on.

There were police cars parked haphazardly in front of the property along with a police van. All their lights were still flashing, as though they had arrived at a speed.

The taxi driver glanced in her rear-view mirror. 'I think there's another vehicle coming up the drive. I'm afraid I need to turn the car around and leave now, otherwise I'll get hemmed in.'

'Okay.' Lili opened the car door. She paid the driver, slipped on her coat and got out of the vehicle, heaving her suitcase off the back seat. She watched the taxi driver do a three-point-turn and pass the unmarked van coming up the drive.

Lili walked the rest of the way, the white van passing her. Nearing the house, she breathed a sigh of relief when she realised there wasn't an ambulance parked outside. However, what she saw surprised her. Police were loading things from the house into the police van. They'd run out of space, so they had started to load up the unmarked van that had just arrived.

Lili stopped and stared at all the activity. Many paintings were being loaded into the vans, some mounted in ornate picture frames. Many looked quite old. They were just the sort of thing she expected to see in a museum or art gallery. She frowned; she didn't recall seeing them hanging anywhere in the house.

Lili didn't see all the paintings being brought out; some were covered in dust sheets, just like the sheet that had protected the picture in the basement – the one she'd told the police about earlier in the day.

'Oh, god!' Lili connected the dots, remembering the two officers rushing out of the interview room the moment she told them where she'd found the landscape painting. She shook her head. It didn't make sense. For starters, there was nothing else in the cellar – unless they hadn't found them all in the house. Her thoughts turned to the old wooden summerhouse in the garden, with the large lock and the curtains closed at the windows so it was impossible to peek inside.

All that time, she'd wondered why it was locked. Now she had her answer. Even so, why were the police so interested in a bunch of old paintings? Joseph was an antiques dealer; it didn't surprise her that he had stored the canvases, waiting to sell them in his shop.

Lili stepped forward and approached an officer in uniform standing by a car.

The police officer must have heard her footsteps on the gravel drive. He turned around. 'Who are you?'

'I'm Lili, a friend of the family.'

At that moment, Joseph appeared at the front door. He was sitting in a wheelchair and was being wheeled outside. Another detective was carrying two walking sticks.

'You can't do this!' Joseph exclaimed. 'You don't understand!'

Lili's eyes went wide when she saw Ray escorted out of the house in handcuffs. 'What did you do?' he shouted at Joseph as an officer led them to a police car.

Lili stepped forward.

The officer held out his arm and barred the way. 'Please stay back.'

'What's going on? Are you arresting them?'

Lili did a double-take when Nate and Sarah emerged, also in handcuffs. They were escorted to the second police car.

The officer looked at the house and lowered his voice. 'We've uncovered one of the largest collections of stolen art in seventy years. I reckon its worth millions.'

'Stolen art?' Lili's mouth dropped open. 'No, there's been some mistake.'

'I'm afraid not.' He glanced at Lili's suitcase on the driveway. 'Were you intending to stay with the family?'

Lili shook her head. 'No, I'm going to stay at The Harbour Inn.' At least, that had been the plan until she'd turned up and discovered what was happening at the house.

'In Aldeburgh?'

Lili nodded.

'Good. If we have questions, we know where to find you.'

'But what about Maisie?'

'Who?'

Lili saw a young female officer walk out of the house, an arm around Maisie's shoulder. She said, 'What about the little girl?'

'Phone social services.'

Lili rushed forward before the officer standing in front of her could stop her. 'I can take her!' she shouted out.

Maisie, her cheeks wet with tears, looked up. 'Lili!'

The female officer tried to grab Maisie's hand.

'Get off me!' Maisie struggled free and ran over to Lili. She threw her arms around Lili's waist. 'Don't let them take me away. I want to stay with you.'

Lili hugged her tight. 'No one is taking you anywhere,' she reassured her.

In the police car, Lili caught Nate's eye. He looked up at the house and mouthed, *William.*

Lili glanced up at the house and understood; they hadn't found William. He was hiding somewhere inside. Lili looked back at Nate and nodded. She saw him close his eyes in relief before the car sped away, whisking him and his mother to the police station. The vehicle taking Ray and Joseph followed. Two officers finished loading Joseph's wheelchair into the van.

The young female officer walked up to Lili. 'Are you a relative?'

'No, but—'

'In that case, I'm sorry, but we can't leave her in your care.'

The word *care* sent shivers down her spine.

The officer reached for Maisie.

Lili turned around, moving Maisie out of her reach.

Her colleague, whom Lili had already spoken to, joined them. 'If you don't want to find yourself arrested too, I suggest you hand her over.'

Lili thought of the prison cell. She knew she couldn't do anything for Maisie if they locked her up too. She had an idea. She prised Maisie's hands away from her waist.

'No!' Maisie protested. 'Don't let them take me.'

Lili smiled. 'I have no intention of that happening, but I need to get my mobile phone out of my pocket.'

The moment Maisie let go of Lili, the officer grabbed her hand.

'Wait!' Lili exclaimed. 'Just wait.'

The two officers exchanged a glance.

Lili made a frantic call. 'Connie, it's Lili. I need your help!' Lili didn't waste any time telling her what was happening; she told her the police were going to phone social services and take her best friend's child away.

'I have a social worker on the phone for you.' Lili handed her phone over to the officer.

Lili stared at Maisie, hoping Connie could persuade one of the officers to release Maisie into her care.

The policewoman kept glancing at Lili as she listened. Then she spoke to Connie. 'I will need to check your credentials and I want it in writing, faxed to the police station, that social services have authorised this child to be temporarily placed in the foster care of Lili Skye.'

Maisie put her arms around Lili's waist again, smiling up at her as though it was a done deal. Lili knew it wasn't – not until they'd seen the fax on official headed paper.

The officer nodded at her colleague. Lili then heard him call dispatch on the car radio. Five minutes later, Lili almost cried when they handed her phone back and told her Maisie could stay.

'Connie?' She was still on the line. 'Thank you, thank you. I can't tell you what this means to me.' Lili knew she had taken a huge risk with her job. She didn't know Maisie or her family circumstances. Despite that, Connie had done as she'd asked.

Lili stood with Maisie, watching the remaining two officers get in their car and follow the last van to leave, full of stolen artwork that Lili guessed was worth millions. Lili was still on the phone with Connie. 'I am so sorry for going off on one over my mum,' she said contritely.

'There is no need to apologise, Lili. I made a mistake – a big mistake – all those years ago, which I will regret to my dying day. I should have been honest and told the Greek authorities that I knew your mother.'

'It wouldn't have changed anything, Connie. They'd still have been dead, whether I found this out years ago or now.'

'Yes, but I robbed you of finding your family, grandparents, aunts and uncles. They might have brought you up.'

'It was for the best.'

'You don't mean that, Lili.'

'I do. Sometimes I feel I had a stronger start in life because of you, Connie. It was you who looked after me and gave me an excellent education. You were always in my corner.'

Lili glanced at Maisie. She didn't want to admit it, but there had been times it had crossed her mind that Maisie would be better off without her mother. Lili's thoughts turned to Maisie's father, grandparents and her great-grandfather. She hadn't known them long. What if they really had stolen that art?

Thinking of Maisie, Lili said, 'You can't choose your family – right? You said yourself that my mum was estranged from her parents. Perhaps she had good reason to keep me away from them.'

'Perhaps,' Connie replied, although she didn't sound convinced. 'You know, there are always two sides to every story.'

Lili thought of Joseph shouting out at the police officers, *you don't understand!*

'Are you saying that my mother was wrong to keep my existence a secret?'

'Not necessarily. I'm just suggesting that you need to discover why they were estranged. You need to find your family and hear their side of the story.'

Lili turned towards the house to watch Maisie run inside, shouting out, 'William! Bella!'

'I went to Corfu,' she said to Connie.

'Did you find anything?'

'I visited my mother's grave.'

Connie fell silent.

'There was a man whose family have been custodians of the cemetery for generations. He kindly gave me the name of my grandparents.'

'Well, that's wonderful news.'

Is it? Lili felt like saying. She was still wary of the reasons why her mother had kept her away from them. She walked into the house and closed the front door.

'Lili, I'm so glad we're on speaking terms again.'

'So am I,' Lili replied, thankful Connie had answered her phone and was prepared to do this for her.

'I've found William!' Maisie shouted out.

'Look, I have to go, Connie.' Lili thanked her again.

'Will you let me know how you get on with finding your family?'

'Yes, I will,' Lili replied, even though just at that moment, as she watched the two children run down the stairs towards her, the issue of her family wasn't at the forefront of her mind. They would want to know why the police had taken everyone away. Lili recalled the paintings being loaded into the unmarked vans and thought, *what the hell did they do?*

36

William ran into Lili's arms. She could see by his tear-stained face that he'd been crying. She knelt and told him that everything was going to be okay.

'Why did the police take everyone away?'

It was a good question. Had they really stolen all that art? She still couldn't quite believe they had.

Maisie ran into the lounge. Lili could hear the television. She took William by the hand and followed Maisie into the room. She glanced at the television. A journalist was reporting for the news about the art haul that the police had discovered. Lili did a double-take when she saw an old photo of The Summerhouse pop up on the screen during the live report.

Crumbs, thought Lili, *news travels fast.* She raced over to the window and pulled the curtains shut, even though there were no journalists outside the house – yet. She nearly slipped on the paperwork and photos that the police had left strewn around as they opened drawers and cupboards and pulled everything out. *God only knows what they were looking for*, thought Lili.

'That's The Summerhouse!' William said, when he saw the photo on the television.

Lili walked over to the sofa, trying to avoid treading on the stuff littering the floor. She sat down in between William and Maisie, putting an arm around each of their shoulders and pulling them close.

The news programme didn't have any further information, apart from that the police had identified the valuable paintings as lost items listed in the Art Loss Register.

When a photograph flashed up of the family that had been arrested, Lili took the remote control out of Maisie's hand and switched off the television. 'Now, listen to me. I'm sure this has all been a big misunderstanding, and the nice police officer will bring them all home soon.'

Maisie looked at Lili. 'Do you promise?'

'Cross my heart,' Lili said, slapping on her biggest smile and hoping it didn't look fake. What if Nate, Ray, Sarah and Joseph really had stolen all that art, like some sort of criminal ring? It sounded ludicrous, but how well did she know them? She'd only just met them around a month ago. And as for Joseph, was that even his real name?

Lili's thoughts turned to her mother and the secret she had discovered which had driven her away to seek a new life abroad. It made her wonder just how much anyone really knew their nearest and dearest. It sent shivers down her spine to think that her mum had felt so strongly about something that she'd kept the knowledge of her own daughter's existence from her parents. Why? Lili was hesitant about the thought of finding her grand-parents.

'When are they coming home?' William whined.

'Ray said they arrested Mummy. That's why I'm staying here. When is *she* coming home?'

Lili looked from Maisie to William. 'Honestly, I don't know.'

William looked about him. 'Where's Bella?'

'I think she went into hiding too, just like you.' She was very surprised the dog hadn't appeared. She'd imagined that in those circumstances, Bella would growl at all the police officers and stand her ground, guarding the house, but she guessed that in reality, Bella had been spooked by all the cars and flashing lights, and had run off. Lili hoped that was the case. She didn't want them to find Bella and take her away too, or – heaven forbid – put her down.

Lili stood up. She cast her gaze around the room at the mess she ought to clear up. 'Let's find her. I'm sure she won't have gone far.'

They all convened in the hall five minutes later. They had each taken a floor of the house to search for her. Lili could hear the two children calling the dog's name while she searched downstairs.

Lili put her hands on her hips. 'Right, where next?'

'She must be in the garden,' suggested Maisie.

'Let's call her from the back door,' suggested Lili. 'It's getting dark outside.'

William ran into the kitchen and returned with a large torch. He switched it on. Lili looked at it. 'Great – but we'll have to stick together this time.'

They all left the house through the back entrance. William shone the torch around the garden, calling out, 'Bella!'

Lili and Maisie joined in. 'Bella! Here, girl!'

'What about in there?' Maisie pointed at the old summer-house.

They made their way down the garden and stepped onto the

wooden veranda. They all stopped and stared at the open doorway.

William shook his head. 'We're not allowed in there.'

Lili turned to him. She knew the property had always been kept locked, but now the lock was broken and the door was wide open. 'Who made that rule, William?'

'Great-grandad.'

'I see. Well, Joseph isn't around right now, and we want to find Bella.'

'She might be inside,' Maisie added.

'All right.' William stepped forward.

Lili and Maisie followed him inside.

'Clever boy!' exclaimed Lili when William shone the torch on a light switch. Lili switched on the lights.

'Wow!' Lili said, standing there in amazement.

'This is *so* cool!'

Lili smiled. She'd missed Maisie so much.

The cabin appeared bigger inside. It reminded Lili of a log cabin she'd seen in a movie once; it had a huge fireplace on one side with a log burner, and oak kitchen units running along the wall on the other side. There was a large L-shaped leather sofa, two matching chairs, and a rug covering the wooden floor in the centre of the room. Above them, there was a mezzanine, which could be reached via a spiral staircase.

'This is where my great-great-granddad used to live.'

Maisie and Lili turned to look at William. He glanced at them and shrugged. 'I asked Daddy once. I've never been inside before. He said that this was where they lived while they built the new house.'

Maisie called out, 'Bella!'

Lili thought she heard something. 'Shh! Do you hear that?' She heard a whine. 'Bella?' she shouted. She started up the stairs. The children followed. On the mezzanine level, there was a bedroom in the eaves with two single divans made up with quilts and pillows that looked old and threadbare.

Maisie ran over and jumped on a bed. They heard the dog whimper. Lili knelt down and shifted the valance to see under the bed. Two brown eyes stared at her in the darkness. 'Bella? It's okay, it's me.'

Bella barked in Lili's face.

Behind Lili, William and Maisie were jumping up and down, chanting, 'We found her, we found Bella!'

Bella, not a small dog, needed help to get out from her hiding place. 'You are a silly, silly dog,' said Maisie, flinging her arms around the dog's neck.

Bella licked both her face and William's when he sat on the floor to stroke her head.

Lili stayed at arm's length. 'Oh, no. I don't want a kiss too.'

'Yes, you do,' squealed the children, and pulled Lili by the arm, making her kneel and give Bella a fuss, getting a doggy kiss in return. They fell about giggling. Then Lili noticed that William wasn't laughing any more. He stood there, looking about him. They all did. In the mezzanine room, and the room below, there were lots of empty hooks where paintings had hung, and several easels, just like Maisie's, where canvases had been stored.

William turned to Lili. 'Is Daddy going to prison for a long time?' His eyes filled with tears.

Maisie put her arms around William. 'It will be okay. I promise. Remember what Daddy told you? I'm your big sister now. I'll look after you.'

Lili looked at Maisie. So, Nate had told Maisie he was her father, and little William was her brother.

Lili put her arms around both of them. 'And I am going to look after both of you. Now, come on. Bella must be hungry. Let's take her back to the house.'

'I'm hungry too,' said William.

'So am I,' Maisie added.

Lili smiled as she watched the two children walk down the spiral staircase with Bella leading the way. Her smiled faded when she thought of what William had said. Despite appearing optimistic for the sake of the children, there was no telling when or if the family would be released.

Lili was about to follow when she saw some photos scattered on the floor beside an upturned drawer which belonged to the desk. She stooped to gather up the prints and was about to pick up the drawer and slip them back inside when something caught her eye. The woman in one photo seemed familiar.

Lili took a closer look. 'It can't be!' It was her mother. She was standing in this very room, with the same curtains up at the window and the same coverlets on the twin beds, except they were not so threadbare. In her arms was a toddler. Lili stared at the first ever photo she'd seen of herself with her mum. Maisie appeared at the top of the stairs, and said, 'Lili, why are you crying?' She ran up to Lili and looked at the image in her hand. 'Who's that?'

'That's my mother, and this is me.'

Maisie studied the photo. 'You were here with your mum.' She looked at Lili. 'Are we related?'

'I don't know, Maisie.'

'Who's that man?' Maisie pointed at the elderly gentleman

standing behind her mother with a hand on her shoulder. He appeared around Joseph's age, if not older in the print.

William ran up the stairs and joined them, asking, 'When are we going back to the house? I'm hungry.' He looked at the photo. 'What's that?'

'It's a picture of me as a young child with my mother.' Lili pointed at the man in the photo. 'But I don't know who this is.'

'Oh, I know,' William said nonchalantly. 'I've seen him in pictures before. That's great-great grandpapa.'

'Joseph's father?'

'Yes, I told you, great-great grandpapa. Now, come on!' William grabbed Lili's hand. 'I want to go now.'

Lili didn't want to be dragged away. She wanted to look through more photos and any paperwork she could lay her hands on. She decided she would return to the summerhouse later when the children were asleep. Now she was desperate to speak to Joseph. Why was there a photo of her and her mum with Joseph's father? She still couldn't believe she'd been there before, in that very room, with her mother.

Lili closed the cabin door behind her and stood there for a moment, staring at the broken latch. Was it just the priceless art that had been hidden under lock and key from the world? Or was it something more? What secret had her mother uncovered? Lili was thinking of the gravestones of a young man and his son.

37

The old lady rang the doorbell. As she stood there on the doorstep, a memory came flooding back, as vivid as if it had been formed the day before, even though it had been many years since Joseph had carried her over the threshold into their new home. The house hadn't changed.

Maisie answered the door. 'Hello.'

'Well, hello there. And who might you be?'

'I'm Maisie.'

She'd never seen this child before and wondered if Joseph still had a cleaner or a gardener and whether Maisie was there with her parent. 'Is your mother or father around?'

Maisie frowned and shook her head. 'They were arrested yesterday.'

'Oh, I see.'

Maisie showed the old lady the small spray can in her hand. 'I'm watering Joseph's orchids. Would you like to see them?'

'Yes, please.' She followed Maisie into the house and through the door into the conservatory. Taking a seat in one of the wicker chairs, she looked around the greenhouse. The inside of the house hadn't changed either. Her gaze shifted to the young girl. She wondered why the child was there alone. 'So, where is everyone?'

'William and Lili are upstairs, but the police arrested my family and took them all away.'

'I know. I heard it on the news.' She stopped and took a closer look at Maisie. 'Your father is Nathaniel?'

'Yes. My mum wouldn't tell me who my real dad was, then I found out when I came on holiday here with Lili.'

'I see.' She didn't, not really, but didn't know what else to say to that. 'Is Lili your mum?'

Lili was towel-drying her hair when she heard Maisie talking downstairs. She walked to the bedroom door, wondering who Maisie was chatting to. Bella was lying on her bed, and William was in the bathroom.

Lili had a sudden thought. Were they back? Had Alex got them all released? Lili had swallowed her pride and phoned him the previous night. She'd thought he'd be in Washington by now, but he wasn't, thank goodness – she needed his help. He'd been vague when she'd asked him when he was leaving, but not when she'd asked for his help. He was going to do all that he could to get her friends released.

Lili dropped the towel and ran out of the bedroom. William had emerged from the bathroom and glanced at her. 'Who is Maisie talking to?' he asked. He'd heard her too. 'Is Daddy back?'

Lili ran down the stairs with William hot on her heels. They both walked into the conservatory. She looked at Maisie, who was still watering the plants. 'Who were you chatting to?'

Lili followed Maisie's gaze to a lady of advancing years. She was very slim, dressed in dark blue slacks, a sweater over a blouse and a tweed jacket. It was hard to gauge her age, although with her grey-white hair and slight stoop, Lili guessed she was at least in her late seventies.

William spotted her too. 'Great-grandma!' He rushed over to her.

'William!'

Lili frowned. 'Great-grandma? Are you Joseph's wife?' Lili assumed she had died some years ago.

'Ex-wife. I'm Elspeth.' She gave William a hug. When William drew back, he said, 'Maisie is my sister.'

'Half-sister,' Maisie corrected him. 'We have different mums, remember.'

Elspeth stood up and smiled. 'You have your daddy's eyes. Come over here and give your great-grandma a hug.'

Maisie put down the watering can and ran over into her arms.

Lili caught Elspeth looking her way. 'And you must be Lili.'

'I'm a family friend, not Maisie's mum.'

Maisie piped up, 'Mum's in jail too.'

Lili rolled her eyes at Maisie. It sounded as though she had put Elspeth in the picture regarding where the rest of her family were. Lili didn't fancy getting into what had happened in Joseph's shop and why they'd arrested Hannah.

William said, 'The police came yesterday and took lots of pictures away.'

'They were paintings, William,' Maisie corrected him.

Elspeth nodded.

'They took Daddy, and … and all of them away too.'

Lili glanced at William. She realised that the events of the previous day must be the reason that Elspeth had turned up. She didn't seem surprised about the paintings, Lili noticed.

Maisie took Elspeth's hand. 'You must see the old summerhouse in the garden. It's amazing.'

'Yes, come on.' William took her other hand. 'The police broke the lock, so I got to see inside.'

Something told Lili that Elspeth knew all about the summerhouse.

Lili joined them. She had questions about the artefacts, about Joseph, about her mum. She still had the photo in her pocket that she'd found the night before.

Lili caught sight of Elspeth staring at the flowerbeds as they walked towards the summerhouse. 'This isn't what I expected,' she commented. 'Joseph always loved his orchids, but he was never one for gardening. I assumed that when I left, it would—'

'Lili is a horticulturist,' Maisie said, sounding very grown up.

'She looks after the garden.'

Lili thought she saw tears in Elspeth's eyes. 'You've done an amazing job.'

Lili shrugged. 'Not as much as I would have liked. I wasn't here long, so I feel I only just got started. There's so much more to do.'

Elspeth smiled. 'I can see that, but what you've achieved is wonderful. I never had a chance to make something of the garden before …' She trailed off.

Lili had many unanswered questions she wanted to ask, especially about why they had divorced. Curiosity got the better of her. 'What happened?' Lili asked in a small voice, aware that it was none of her business. She didn't expect Elspeth to tell her.

Elspeth fell silent.

As they approached the summerhouse, the two children ran ahead.

Elspeth turned to Lili. 'I'm afraid I felt I had no choice but to leave Joseph. I didn't want to get sucked into it.'

'Into what?'

She hesitated as though it was something she wasn't sure she should share with Lili. 'Who are you, exactly?'

'I'm a friend of Maisie's mother. She's my best friend.' *At least, she was until she took advantage of me*, she thought. She changed the subject. 'I knew Nate a long time ago. We went to the same school, but I was a boarder. So was Hannah.'

'Hannah?'

'Maisie's mum. She got to know Nate at a house party here when we were all in sixth form.' Lili hoped Elspeth understood the euphemism, so that she didn't have to spell out that they'd had drunken sex at the party.

Elspeth nodded her head. 'I see.' Lili guessed that she got the picture.

As they approached the summerhouse, Elspeth said, 'I heard about the arrests on the news and was worried about William. That's why I came. I live in London, so I see William often. Imagine my surprised when my grandson decided to relocate here. I never envisaged Nathaniel would move back into the house.'

'He's looking for somewhere else to live.' Lili added in a hushed voice, 'I imagine The Summerhouse reminds him of when his parents sent him away to live with his grandfather.'

Elspeth shook her head. 'I'm afraid my daughter was too intent on righting the wrongs of the past. I told her not to work at the Art Loss Register, chasing ghosts. It wouldn't bring them back.'

'Who?'

Elspeth looked at her in surprise. 'The Jews, of course, the ones whose paintings and antiques were confiscated by the Nazis. I'm glad Nate didn't go into the family business.'

'The family business?'

'Stolen art.'

'You mean Sarah, Ray, and Nate stole—?'

'Of course not!'

Lili breathed a sigh of relief. For a moment, she wondered what she'd got Alex involved in.

'I'm talking about Joseph and Otto. I mean George.'

As they stepped into the old wooden summerhouse, Lili turned to Elspeth. 'Who is Otto?'

Elspeth quickly shook her head. 'Forget I said that. It was a mistake.'

Lili eyed her. She was hiding something.

Elspeth stood in the room, gazing around the cabin.

Lili could hear the children playing upstairs on the mezzanine. She glanced at Elspeth, and said, 'I know about Corfu.'

Elspeth shot her a look. 'What are you talking about?'

'Sarah told me that Joseph and his parents, who were artists, were visiting friends on the island of Corfu when they were caught up in the Nazi invasion of the Ionian Islands. She said her grandfather and father escaped the island. Joseph never went into detail about how they escaped or what happened to his mother – Sarah's paternal grandmother.'

Lili took a breath before continuing, 'Apparently, he wouldn't speak of it. After the war, they returned to England. With no friends and family who had survived the war, and their London home turned to rubble, they had nothing left but the old, abandoned summerhouse in Suffolk where, eventually, Sarah's grandfather built another house in the grounds.' Lili chewed her fingernail, avoiding eye contact while she was telling Elspeth all this. There was something else on Lili's mind – the two gravestones she'd stumbled across in the British Cemetery on Corfu. She still couldn't make sense of it.

There was only one obvious explanation: the two people who returned from Corfu after the war to live in the summerhouse were not Joseph and George. Did Elspeth know the truth?

'Are you all right?' Elspeth asked Lili. 'You've gone awfully quiet.'

Lili stared at her, wondering how much she knew. And if she had no clue, then how would she tell her that her ex-husband and father-in-law had stolen identities and had been living under assumed names for decades? She didn't know who they were, but she knew who they weren't.

Elspeth sat down on the leather sofa beside the fireplace.

Lili joined her. Before she'd brought that up, there had been something else, something more pressing, on her mind. She cut to the chase. 'Can you tell me who Alena is?'

'Alena?' Elspeth blurted. 'How do you know that name?'

'Joseph was in hospital suffering from delirium.'

Elspeth nodded. 'Yes, Sarah told me.'

'He called me Alena. I must look a lot like her. Please tell me what you know.' Lili reached into her pocket. 'I think I have some connection to Joseph, to your family, but I don't know what it is.' Lili told her all about being found wandering alone on a beach in Corfu when she was little, her parents' fatal trip to another Greek island, and her mother's apparent estrangement from her family.

'Ray was helping me trace my relatives, but if you know something … anything …' Lili trailed off. 'I can't make sense of it. But I found this.' Lili handed Elspeth the old photo. If she couldn't ask Joseph, then perhaps his ex-wife might know something.

Elspeth took the photograph.

'That's me with my mother. This photo was taken upstairs in the mezzanine. I have a fleeting memory of this place, but I don't know this man.' She pointed.

Elspeth stared at her, speechless. When she found her voice, she said, 'You are this child in the photograph?'

Lili nodded. 'Yes, that's me.' Hanging around the toddler's neck was a necklace with a ring on the end. Lili showed Elspeth her the pendant with the Hebrew wedding band. My mother died not long after this photo was taken. I never knew either of my parents. I've only just learned about them.'

'And it led you back here?'

'Well, not exactly. It's a long story.' Lili didn't want to get into the details about Connie and how she'd met Lili's mother on Corfu. 'I remember being at the party here when I was in sixth form and thinking the place seemed familiar…'

She was about to ask Elspeth whether she'd known her mum when she heard footsteps outside on the wooden veranda, and Nate's voice calling out, 'William? Maisie? Are you in there?'

Lili turned in her seat as the children thundered down the spiral staircase at the sound of their father's voice.

Nate walked in. William and Maisie ran up to him and flung their arms around his waist. He was followed by Ray and Sarah.

Lili rose from her seat when she saw them.

'I wondered where you two were,' said Nate.

The last one in the door was Alex.

'Alex!' Lili exclaimed, shocked to see him. 'What's going on?'

He smiled at her.

Ray said, 'We've been released without charge.'

'Does that mean you're not going to prison again?' William asked as he ran up to his grandfather.

'That's right. All thanks to Lili and an exceptionally good solicitor friend, called Alex.' Ray hugged Maisie too.

Lili ran up to Alex and hugged him. 'Oh, my god, I don't know what you did, but thank you, thank you!' She hadn't expected him travel to Suffolk after her call the previous night and sort things out straight away. For a moment, she forgot herself, and was about to apologise and step away, when she felt his arms close around her waist. He whispered, 'I'm sorry. It was the least I could do for being such an idiot.'

When he released her, she turned around and caught Nate giving Alex a nasty look. *Was that a pang of jealousy?* she wondered. Nate wasn't the only one giving Alex sour looks, though. Maisie sidled over to her dad and got another big hug for her troubles.

Lili grinned. It was lovely to see Maisie enveloped in the love and warm embrace of her dad and grandparents.

Alex whispered to Lili, 'What is Maisie doing here? I thought with her mother being in prison, social services would have taken her.'

'I pulled some strings – or rather, my old social worker did. Maisie was staying with me.' Lili raised an eyebrow. 'But don't worry, she won't be with me any longer. She has her dad and grandparents now.'

'That's her dad and grandparents?'

Lili nodded. 'It's a long story.'

Alex whispered, 'Perhaps you could tell me all about it over dinner?'

Lili looked at him in surprise. After all that had happened, was he asking her out on a date? 'I thought you were going to Washington?'

Alex didn't answer. She wondered if he'd had a change of heart about the move.

Nobody had noticed Elspeth sitting quietly on the sofa. She overheard Lili talking about Maisie with her dad and grandparents. 'Don't forget her great-grandmother.'

Sarah turned around at the sound of her mother's voice and spotted her on the sofa. 'Mum?' She exclaimed in surprise. 'I thought you were on holiday?'

'I was about to leave when I heard the news.' She looked past them all to the door of the cabin. 'Well, where is he? Where's Joseph?'

Lili looked at Alex. 'Where's Joseph?'

Alex took a deep breath. 'Although they haven't charged him with anything yet, they wouldn't release him. I'm afraid the police have found an irregularity.'

Lili asked, 'What does that mean?'

'I'm not sure myself. I've yet to get to the bottom of it. They have called in a genealogist.'

Ray stepped forward. 'I wonder what that's about? Why do they want to look into Joseph's family tree?'

Sarah looked at Ray. 'I don't know. '

Elspeth sighed and said, 'I do.'

38

They all took a seat, everyone's eyes on Elspeth, waiting for an explanation.

She sighed and glanced at the photo in her hand; the one Lili had just given her. She looked across at her son-in-law. 'On the subject of tracing family trees, you have outdone yourself this time, Ray.'

'What do you mean?'

Sarah stared at her mother. 'What's this got to do with Ray?'

'He has done you and Nate out of your inheritance.'

'What inheritance?'

Elspeth looked about her.

'What – this old place?'

Elspeth nodded. 'The Summerhouse too.'

'What on earth are you talking about, Mum?'

Elspeth turned to Lili. 'That's what you're here for, aren't you? To get what's rightfully yours when Joseph pops off this mortal coil.'

Sarah wasn't the only one looking at Elspeth as though she'd lost her marbles. Lili didn't have the first clue what she was on about. 'I have no clue what you're talking about.'

'Very clever of you to enlist Ray's help.' She glanced at her son-in-law. 'You fool.'

Ray stared at his mother-in-law. 'I have no idea either.'

'Of course, you don't, otherwise you would never have helped *her*.' Elspeth pointed at Lili.

Maisie spoke up, the tension in the room going over her head. 'Why does Great-granddad need a genie, a genie—'

Elspeth turned to Maisie. 'A genealogist. Because a clever police officer has unearthed an incongruity they are looking into, a mystery about your great-grandfather's past.'

Maisie looked puzzled but was clearly longing to discover what the mystery was.

Elspeth caught Lili's expression. 'You know, don't you?' It wasn't a question.

Everyone's eyes were on Lili.

Lili stared at her. Elspeth was right: she had an idea. She was thinking of the graves in Corfu. Had someone figured out that Joseph and his father might have been living under assumed names?

Lili took a deep breath. 'Look, all I know is that I saw the gravestones in the British Cemetery in Corfu.'

'What are you talking about?' Sarah interrupted. 'What's this got to do with graves in a cemetery in Corfu?'

Lili kept her gaze fixed on Elspeth.

Alex frowned. 'Will someone please explain what's going on? If you know anything I should be aware of, as Joseph's solicitor you must tell me.' He directed that comment at Elspeth.

Elspeth sighed. 'Where to begin?'

'At the beginning?' ventured Maisie.

Nate almost hid behind his daughter on the sofa. He had

always been a little afraid of his grandmother. She was quite a formidable woman. However, he knew, from what Joseph had told him, that the couple had been very much in love. Nate suspected that, just like with his own parents, the past and his family's obsession with art had driven a wedge between them and led to their divorce.

Elspeth smiled at Maisie. 'You are quite correct, Maisie. I shall start at the beginning. But first I need a cup of tea.'

A few minutes later, after refreshments had been brought down from the house, everyone took their seats again. Nate, Sarah, Lili and Ray sat on the two sofas. Elspeth had a seat on the only upholstered chair by the fireplace, and Maisie was seated on a cushion on the floor. William settled on his father's lap.

Alex hovered in the background, standing behind Lili. 'Um, look, this is a family thing. I guess I'd better go.'

Lili turned around and reached for his hand. 'You're Joseph's legal representative. I think you should stay.'

Elspeth seconded that motion. 'He's going to need you.'

Alex looked at Lili. 'Is that the only reason you want me to stay – for Joseph?'

The question embarrassed her. There was an uncomfortable silence in which Lili caught Nate staring at her.

Ray was still annoyed that Elspeth had told him off earlier, for reasons he couldn't quite fathom. He frowned at her. 'I still don't know why you suggested I have done Nate and Sarah out of their inheritance?'

Elspeth's eyes flicked to the photo in her hand. Ray was about to say something when Elspeth held up her hand. Nate whispered in Lili's ear, 'No prizes for what her profession used to be.'

Lili smiled. She felt like she was back at school when the headmistress walked into the room and everyone fell silent.

'Joseph is the best person to tell this story,' said Elspeth.

They all breathed a sigh of disappointment.

'But as he isn't here right now, I will tell it, and all will become clear.' She held up a finger. 'But no interruptions.'

'But—'

She threw a stern look at Ray. 'That goes for you too.'

Ray shut his mouth.

'Otto …'

'Who's Otto?' Maisie asked. No one else dared.

Elspeth's expression softened. She glanced around the room. 'A long time ago, when George was a young man, before he came to live at the summerhouse with Joseph, he had another name. He was called Otto.'

While the group exchanged surprised glances, Alex groaned loudly. He now had a good idea what the irregularity about his client was – it had something to do with Joseph's father's past.

Maisie just nodded her head and smiled at the old lady who, it turned out, was family. She looked at her dad and her grandparents and Lili. The horrible feeling that she had carried around in her tummy all the time, the sense of dread – as though something bad was going to happen – had gone.

She didn't have to worry about her mum any more or where they would live, or what food might be in the cupboard; she had all these people to care for her. It was, she decided, the best feeling in the world, having a big family.

The only times she had felt like this before had been when she was with Lili. That was why she had loved staying with Lili and Alex. She knew Alex didn't want her around. He didn't play with her and talk to her like her own daddy now did, but he never said bad things to her and told her to go away like her pretend daddies – her mum's boyfriends.

'So, back to my story, or George's story … or Otto's, as he was then known.' She paused. 'Is everyone with me so far?'

There were murmurs of *yes, kind of*.

Sarah had a question. 'Otto doesn't sound like an English name. I thought my grandparents were from London?'

Ray exchanged a glance with Sarah.

Elspeth frowned. 'Just be patient, Sarah, I'm getting to that. Like Maisie said, I should start at the beginning …' She paused for a moment and glanced at Lili. 'It all started on the island of Corfu.'

'Corfu?' Ray glanced at Lili with a question he had kept to himself for now. Lili caught him looking at her and guessed what he was thinking: what did this have to do with her? She thought of the photo Elspeth was still holding and wondered what her connection was to this family. She looked around the room. Were *they* her relatives? Oh, how she wished that would turn out to be true. She loved them like her own.

Elspeth continued, 'Joseph's parents were artists. They lived in London and travelled abroad a lot to visit friends.'

Lili stared at Elspeth, thinking, *but who was he really?* She knew he wasn't the boy on the gravestone. 'But who was—'

Elspeth held up her hand. 'Lili, let me continue, please.'

'Okay.' Lili sunk back into her seat.

'They loved the Ionian Islands and would spend weeks, sometimes months, there at a time with good friends who owned a plantation in the hills above Corfu. This was the 1930s. When Joseph was born in the mid-thirties, that didn't stop them travelling there too with their young son. The wealthy Corfiot family, one of the wealthiest families on the island, welcomed people of all nationalities into their home. They had three sons and a daughter – Alena.' She looked at Lili.

Everyone followed their gaze.

'So, George used to be called Otto?' Ray clarified.

Everybody sighed.

'What? I just want to get the facts straight.'

The look on Alex's face said he wanted to do that too.

'Wasn't that the woman my father mistook you for, Alena?' interrupted Sarah. 'If you resemble her, and your relatives on your mother's side are originally from Corfu, you could be related to the Greek family who my father and grandparents stayed with all those years ago.'

Everyone nodded, staring at Lili, making her feel self-conscious.

Lili nodded too. That's what she thought. 'I think my mother was in Corfu looking for her family's roots.'

'Right, back to the story.' Elspeth looked at them all, as would a schoolteacher surveying a naughty class.

They fell silent. Even Bella, who had been licking her fur as she lay on the rug in front of the fireplace, stopped what she was doing. She had woken from her doze on the sofa up at the house when they all trooped inside to make tea, coffee and squash. Excited that everyone was home, she had followed them all back to the old summerhouse.

'From what Joseph recalled about some of his childhood spent abroad—'

'You mean in Corfu …'

Elspeth fixed her gaze on Ray. 'Yes, Corfu.' She raised her

eyebrows at Ray. 'May I continue?'

Lili resisted the urge to smile. Ray's relationship with his mother-in-law appeared decidedly frosty.

'Yes, please do,' Ray replied, a hint of sarcasm in his voice.

Elspeth gave him a look before continuing. 'Alena made quite an impression on Joseph. Although he must have been five or six years old, he was smitten with the beautiful young woman. She *was* still a teenager. She'd take him for walks in the countryside and paddling in secluded coves. However, I imagine there was an ulterior motive for taking him along. I think he was a decoy. Joseph talked of a young man, one of his parents' friends, who would join them. I believe she was meeting him covertly.'

'A secret liaison?'

Elspeth looked across the room at her grandson, 'Yes, Nate, that's correct.'

Alex was staring at the doctor, wishing he wasn't quite so tall, dark, and handsome and wasn't sitting next to Lili with his arm resting on the back of the sofa, inches from her shoulders.

'So, why did they have to meet in secret?' asked Ray. 'Was it because he wasn't Greek?'

Elspeth shook her head. 'No, of course not. Their friends came from different countries, with a shared interest, a passion for all things artistic. Religion – that was the problem. You see, Alena's family were Greek Orthodox Jew. He was not.'

Lili leaned forward in her seat. 'What happened to them?'

'The inevitable. She fell pregnant. It was scandalous in those days. So, her parents sent her away to have the baby. Fortunately, they had good friends in England who had a summerhouse where she could stay.'

Ray and Sarah exchanged glances.

'That's right – this is the summerhouse. Joseph's parents took Alena back to England with them. I believe the idea was that they would adopt the child and bring her up as a sister for Joseph.'

'But that didn't happen,' Sarah said flatly. She knew her father was an only child.

'With rumours of war, it's ironic that Joseph's parents thought it would be safer for them to return to Corfu than remain in England. Joseph, along with his father, his mother, Alena and the baby, went back to Corfu, where Joseph's mother pretended the infant was hers.'

Lili remembered what the old man who worked at the cemetery had told her and her guide about the rumours. So, they were true – the baby had been Alena's.

'What happened to the baby?' Maisie asked.

'That's a good question, sweetheart.' Nate smiled at his attentive daughter, wishing he'd known about her before and hadn't missed the first eight years of her life. But she was finally there – and all because of Lili. He glanced at Lili and caught Alex out of the corner of his eye, scowling. He got the impression that Alex was none too happy he was sitting next to her. Nate thought Alex and Lili were finished, over. He hoped they were.

'Three years into the war, they'd survived the Italian occupation, but then the Germans arrived on the Ionian Islands.' Elspeth glanced at the children. So did Nate. Whatever Elspeth was going to say next involving the Nazi occupation of Corfu was not for their ears.

Lili already knew about the death boats. It wasn't something she wanted Maisie to be privy to – not at her age. 'Sorry to interrupt, Elspeth, but I think Bella needs a toilet break.' She turned to Maisie. 'Could you do me a *huge* favour, Maisie, and take Bella outside to do her business?'

Nate cottoned on to what she was doing. He lifted William off his lap. 'Be a good sport and help Maisie. I think Bella might need feeding too. How about it, son? Take the dog back up to the house, will you?'

William frowned. 'Oh, all right.'

'Good lad.'

Maisie wasn't so easily persuaded. 'But I want to hear the rest of the story.'

Nate smiled at her. 'I know, but I'll tell you what, if you look after Bella, then how about some pocket money for being a good dog owner?'

'Is Bella *my* dog now?'

'Well, Joseph can't care for her at the moment, so yes, I guess so.'

'Is that because he's in prison?'

'Hopefully, he'll get out soon.' Nate glanced at Alex, hoping he was one hell of a lawyer because by the sound of what Elspeth had said, his grandfather had been living under an assumed name for decades.

Nate shifted his attention to Maisie. 'How about it, eh? You can start earning that pocket money right now?'

Maisie looked at Lili.

She gave her a nod of encouragement that she should accept the deal.

'I want pocket money too!'

Nate turned to William. 'How about you tidy your room?'

'That's not fun.'

'Well, neither is picking up dog poop.'

Maisie's grin faded.

Lili stifled a smile. Maisie hadn't thought of that.

After cleverly negotiating how much money she would get, Maisie sprang to her feet. Bella followed closely at her heels. 'Good girl,' she said to Bella. 'You know, you're my dog now.' Maisie stopped in her tracks halfway to the door. She turned around. 'Do you think I can teach Bella some more tricks?'

'I don't see why not. Why don't you play outside, see what you can teach her?' suggested Nate.

'Can I come back and show you afterwards?'

'In a little while.'

'Cool.'

Lili smiled. *Cool.*

When she'd closed the door, everyone turned to Elspeth, enraptured by the story and what would follow.

39

'Now, where was I?'

'Three years into the war, and the Germans had arrived,' Lili reminded her.

'That's right. They were there to round up the Jews.' She fell silent for a moment. 'Like other islands, the villagers tried to hide their Jewish neighbours, but on Corfu a lot were found and sent on the death boats to Auschwitz.'

Lili had heard this story before when she had visited the British Cemetery in Corfu. She leaned forward in her seat. 'So, do you think Alena was on one of those boats?' she asked in a small voice.

'Yes, I believe your great-grandmother was on one, along with Joseph's mother.'

Lili looked at Elspeth in surprise when she called Alena her great-grandmother. 'How can you be so sure Alena was my great-grandmother?'

Elspeth held up the photo. 'Do you still have this ring?'

'She does, yes.' Sarah blurted. 'Was that photo taken in …?'

'In this very summerhouse.' Elspeth nodded as she handed Sarah the print to inspect.

'Can I see the photo?'

Sarah passed it to Ray.

'You were here when you were a toddler?' Nate said in surprise.

Lili glanced at Nate as she held up the ring. 'I still have it.'

Elspeth sighed. 'You really have no idea who you are – what your connection is to this house – do you?'

Lili shook her head. 'Despite what you may think, I don't know what you were talking about earlier.'

The look on Elspeth's face said she believed her.

Lili fingered her ring. 'So, Alena's child survived.' It wasn't a question; she knew she wouldn't be there at all if that hadn't been the case. 'Did you know her daughter's name?'

'I did. She was called Miriam.'

If Lili needed any further proof that Alena had been her great-grandmother, hearing the name *Miriam* confirmed it. That was the name of the woman who the old man had recorded in his register after she had attended the funeral of Lili's mother on Corfu.

Ray had a question. 'With so many Jews rounded up and put on the death boats, how did any of them escape the island?'

Elspeth paused. 'The Nazis weren't just after the Jews. They also confiscated the families' assets.'

'You didn't answer Ray's question,' said Sarah.

'I'm getting to it …'

Sarah wasn't the only one becoming frustrated. Alex said, 'But I don't see what stolen art has to do with—?'

'It has *everything* to do with it. You see, Alena had fallen in love with a young man, an aspiring artist. If it hadn't been for him, the children would never have survived. He was fresh out of university. He loved the Ionian Islands. During his student days, before the war, he had travelled there often, staying with Alena's family and becoming great friends with the other visitors to the wealthy family's estate – especially Joseph's parents. He'd even visited England and stayed in their summerhouse.'

'You're talking about Alena's sweetheart, and Miriam's father,' said Lili. 'Do you know who he was? Do you have a name?' Lili was excited because Elspeth was talking about her great-grandfather.

'I don't get why Joseph's father changed his name,' commented Alex. 'If he wasn't George, but a man named Otto, then what about Joseph? Is that even his real name?'

Lili turned in her seat and looked at Alex. That was the question that had been on the tip of her tongue.

Sarah was staring at Alex too. She turned to Elspeth. 'Mum, I am really confused. Please can you tell me what this is all about?'

Elspeth glanced at Alex, then Sarah, but didn't answer their questions. 'He saved them, you know. He came back during the war to find Alena, but he found two children instead – Joseph and Miriam.'

'What's this got to do with stolen art?' Ray asked, repeating Alex' question.

'Otto was an art officer.'

'What is an art officer?' asked Lili.

Ray told them about Hitler's obsession with valuable pieces of art and the officers whose task it was to find and confiscate those paintings from the Jews.

Elspeth stepped in when Ray had finished. 'You must understand, during the war it was the only way he could think of to return to the Ionian Islands to find her – to find Alena. He didn't know he had a child until he found Joseph and Miriam hiding with the family's servant in the house while he was valuing and having the paintings removed. Joseph had recognised Otto. He told Otto that Alena had lived with him and his parents for many months at the summerhouse in England and that Miriam was going to be his sister.' Elspeth looked around the room. 'That's when he guessed the truth – that he had an illegitimate daughter.' Elspeth continued, 'The servant, hiding with the children, told Otto that the other members of the family had been rounded up and shipped off the island. So he used his position as an art officer to smuggle the children and the servant to a neighbouring island, on a boat in crates full of artefacts.'

'Zakynthos,' said Lili.

Elspeth smiled. 'That's correct. He went back after the war to continue his search for Alena, never giving up hope that she had evaded the death boats and was still alive, but he never found her. Or saw his daughter again. A Greek family on Zakynthos had taken in his daughter, Miriam. By the time he returned, after the war, they had left the Ionian Islands. He didn't know where they were.'

'Israel.'

All eyes were on Lili.

Lili explained, 'A lot of Greeks settled in the then newly created state of Israel.' Lili stared at Elspeth for a long moment. Her mouth dropped open when it hit her. 'Are you saying my great-grandfather, Otto, was a German art officer – a *Nazi*?'

'Yes, but he was also a young man caught up in a conflict, trying to find the woman he loved.'

Sarah commented, 'So, he saved my father and the little girl, Miriam, Lili's grandmother?'

Elspeth nodded. 'That's right.'

Lili noticed that Elspeth had fallen silent. There was something she was holding back.

Ray glanced at Lili. 'What happened to him, the German art officer?'

That question had been on the tip of Lili's tongue.

Elspeth stared at the photo in her hand. 'He lived a long and innocuous life. Along with saving the two children, he also saved Alena's family's incredible art collection, worth millions today. I suspect it was the largest collection of art looted from one family by the Nazis outside of the Rothschilds, and the largest collection of confiscated art in a private collection today.'

Elspeth sighed. 'Despite sitting on all that wealth, the sad part was he'd amassed a substantial fortune, but he never found the most precious thing in the world to him.'

Lili knew what it was. 'Alena.'

Ray asked Elspeth, 'How do you know he lived a long and innocuous life and he kept hold of that art?'

Elspeth turned to him. 'I thought you would have guessed.' She took a deep breath before she revealed what she had been building up to. She looked at the photo. 'His name was Otto, but…' Elspeth held up the image. 'You all knew him as George.'

Sarah looked at the photograph, then at her mother as if she'd gone stark, raving mad. 'But that's granddad.'

'Not exactly.'

Nate stepped in. 'What do you mean, *not exactly*?'

Ray glanced around the old summerhouse at the hooks on the wall where all the artwork, taken by the police, had hung. Sarah was doing the same. Their eyes locked in silent, shocked understanding. They had spent decades looking for artefacts belonging to Jews which were confiscated by the Nazis during World War Two. It had been their life's work to find some of that art, confirm its true provenance, and return it to the Jewish families it had been plundered from. Neither Ray nor Sarah could get over the irony. All this time, one of the biggest collections of stolen paintings was right on their doorstep, along with the Nazi officer who had taken them.

Ray fixed his gaze on Elspeth. 'But where did all this come from?' he asked, referring to the works of art that had hung on the walls.

'Some of the pieces were hidden with the family in Zakynthos who took the children in, and he shipped them back to England after the war. The rest he accumulated over time, looking out for when they resurfaced – sometimes they were sold by private individuals, and others came up for sale at auctions around the world.'

Ray looked from Sarah to Elspeth. The news was incredible.

Sarah was shaking her head. She was not concerned with the paintings, but with something else. 'This makes no sense. Are you saying my grandfather was a Nazi German art officer?'

'Sarah, let me finish. All will be revealed, I promise. When Otto returned to Zakynthos, soon after the war, to be reunited with the children, remember I told you that Miriam was gone, taken away to live in Israel with the Greek family who'd given them refuge. So, he only found Joseph, the little English boy who no one wanted to adopt. They both had nobody left after the war. They were both so alone.'

Lili stared at Elspeth.

'Alena had disappeared, although Otto would never acknowledge that she ended up on a death boat with Joseph's mother. Miriam was gone, taken off the island with a Greek family to start a new life abroad. Even so, Otto took Joseph with him in search of Miriam and Alena on Corfu, and that's when they ventured into the cemetery and Otto showed Joseph his father's final resting place. George died on the island trying to stop the Nazis taking his friends and family. And that's when Otto told Joseph his plans for their future.'

Elspeth had kept this secret for decades. Now it was time to reveal the truth. 'Otto needed a new identity. He was a German art officer, a Nazi. And Joseph needed *him*. So, Otto assumed George's identity and together they returned to the summerhouse on the East Coast of England after the war to start a new life.'

Lili frowned. She had to say something. 'So, if Joseph was still alive, why was there a small gravestone erected next to his father saying he'd died?'

Elspeth nodded. 'It wasn't official. The family who had looked after the cemetery for generations knew the two children had been smuggled off the island. The Germans had lists. Joseph's name was on it. So, to protect him, they erected the gravestone next to his father's and told the Nazis he was dead.'

Elspeth paused for a moment and gazed around the old cabin before continuing. 'This is where they came to live after the war. The summerhouse had been abandoned during those war years. The family who owned it, Joseph's parents, weren't well-known in the local community. They were outsiders from London who only spent the summer there and kept themselves to themselves. So, when a young man and his son moved into the abandoned place, nobody batted an eyelid. They assumed they had returned. No one in the town remembered George and his family who used to come down from London to their summer-house by the lake.'

Everyone sat in stunned silence.

Elspeth continued, 'Otto opened a shop in the town, and he was an immensely popular and well-liked character. He'd arrived in England using false documents, and to the world at large – not to mention the small community of Aldeburgh – he was just George, the owner of the local antique shop.'

She cast her gaze over to Nate and Sarah. 'I think that by now, you realise that you were no blood relation of this man whatsoever.'

Sarah looked at Elspeth in shock. 'You mean, all these years the man I thought was my grandfather …?'

'He died in the war, Sarah. I'm so sorry.'

Sarah stared at her.

Ray was staring at her too, as was Alex, who rubbed his forehead. 'So, let me get this straight. Otto didn't just pass himself off as George; he had, in fact, stolen Joseph's father's identity?'

Elspeth nodded. 'In a nutshell.'

Sarah said, 'How is that even possible?'

This time Ray stepped in. 'I've never come across this type of identity theft before in all my years on the force, but I have heard of it. It's a type of identity theft called *ghosting*.'

'Ghosting?' Sarah had never heard of the term before.

Ray leaned forward in his seat and explained. 'You hear about identity theft in the news all the time – the type that is carried out for short-term financial gain, stealing from people's bank accounts, that sort of thing. But in Otto's case, he needed a new identity to start over after the war; one that he could acquire that would give him an air of respectability and he could use for years without suspicion. So, he stole the identity of a person who had died – the ghost, hence the term. Now what's important here is that the person's death has …' Ray was searching for the right words. 'I wouldn't say gone entirely unnoticed, but perhaps not a lot of people are aware of this person's passing.'

Alex nodded. 'Joseph's relatives had perished in the London Blitz. There would've been nobody alive who'd have known George after the war.'

'Apart from a little boy,' commented Elspeth. 'And let's not forget,' she added, 'that George died on Corfu. I suppose the Mediterranean island is at least a thousand miles away. And it happened in the midst of war.'

Sarah was getting the picture.

So was Lili as she listened to all this intently.

Ray nodded. 'Not to state the obvious, but the ghoster, if you like, would have to be around the same age that the deceased person would have been if they had lived.'

Sarah frowned. 'I don't understand. How did he get away with it? Surely, he should have got caught out by somebody in officialdom like a government agency or something because he was using false documents?'

'Ah, that's where you're confusing identity theft with creating a false identity. If you do the latter, you're quite right, Sarah – at some point, you're going to get caught out. But in this case, it wouldn't happen. There was a reason Otto could pull it off, and it wasn't just because George's friends and relatives were gone, save for his son, and because George had died on an Ionian Island in the midst of war in the middle of the Mediterranean. You see, Otto didn't have a false identity he'd made up, with forged documents. At some point, he must have acquired George's birth certificate.'

'But how?' Lili asked.

Alex stepped in. 'It would have been very straightforward, to be honest. Before computers and databases full of personal information at government agencies' fingertips, taking a dead person's identity was easy – especially in this country.'

'Why in this country?' asked Sarah.

Ray replied, 'Because here copies of someone's birth certificate can be acquired for a small fee, as long as you have the person's date of birth.'

Lili stared at Ray. 'You're joking.'

'Nope. And once you've got the birth certificate, therein lies the foundation of your new identity. Otto became George – and the rest is history.'

Sarah stared at Ray for a long moment before turning to her mother. 'You knew the truth all this time and let me believe …?'

Elspeth sighed. 'It was one reason Joseph and I divorced. I thought there were no secrets between us, but then, one day, I stumbled on the old summerhouse at the bottom of the garden. It was normally locked. Joseph had told me that he and his father had once lived there, but that when they'd built the new house in the grounds, they'd started to use it as storage for their antiques business. I believed them. There was no reason not to. What he didn't tell me was what they were storing in there or why he kept it under lock and key. Then, one day, one of them hadn't secured the latch properly. Curious, I opened the door …'

Elspeth paused, remembering that day vividly. She knew immediately that she had stumbled on something important. 'If I could go back in time, I wish curiosity hadn't got the better of me, and that I hadn't opened that door. But there you have it. That was the end of my relationship with Joseph, the love of my life. But everything made sense; the way Joseph discouraged friends from visiting the house. The antique shop was a front for Joseph's travels abroad in search of lost art. In search of Alena.'

Elspeth sighed. 'For Joseph, he had to keep the secret of who his so-called father really was. In the years following the war, the search for Nazis began, and over time it just intensified. Otto wasn't a Nazi in the sense that he didn't send people to their deaths, but he was on those islands when people were being rounded up and put on those boats to be transported to the camps. I don't know what would have happened to him if his true identity had ever come to light. There was also a tremendous interest in discovering the depositories of lost art. He didn't know where they were. The art officers weren't told their eventual destination, but he had meticulously recorded those paintings and other assets, and who they belonged to. The ones he was involved in requisitioning.'

Ray sat bolt upright. 'You mean those records still exist?'

Sarah was leaning forward in her seat too. 'They would be invaluable.'

Elspeth nodded and continued, 'Joseph said he owed Otto for saving his life and that I must keep Otto's secret. So, I did, because I loved Joseph and I didn't want to destroy his little world. But it destroyed *us*.'

She looked pointedly at Ray and Sarah. 'Do you know how disappointed I was when you told me you were going to work for the Art Loss Register, and to cap it all that you'd fallen in love with an art cop? I knew that the writing was on the wall – to borrow a phrase. The obsession with finding lost artefacts would eventually come between you. It was inevitable, and I knew the repercussions for your son.'

Nate shifted in his seat.

Sarah said, 'Why didn't you just tell me the truth?'

'I wanted them to tell you the truth, but they weren't having any of it – especially Joseph. He was afraid—'

'The secret would come out about George's identity, the Nazi art officer, Otto.' Ray understood. It was only recently, as time had marched on, that the search for Nazis and uncovering the identities of those who had lived under assumed names, in adopted countries for decades, had stopped. 'He would have been arrested,' said Ray.

Elspeth looked at Ray. 'Yes, he would have been.'

'And you were afraid of being implicated.'

Elspeth nodded. 'Very much so. The fact that he'd kept all the evidence of his past so-called war crimes right here made it worse. It meant, if it had been discovered, that we'd all have gone to prison.'

Ray cast his gaze around at the empty walls that had housed one of the biggest depositories of lost art in a single private collection – now crated and housed in the bowels of the local nick. The news reporters were having a field day. The camera crews had accosted Ray, Nate and Sarah as they'd left the little police station. How word had got out so quickly, they did not know.

Even up at the house, while they had been making some tea, coffee, and juice before they returned to the old summerhouse, there had been news teams camped out on the front lawn. Everyone in the house had ignored them. It was something they knew would have to be dealt with later, but for now they were safely away from prying eyes in the privacy of Otto's cabin at the end of the garden – or so they thought.

40

Elspeth gazed around the place, taking in the bare walls of the summerhouse. They had just settled back into their seats after sitting out on the wooden decking of the summerhouse overlooking the lake, eating sandwiches and drinking lemonade.

They were intending to remain outside on the deck in the afternoon sunshine while Elspeth finished her story. Unfortunately, a lone photographer had hired a rowing boat. He floated past, snapping their picture with a zoom lens. They knew that where there was one, there were bound to be others; the rest would soon figure out that the rear of the house could be seen from the lake, where you could hire rowboats and canoes. It was the group's cue to scuttle back inside and shut the door.

'Would the police believe me if I said I knew nothing of all this, even though it was right under my nose at the end of the garden, in the grounds of my marital home?' asked Elspeth.

Lili stared at her. She was thinking of the previous day, when she had returned to the house to find artworks she'd never seen before being taken away and Joseph's entire family being arrested. It was lucky for everyone in the room that they had a brilliant solicitor. She turned in her seat and smiled at Alex. He'd dropped everything and come to their rescue. She hadn't expected that – at all.

'It wasn't about me, though,' Elspeth continued. 'I was afraid I'd lose you, Sarah, and couldn't live with the anxiety that someone else might stumble upon the secret. I wanted Otto to inform the authorities. I begged him to let the collection go, but he said he'd done nothing wrong. I knew he was no criminal, just a broken-hearted young man, swept up in the horror of war, who'd signed up to be a Nazi art officer to save the woman he loved. Otto had taken the artefacts, it was true, and he wouldn't give them up. He wanted the collection to stay together so he could hand it over to—'

'Quick question, excuse me for interrupting,' Alex apologised. 'If Otto was so concerned about his past catching up with him, why take the risk of returning to the summerhouse? What if someone had recognised Joseph? A curious, nosy neighbour, perhaps. Who knows where that might have led?'

Elspeth turned in her seat to look at Alex, perched on a stool from the kitchen. 'Yes, he took a risk, you're quite right. But there was a reason for that. Joseph told me that Otto and Alena had made a secret pact. If the worst – the unthinkable – happened, and they were separated by war, then they would find their way back to each other and meet at their English friends' summerhouse.'

Elspeth frowned. 'Although I believed Alena had been taken on a death boat and had died – and that Joseph had too – Otto could never come to terms with that possibility. He never gave up hope that one day they would find each other again. He even had the Hebrew betrothal rings made, and he converted to Judaism, intent on marrying her when she returned.'

'That is so sad,' Lili commented, fingering the ring on the chain around her neck, now understanding its significance.

'Yes, it was,' Elspeth agreed. 'That was why he would never demolish this old cabin, and it was the reason he stored this precious art collection that once belonged to Alena's parents here.'

Sarah and Ray exchanged a glance. Ray said what they were both thinking. 'He wanted to return it to the family whence it came. It was her legacy.'

Elspeth frowned. 'It was his dying wish.'

There was a long silence. Everyone was taking a moment for all of it to sink in – especially Lili when she realised that she wasn't related to this family, not by blood, but that she was bound to them in the most extraordinary way. That meant the world to her.

Lili could hear the children playing with Bella in the garden. She turned to Elspeth. 'Do you know how my mother found out about Otto?'

'I'm not entirely sure. Joseph may have mentioned it once, but I'm afraid I don't recall. We kept in touch over the years.'

'All I know is that my mum was estranged from my grandmother, Miriam,' Lili added.

'I'm afraid that was true.'

'Was it because of Otto?'

'Yes. The Greek family who took Miriam in, they'd heard the rumours about Alena and her friendship with a German artist friend of her family. I believe it was a member of staff at the house, a cook or a cleaner, who recognised the Nazi officer who came to take the family's collection. She looked at Miriam and put two and two together. So did Otto when he first set eyes on the toddler. It was with the aid of that loyal employee that they got the children out of Corfu and into the hands of another Greek family on the island of Zakynthos.'

Lili sat there thinking about the old man in the British Cemetery. His mother had told him the two children he had once played with were safe. How had she been so sure, unless she was the loyal employee who had helped in their escape? Was it some of her relations in Zakynthos who had taken them in and knew the truth about Miriam's parentage? Lili suspected it was. She also had an idea that her grandmother had found out later in life about her true parentage but had kept her father's identity a secret from her daughter.

Lili asked Elspeth if this was the case.

'From what Joseph told me about your mother's visit, I gather Miriam wanted nothing to do with Otto. He'd been a Nazi officer, after all. Don't forget, Miriam had been brought up by a Greek family who'd felt forced to give up their country, their roots, and start again in Israel – all because of the German occupation.'

Lili understood. Her grandmother would have thought it was a betrayal of her adopted family if she contacted her father. 'But my mother didn't see it that way?'

'When she found out about her grandfather, she wanted to visit him and give him a chance to tell his side of the story.'

Lili was confused. She knew her mum had already located her grandfather, which was clear from this photo. She had made the trip to England so that Otto could meet his great-grandchild. So, what had she been doing on Zakynthos the day she and Lili's father died? Lili asked Elspeth the question, wondering if she knew.

'I think she was visiting some descendants of the Greek family who had looked after her mother and the little English boy during the war. Not all the relatives moved to Israel.' Elspeth fixed her gaze on Lili. 'Joseph told me it was the happiest day of Otto's life when your mother turned up. Otto had written a letter, sealed in an envelope, tucked in little Miriam's dress. The family who took her in must have given it to Miriam at some point when she was older. That's how your mother found out about the summerhouse in England. He'd written in the note, their rendezvous place in England, in case his daughter ever wanted to seek him out.'

Elspeth breathed a sigh. 'I suspect your mum came across that letter. That's how she discovered the secret of the summer-house.'

'The secret of the summerhouse,' Lili repeated. 'Are you talking about Otto?'

Elspeth smiled at Lili. 'I am indeed. When your mother turned up, that's when Otto knew that his daughter, Miriam, had survived.' Elspeth handed the photo back to Lili. 'It wasn't the first time your mum had visited, but it was to be the last. It couldn't have been long after this picture was taken that …' Elspeth trailed off.

'She died,' said Lili.

Elspeth had a thought. 'Perhaps it was a blessing that Otto never knew about that motorcycle accident. He passed away a very happy man indeed. You see, Alena had returned after all.'

Lili furrowed her brow. 'Pardon me?'

Everyone else who had been listening intently – Ray, Sarah and Alex, even the two children, who had wandered back into the summerhouse with Bella and taken a seat together on cushions on the rug – all looked at Elspeth with perplexed expressions. Wasn't Alena dead?

Before anyone asked what she was talking about, Elspeth said to Lili, 'Look at the photo. He is holding her in his arms.'

'But that's me.'

'Yes, his great-granddaughter, Alena.'

'No, my name is—'

'Lili is your middle name,' Elspeth explained. 'Your mother named you after your great-grandmother, who perished in the war. Your first name is, in fact, Alena.'

'Alena,' Lili repeated, stunned. It made her wonder if Joseph hadn't mistaken her for her great-grandmother, but knew she was the little girl who had once visited with her mum years ago.

'And this …' Elspeth turned and flung her arm around the room, 'is now yours. Well, when the police establish the provenance of the paintings and return them.'

Talking of which,' Elspeth added, 'I imagine Joseph is telling the police about the collection of artworks waiting for its rightful owner, as we speak. That's you, Lili.'

'That's assuming Miriam isn't alive,' Ray butted in, putting his heir-hunting hat on.

Lili turned to look at Ray. She didn't want the paintings or a fortune to fall in her lap; she'd give it all up to see her great-grandmother. She wanted her to be alive. She wished she could see her face when she found out her father had, over the years, put her families' collection of art back together, waiting to return it. Although she was Otto's great-grandchild, Lili knew in her heart that it was Miriam to whom these paintings should be returned.

Elspeth turned to her daughter. 'Expect a phone call from

the police, Sarah, to confirm the provenance. There's a safe behind the painting above the fireplace. It contains records of all the paintings and artefacts that Otto and his team stole during the war and who they belonged to, including those that were stored here.'

Everyone turned to look at the large watercolour portrait of a beautiful young woman.

Maisie asked the question everybody was thinking. 'Why didn't they take *that* painting?'

Lili smiled at Maisie's pertinent question. Lili had seen other paintings hanging on the walls up at the house that the police hadn't seemed interested in either.

Elspeth looked at her great-granddaughter. 'A famous artist did not paint it, Maisie. Perhaps in another life he might have become a renowned artist, if it weren't for the war, but it was not to be.'

Lili stared at the canvas. 'That's Alena.' Lili knew this because she bore a striking resemblance to the woman in the picture. 'Otto painted that portrait – didn't he?'

'I'm glad you got to meet him, Lili, even though you were so young.'

Lili stared at Elspeth. 'You were here, weren't you? You took the photo?'

'Yes. Your great-grandfather was a gentle soul,' commented Elspeth, turning in her seat to look at the painting.

Nate nodded, remembering the person he had thought was his great-grandfather. Nate recalled he had indeed been a kind man with a mischievous, fun-loving streak. Even though he'd just found out about Otto's background, his role in the war, Nate didn't feel any animosity toward the old fellow he had known and loved as a child. He understood the conflicts Miriam must have felt when she had discovered the truth about her father. If only she'd met him and listened to his story, as they all were now, then perhaps everything would have played out differently.

Nate was thinking of Lili and her parents. Maybe if they had all been together visiting Zakynthos – Lili, her parents, her grandparents – then they would have been travelling in a car, not a motorcycle. Perhaps the accident would never have happened. But then again, maybe it would have, and they would all have perished. Who knew what fate ever had in store? Then the woman he'd fallen in love with wouldn't be sitting there, making it hard to concentrate because all he could think about was putting his arm around her shoulders, leaning in close and kissing her.

Nate tried to focus on his grandmother. She was still talking.

'All he ever wanted to be was an artist. You are quite correct, Lili – he painted that portrait, and others hanging in the house, but he would never be recognised as a gifted artist. I think being unable to show the world at large his work affected him greatly, but that was the price he paid to keep his secret.'

Lili frowned as she cast her gaze around the empty walls. She was thinking back to something Elspeth had said a while earlier, when they had all first sat down together to listen to what she had to say. Lili recalled that Elspeth had admonished Ray, saying something about tracing family trees and Sarah and Nate's inheritance. Elspeth had then implied that she was there to claim what was rightfully hers when Joseph died.

Lili recalled her strange comment, *That's what you're here for, aren't you? To get what's rightfully yours when Joseph pops off this mortal coil.*

Lili didn't want to bring that up again, and cause another argument, but there was something about that comment that made Lili think there was more to tell, and that Elspeth hadn't finished her story.

'Elspeth, what did you mean when you said I was here to claim what was rightfully mine? You were talking about the paintings – weren't you?'

Elspeth cast her gaze around the cabin. 'As you are all here, I might as well tell you. I think it's time you all knew, especially Lili. Sooner rather than later you're going to find out anyway.'

Sarah frowned. 'Find out what, Mum?'

'One day soon, this cabin and The Summerhouse will belong to Lili.'

'Mum, what are you talking about?'

Lili glanced at Sarah. That's what she wanted to know, too. She eyed Elspeth. 'You must be mistaken.'

'I can assure you, I'm not. This was the other reason I left Joseph. We had a huge falling out over his will. Lili, with your mother deceased, you are the sole heir to Otto's fortune.'

Lili shook her head. 'But Otto's fortune is the paintings.'

Ray stepped in agreeing with Lili. 'Joseph owns The Summerhouse.' He could understand why Otto left the paintings to Alena's descendants, but not The Summerhouse.

'And that's where *you* are mistaken, Ray.' Elspeth shook her head at him. 'You search for lost descendants. Well, congratulations, you found one, and she is the sole beneficiary.'

'Of The Summerhouse?' Sarah got out of her seat and turned to Ray. 'How can that be?'

He shrugged his shoulders just as flummoxed as she was.

Elspeth sighed. 'Otto's will has nothing to do with the paintings. Although he acquired some of the collection, over time, from private sellers in different countries when they resurfaced for sale, they were never his to bequest. Their provenance proves that.'

Ray nodded. He understood that. How could you leave something in your will that never rightfully belonged to you in the first place? He wasn't just thinking of the art collection. That was why he was confused over The Summerhouse.

Elspeth breathed a sigh. 'There was a codicil in Otto's will. Joseph can remain living in the house until he dies, but then the property reverts to Otto's heir, whom he named as Lili's mother.' Elspeth turned to face Lili. 'Otto changed his will after your last visit when you were a small child. In the event of your mother's death, Otto's estate passes, in its entirety, to you.'

Lili couldn't believe what she was hearing.

'I have asked Joseph many times to challenge the will, but he refused.' Elspeth sighed. 'It doesn't surprise me that he was loyal to Otto until the bitter end. However, when Joseph didn't hear from your mother again, I presumed something must have happened. Who wouldn't turn up to claim The Summerhouse if they were still alive? In that case, the house would be left to Joseph and his descendants.'

Elspeth looked over at her son-in-law seated next to her daughter. She wondered when they were going to get on with it and sign those divorce papers; she knew they had been hanging around for almost five years. Just then, Elspeth was looking forward to Ray being her *ex*-son-in-law. She threw him a sour look as she said, 'I gather it was Ray who tracked down Lili's parents, and … well, here she is – Otto's heir.' Elspeth clapped. 'Well done, Ray. Quite ironic, isn't it, that our very own heir-hunter has done his own family out of their inheritance?'

Sarah turned to Ray, repeating Elspeth's words, 'You fool!'

Ray shrugged. 'How was I supposed to know?'

Lili looked from Sarah to Ray, her eyes settling on Elspeth. She was having a hard time wrapping her head around what Elspeth had just told her. 'I'm sorry, what does this mean?'

'It means,' replied Elspeth, 'that you stand to inherit The Summerhouse, along with the art collection too, assuming – as Ray pointed out – that Miriam is no longer with us. That means you will be a very wealthy young lady.'

Lili glanced around the room. All eyes were on her. She turned to Nate sitting next to her on the couch.

He stood up. 'So, Elspeth was right. That's what you came back here for, to check out the house and get what's yours.' He stormed out.

'Nate?' Lili called after him. As she rose from her chair, she felt Alex's hand on her shoulder.

Ray reached out to Sarah. 'I'm sor—'

Sarah flicked his hand away and stood up. She stormed out of the summerhouse too, Ray following in her wake with more lame apologies, his voice growing faint, as he followed her up the garden towards the house.

Elspeth clapped her hands together. 'Well, I wouldn't exactly call it a fun afternoon, but I for one feel so much better getting all that is off my chest.' She breathed an enormous sigh. 'I've been carrying the secret of the summerhouse around for too long.'

'Are you mad at me?' Lili asked Elspeth in a small voice. It was a dumb question; of course, she was. Lili's very existence had cheated her descendants out of all this.

Alex walked over and sat down next to her, slipping a comforting arm around her shoulders.

Maisie and William, still sitting cross-legged on cushions on the floor in front of their great-grandmother, stood up and ran over to the sofa, vying with each other over who would sit next to Lili. Maisie got the spot beside Lili first, but William went one better by climbing onto Lili's lap for a cuddle. He put his hands around her neck. 'I'm not mad at you. I love you.'

'Oh, William, that is so sweet. I love you too.' Lili could feel her eyes welling up.

Maisie looked at her brother. 'I'm not mad at you either, Lili.'

Lili smiled. 'I know, sweetheart.' She guessed they were too young to understand what had just transpired.

Lili raised her eyes to look at Elspeth.

Elspeth smiled at her great-grandchildren before turning her attention on Lili. 'This isn't your fault, Lili. What happened … all this played out a long, long time ago, before you were born.'

She paused, as if choosing her words carefully. 'Ray once told me that although he enjoyed his new job as an heir hunter, there is a downside to seeking descendants and finding lost heirs who have relations they never knew existed; for some people, like yourself, he has uncovered vast wealth, but it often comes at a price. Sometimes he uncovers more than they bargained for.'

'You're talking about family secrets.' Lili swallowed as she looked around the old summerhouse. She didn't want to lose her friends. They were more than friends. In the brief space of time she'd known them – Lili looked at the little boy sitting on her lap, his hand in hers – they'd become the extended family she'd never had. She realised Elspeth understood that too.

'What should I do?'

'I can't answer that, Lili. You will inherit, that is a given. What you do after that …' Elspeth trailed off.

Lili cast her gaze towards the door. 'What about them?'

'They'll just have to learn to live with it.'

Alex, who had remained silent, spoke up. There was something on his mind. 'I told you earlier that the police were looking into Joseph's past. That's why they haven't released him.'

Elspeth nodded. 'You mentioned a genealogist.'

'Yes.'

Elspeth frowned. 'Before you say another word, I know where you're going with this.' She shook her head. 'Even if someone suspected something amiss, and I'm talking about Otto's real identity, and this ghosting that Ray was talking about, Joseph isn't going to tell the police the truth – that his father is buried in a little grave in the British Cemetery on Corfu.'

'But you could.'

Elspeth shook her head at Alex. 'No, I can't do that to Joseph.'

Lili stared at Elspeth. 'So, if it came to light that Otto wasn't really George then Otto's will, posing as George, could be contested. As Otto's descendant, I wouldn't stand to inherit The Summerhouse.' Lili glanced at Alex for confirmation this would be the case.

He nodded.

Lili thought this through. 'The house and land must be in Joseph's late fathers' name. His direct descendant is Joseph and his family – not me. So, if I told the police—'

Elspeth interrupted, 'But you can't do it, Lili.'

'Why not?'

'For the same reason I can't. Joseph made a promise he

would never divulge Otto's identity. It would break his heart if we went against his wishes.'

Alex shrugged. 'Not to state the obvious, but Otto is dead. He has been for years. What does it matter now?'

'It matters to Joseph. He wouldn't want Otto's name blasted in the papers. Can you imagine the headlines? *Nazi lived for years under an assumed name in deepest Suffolk*.'

Lili thought of the press camped on the front lawn waiting for their big story. She was starting to understand where Elspeth was coming from. Otto was, after all, her great-grandfather. Is that what she really wanted, to see Otto portrayed in the press as a Nazi war criminal? That would be the conclusion they all jumped to when they discovered he had lived under a false identity for decades. On the other hand, Alex was right: Otto was long gone.

Elspeth added, 'Besides, they'd probably want to exhume his father's body to do DNA testing – do you really think Joseph would want that?'

Lili shook her head even though she wondered if DNA testing was even a possibility, considering the length of time that he had been dead. She said, 'So, I still stand to inherit The Summerhouse after Joseph dies, even if I don't want to?'

Elspeth nodded. 'I'm afraid so.'

Lili fell silent until William fidgeted on her lap. 'I'm hungry.'

Elspeth looked at her great-grandson. 'Why don't you two run up to the house and ask your dad for a snack?' The children nodded at Elspeth, then gave Lili a cuddle before heading outside. William ran out first. Maisie was following him, but she stopped in the doorway and turned around. 'Lili, does this mean you are going to come and live here when Joseph dies?'

Lili looked at her in surprise. She'd understood more than Lili gave her credit for. 'I don't know, sweetheart. Besides, Joseph isn't going anywhere, anytime soon.'

41

Lili opened the letter. She stared at it for so long that Alex eventually appeared. 'Is something the matter?' He walked up the hallway and joined her at the front door.

'Joseph passed away.'

'Oh, I'm so sorry to hear that.'

So was Lili. When they had released Joseph without charge, she had returned to Aldeburgh to see him at home. He had still been recovering from his hip operation. It wasn't something she had wanted to do – return to The Summerhouse knowing Nate was there – but she had good reason. Apart from the fact that she had longed to meet up with Joseph and talk to him about Otto and her own visit to the house with her mother years earlier, Lili wanted to hear the story that Elspeth had told her first-hand. But Lili's main purpose for the visit was to persuade Joseph, with her support, to go to his solicitor and challenge the will.

He'd been overjoyed to see her. They had spent a wonderful day together, reminiscing about the past. He talked about his memories of Corfu in the good times with his parents, and the Corfiot family, and all the artist friends his parents used to have before the war. The meeting had been bittersweet for Lili. Elspeth had been quite right when she had said that Joseph would be loyal to Otto to the bitter end; he would not contest Otto's will.

Lili looked at Alex. 'His funeral is next week. The family have invited me.'

'They have?' He appeared just as surprised as Lili. 'Will you go?'

'I'm not sure.'

Alex wasn't surprised by her reticence. He could imagine how she felt at the thought of another funeral. They'd not long attended the memorial service for their good friend, Toby.

Lili said, 'You realise what this means – don't you?'

'You inherit The Summerhouse.'

Lili stared at the invitation.

'Who sent it – do you know?'

'It's from Elspeth.'

'That makes sense.'

'I don't think the rest of the family will want me there.'

'Maybe they'll surprise you.'

Lili doubted it.

'When is it?' Alex asked.

She caught the nervous inflection in his voice before he exhaled in relief at her reply. 'Friday.'

Lili glanced at the suitcases piled up in the hall and the boxes ready to go into storage. They had stripped the rental flat of all their possessions, most of which were Alex's. Lili's were still in the FedEx box she'd retrieved from Ray's boat. They were preparing for their imminent move to Washington.

Lili had persuaded Alex to take the promotion, and this time she was not objecting to going with him. After what had happened at The Summerhouse, she wanted to make a fresh start as far away from Suffolk as possible. Washington would be perfect.

Alex had questioned Lili about her motives. He felt she was running away from the hurt of discovering that the people she had grown close to had rejected her, even though it wasn't her fault that she was going to inherit the property. Nobody had contacted her to see how she was; the letter from Elspeth letting her know that Joseph had died peacefully in his sleep was the first she'd heard from them.

Lili had told Alex that he was mistaken about her motives, although there was a grain of truth to his concerns about why she was leaving the country. She *was* running away, avoiding the inevitable – inheriting The Summerhouse and those priceless paintings.

As a consequence, and not through choice, Lili had become a minor celebrity. She felt as though the paparazzi hounded her wherever she went. The intrusive nature of having her photograph taken without her permission, and articles printed about her in newspapers, was getting to her. Any thoughts that it was fun being the centre of attention were quickly dispelled when Lili found herself in that position.

Although it wasn't her fault, she felt responsible that Otto (still known to the outside world as George) and Joseph, who had spent their whole lives in quiet anonymity, had posthumously been thrust into the limelight with the discovery of the artwork worth millions that they had stored in their old summerhouse in Thorpeness.

And Ray hadn't escaped unscathed either. The former art cop turned heir-hunter was all over the news. He had been inundated by inquiries from people clamouring for his services to see if they, too, were the lost descendants of a secret fortune.

But it wasn't Joseph's or Ray's story that had captured people's imaginations. What had caused such a sensation was the rags-to-riches tale of the little orphaned girl found lost in Corfu; a child who had grown up in care only to become one of the richest women in the country. Lili had become a minor celebrity. She felt as though the paparazzi hounded her wherever she went. The intrusive nature of having her photograph taken without her permission and articles printed about her in newspapers was getting to her. Any thoughts that it might be fun being the centre of attention were quickly dispelled when Lili found herself in that position.

Lili didn't want to be rich. All she wanted was to find her grandmother, Miriam. The paintings were Alena's legacy, which Lili knew should be passed down to her daughter – Lili's grandmother – if she was still alive.

Lili took exception to the way she was being portrayed in the media. She was also worried what any journalist who started really digging into her story might find. So far, her connection to Joseph had been explained through his parents' friendship before the outbreak of war with the Greek family on the island of Corfu, of whom she was a descendant. So far, nobody knew George had really died on Corfu in the war and that Lili's great-grandfather, Otto, had assumed his identity.

That explained why the police – and, Lili imagined, some journalists – were baffled as to why Josephs' father had gone to such lengths, and spent so much money, to piece together his Corfiot friends' art collection over the years. Lili knew that one word from her would reveal everything.

Right now, with all the media hoopla, Lili knew that Elspeth had been right. She didn't trust how her great-grandfather would be portrayed if the truth came to light now.

She hoped the fact that she would now inherit The Summerhouse would slip quietly under the radar, because that could not be as easily explained away. Fortunately, the haul of priceless paintings was of far more interest to people than the house on the shore of the lake in Thorpeness.

Alex had already suggested, on more than one occasion, that if she wasn't happy with what they were saying about her in the media, then she should tell her own story.

Lili had had plenty of offers from newspapers and reality television shows. A publisher had even offered her a book deal to write her memoirs. 'I'm not even thirty, for goodness' sake,' Lili had scoffed. 'Why would I want to write my memoirs?' Besides, if she did that, then the truth about Otto's identity would come out, and she wasn't ready to reveal that. She had enough media attention without the world at large finding out about Otto.

'You know, the truth is going to come out,' Alex had said to her one day, soon after Joseph was released.

Lili really didn't want to think about that. She hadn't asked for all the media attention. She was just a horticulturist who wanted to make her own way and lead a quiet, innocuous life, like her great-grandfather, Otto.

Lili had discovered that Elspeth had been right when she'd told her about the observations Ray had made as an heir-hunter. Although, in his experience, people were thrilled to discover they were lost heirs to an inheritance, with ties to relatives they had never known existed, it often came at a price. One of the unexpected downsides to Lili's apparent newfound wealth, in the form of those priceless paintings, was the media getting wind of her search for the grandparents she had never known.

The number of people, some as far afield as Australia, who had come forward claiming to be her long-lost grandparents was laughable. Except that Lili didn't find it funny; they were all after one thing – her money. She had thought that all the media attention about her story would help her find them, but the reality had been the opposite.

'What are you thinking?' Alex asked.

Lili touched the ring on her necklace. She wished that Otto had never given her the Hebrew wedding band that turned out to be the ring he'd had made for Alena. He must have known he would never see Alena again when he gave it to Lili on the only occasion she'd met her great-grandfather. It was Elspeth who had told Lili this. Lili realised that if it hadn't been for that ring, she would never have discovered her connection with Joseph and his family; a connection that was now irretrievably broken because of Otto's silly will, leaving The Summerhouse to his descendants – to her. He'd had no right to do that. Somehow, she had to make things right – but how?

Lili fingered the other ring on her necklace. During her last meeting with Joseph, he had told her that he'd known she was Otto's great-granddaughter the moment she'd walked into his shop. He had seen the resemblance to her great-grandmother, Alena, and had recalled the first time he and Lili had met, when she was just a toddler visiting The Summerhouse with her mother. He had always wondered why Lili and her mother had never returned; he'd hoped that someday they would. At that last meeting, he had taken off the ring on his finger, Otto's ring, and had given it to her.

Alex stared at the two Hebrew wedding bands on Lili's necklace. It reminded him that he still hadn't proposed to her. He knew why he was holding back; it wasn't just because of all the things that had been going on in her life lately. He was holding out to do it in Washington. There was a reason for that; Alex still wasn't wholly convinced that she was coming too.

A piece of notepaper that Lili hadn't noticed with the invitation dropped out of the envelope and floated to the floor.

Alex knelt and picked it up, his solicitor's eye roving over its contents. 'It's from Ray,' he said in surprise.

'Really?' Lili took the note. She too was surprised he had written to her.

'What does it say?'

Lili skim-read the contents. 'I think I need to sit down.'

'What is it?' said Alex, concerned.

Lili retreated to the kitchen, followed closely by Alex. Perched on a stool at the counter-top, she re-read the note. 'Ray continued the search for my grandmother in Israel.'

'You're joking.'

Lili shook her head. 'It's true.' She remembered to breathe. 'There's more …'

42

Alex took her hand. 'Are you nervous?'

'A little,' Lili replied. It was an understatement. Her stomach was doing backflips at the thought her grandmother would be there. 'I wish I'd had a chance to meet her beforehand.'

'I know, but there wasn't time. You'll have plenty of time to talk to her after the service.'

Alex pulled the hire car to a stop as the funeral cortège reached the entrance to the small cemetery where Otto had been laid to rest years ago.

'That's assuming Miriam comes,' commented Lili.

'Ray said in his letter that she would try to make it to Joseph's funeral. I'm sure she'll be here.' Alex put on the handbrake and turned off the engine.

'Do you think there might be other members of my family from Israel here too?'

'Well, you're about to find out.' People were getting out of the vehicles in front. Alex opened the driver's door. 'I think we walk from here.'

Lili got out of the car. There were at least ten other people in front of them. She stared at the figures; some she recognised, like Joseph's immediate family and Reggie from the music shop, but others she didn't. Lili was looking for an elderly lady of Mediterranean appearance.

'I don't see her,' Lili whispered as they stepped forward. Theirs had been the last vehicle in the cortège to arrive at the cemetery.

'Perhaps she's still in the car.' Alex glanced behind them. 'Or they haven't arrived yet.'

Lili turned around and looked down the empty street. No other cars had been following them. They stood there for a few minutes until Alex said, 'We'd better catch up with the others. We don't want to miss the service.'

Lili nodded, wondering if perhaps Miriam had decided not to make the trip to England after all. She was well into her eighties. Lili hoped ill health hadn't prevented her from coming.

Alex took her hand and squeezed it tight. 'Don't worry. I'm sure she'll be here.'

Lili caught the nuance in his voice. He didn't sound as convinced as he was making out. Perhaps he was thinking the same thing; she was a woman of advancing years; maybe ill health had derailed her plans. Lili didn't want to think about the other explanation; she had decided she didn't wish to travel all this way to meet her granddaughter after all. Lili swallowed. She was the only grandparent that Lili had left.

Despite the countless people coming forward to claim they were her grandparents, and that she was their long-lost grandchild, Ray had found her paternal grandparents too. Lili's father had had an all-too-common surname, *Jones*. Ray remarked that the people trying to pass themselves off as her relatives must be stupid. It was quite straightforward for a genealogist and a DNA test to establish the truth. Even so, it was time-consuming to vet all these dishonest individuals who were claiming to be related to Lili.

It turned out that Ray had ended up with a solid lead. He had received a letter from someone claiming to be Lili's uncle, her father's brother. Inside the note was a photo of himself as a young man with his brother. The photo couldn't lie; it was Lili's father.

He hadn't come forward straight away, even though he was aware of the search for Lili's relatives. His explanation for the delay was that he had wanted to avoid all the media hoopla and attention, although he did want to see his only niece.

They had met secretly at a coffee shop in Aldeburgh the day before Joseph's funeral. Her paternal grandparents hadn't been there. They had died several years earlier. Her uncle told her that his parents, both retired doctors, had wanted their sons to go to medical school. But his younger brother, Lili's father, had dropped out and gone travelling.

Although there was no question in Lili's mind that the retired doctor was her uncle, Ray had still insisted on a DNA test. However, it was the details he knew that were not in the public arena that had convinced Lili they didn't need to take a test to prove they were related.

Her uncle had told her that his brother had lived in a kibbutz in Israel. That was where he'd met Lili's mother. The only other person outside the immediate family who knew that was Connie, and she had her own reasons for staying away from the media fray that had become part of Lili's life.

The reason the press hadn't descended on Joseph's funeral, and turned it into a circus, was Elspeth's foresight in keeping the arrangements under wraps. Anyone attending was sworn to secrecy. Speaking to her uncle, Lili had found something out. Her father had told him about her – kind of. Lili recalled what her uncle had said:

I'd been travelling. I was in Africa when he died. Just before the motorcycle accident, he told me he had someone he wanted me to meet. After his death, I assumed he'd meant your mother; I knew she'd died in the motorcycle accident too. I didn't know he was talking about his child – you, Lili. It's my biggest regret. If I'd known about you, I would have brought you up.'

Her uncle had married but didn't have any children. It turned out he'd returned from his stint abroad and opened a GP practice in another London borough, where he'd worked until he retired.

Lili thought about how ironic it was that all that time, she'd had family virtually on her doorstep.

❖

Alex went to fetch Lili a drink and a plate of nibbles from the spread Elspeth had laid out in the kitchen. She wasn't happy; he knew that. Miriam hadn't turned up.

He made his way through the lounge, which was filled with people from the local community who had come to the wake to pay their respects. Although Joseph had had few close friends, the antiques business had been a stalwart of the local community for decades. Even so, Alex hadn't expected so many people, but he guessed most of them had seen the news, and the notoriety had something to do with it. He expected the press to turn up at any moment, but it appeared that nobody, not even the locals, had alerted them, out of respect for Joseph and his family.

It took some time for him to find Lili. She was in the lounge, but she had retreated to the conservatory and was sitting in a wicker chair on her own, staring at Joseph's prize orchids. Bella growled at Alex as he walked in.

'Whoa! I come bearing gifts.' Alex presented the dog with a peace offering in the form of a sausage roll off the plate.

'You shouldn't feed her those,' Lili commented. 'She'll be sick.'

'Too late now. I'm not putting my hand anywhere near those jaws to retrieve it.'

'She won't bite. She's a sweetheart.' Lili stroked her head. 'She just needs to get to know you first.'

'I'll take your word for it.' Alex gave the German shepherd a wide berth and passed Lili the plate.

'I'm not hungry, Alex.'

'It was a nice service, wasn't it?'

Lili nodded, her gaze distant. She glanced at Alex. 'Would you mind if I had some time on my own?'

'Of course.' Alex looked at the plate. 'Shall I take this away?'

Lili nodded. 'Please.'

'I'll let you know if your grandmother arrives.'

'If you like,' Lili replied.

Alex got the impression she'd given up on the idea that her grandmother was coming.

He had just walked out of the door, followed by a German shepherd after another sausage roll, when a young couple Lili didn't recognise wandered in.

'Wow, this room is amazing,' the woman said. 'Do you think these are Joseph's prize orchids?'

The two locals were accompanied by several more people

having a nose around the house. They hadn't noticed Lili sitting in the corner of the conservatory. She sighed.

'Oh, sorry – didn't see you there,' one of them said when they spotted Lili. 'Hey, aren't you the heir to those paintings worth like millions they found in the old summerhouse?'

Lili rolled her eyes. This was all she needed. She shook her head. But one of the other guests overheard. 'Yes, that's her. I saw her photo in a news article just the other day.'

And that was her cue to leave. Everyone was staring at her. She felt like an exhibit in a museum. She rushed outside. All the places she went, the hall, the kitchen, the lounge, were full of people. She ran down the hall and out of the back door. She was already halfway down the garden before she slowed her pace near the path that led round to the front of the old summerhouse. She was about to take a breather on the porch when she noticed the door was ajar. She stared at it in surprise. With all the people arriving for the wake, she had thought the cabin would be locked.

Lili gingerly stepped inside. 'My god!' She cast her gaze around the walls, which were covered in beautiful paintings of the Suffolk coast, towns and villages.'

'They're quite something, aren't they?'

Lili looked at Nate, who was seated on the sofa. She agreed. 'He certainly captured the landscape and the beautiful sunrises in this part of the world.'

They both knew who the artist was behind these paintings – Otto.

Lili recognised some of them. 'Who brought them here from the house?' she asked. With all the people around, and other things on her mind, notably Miriam's absence, she hadn't noticed they were missing.

'I brought them down here before the funeral.'

Lili looked at him. Before she could ask why, he said, 'I was worried that so many people might descend on us during the wake that one of them might get damaged. I was going to put them in the basement, but I thought, why hide them away? Why not hang them here?'

Lili agreed. 'I didn't know he had painted so many. I don't remember seeing all these up at the house.'

'They must have been stored in the attic. It appears he was quite prolific. The police took the lot away, but when they realised these were by an unknown artist, and weren't valuable, they returned them. Rather than putting them back in the attic, I hung them all here instead.'

'They're valuable to me,' commented Lili, gazing at the beautiful creations at the hand of an artist she would love to have known.

'Sorry, I know I shouldn't be here,' Nate apologised, 'but I just had to get away from all that.' He glanced in the direction of the house.

Lili smiled. She knew what he was talking about. 'Me too.'

There was an uncomfortable silence.

Nate stood up. 'I'd better go.'

'Please don't leave on my account.'

Nate shrugged and sat down.

Lili took a seat on the sofa opposite Nate, avoiding eye contact. She wanted to ask him about Otto. He'd known her grandfather and had spent time with him. It sounded as though they'd had a lovely relationship, from the little Nate had told her. She wanted him to tell her more but doubted he would be very receptive; not after the way they had parted the last time they'd seen each other, with Nate storming out of the cabin when Elspeth had told them all what Lili stood to inherit.

She could feel Nate staring at her. 'So, where are the other paintings?' he asked.

The police had advised Lili not to return the paintings to the cabin. With all the media attention, the chances that it would be broken into, and the pictures stolen, was an insurance company's nightmare. The police station didn't have the room or the conditions for them to remain there.

'A museum in London is temporarily storing them in their vault while I figure out what to do with them.'

Nate nodded. 'That makes sense.'

Does it? thought Lili. What she wanted to do with them was hand them over to Miriam, but she hadn't turned up.

'I heard what you tried to do on your last visit here.'

Lili looked at him sharply. 'I don't know what you mean,' she said defensively.

'You attempted to persuade Joseph to challenge the will.'

'Oh, that,' Lili said offhand. 'It was stupid of me to think he would do it.' Lili was still staring around the room. 'Then I realised I didn't need his permission or his solicitors.' Lili glanced at Nate. 'I can make the changes myself.'

Nate leaned forward in his seat. 'What are you talking about?'

'All this,' Lili held up her hand, gesturing at the artwork adorning the walls of the summerhouse. 'This is ridiculous.'

Nate frowned. 'What do you mean?'

'The paintings that were here, but are now sitting in a vault, shouldn't be in a private collection. Those masterpieces have been under lock and key for far too long. I want them to be seen and enjoyed by all, not just one person.'

Nate stared at Lili. 'Just what are you proposing to do?'

Lili wasn't proposing anything; she had already made up her mind. 'I want to donate them to the museum, with one proviso: that they hang them in a gallery dedicated to my great-grandfather.' She knew it would be controversial, telling the story of a Nazi art officer, but she didn't want him or his legacy to be hidden any longer. 'I want to encourage others to search out the human story that is so often concealed behind emblems and labels and …'

'… swastikas,' Nate added.

Lili turned to him. She didn't need his permission or to seek his approval, but as a friend, she would have liked his opinion. She imagined he thought she was crazy to give up this immense wealth, but Lili still thought they weren't hers to keep, even if her grandmother wasn't alive.

Nate stared at her. He shook his head. 'You are crazy – do you know that?' His face broke out in a wide grin. 'But you are also amazing.'

'I am?'

'Yes. I imagine very few people would give them up for posterity rather than sell the paintings and make a fortune.'

'I know it's the right thing to do, Nate.' She just wasn't sure if Miriam would agree. Lili was aware it wasn't her decision to make, not yet, not unless Miriam was …

Lili didn't want to think about that – the fact that she'd been waiting all day and her grandmother hadn't come. Why hadn't she turned up? Had something happened? Lili tried to dismiss where that train of thought led; to the possibility that perhaps she would never get to meet her.

She said to Nate, 'I know Otto kept these for Alena. They

belonged to her family. But I think he would have approved.'

'I think Joseph would have approved too.' Nate's expression turned serious. He leaned forward in his seat and placed some keys on the coffee table in front of Lili. 'These belong to you now. There's no point waiting for the reading of the will. We all know what it says.'

Lili stared at the keys to the house. 'I'm not taking those.'

'You haven't got a choice, Lili. You heard Elspeth, it's what Otto wanted.'

'Ah, but that's where you're wrong.' Lili smiled. 'I *have* got a choice. Besides, what about what I want?'

'But Otto wanted this house to remain in his family – *your* family.'

Lili was still smiling. 'And it will. Joseph and his descendants are just as much a part of Otto's family as Alena and her descendants …' Lili trailed off, a lump in her throat. She took a breath and continued, 'Our families,' She glanced around the summerhouse, 'are inextricably linked through a kind, passionate man who saved not one, but two children all those years ago.'

Nate stared at her. 'What are you saying?'

'We are family, Nate. That is Otto's legacy. I don't need that big old house, but *you* do. You have children who need a home, and, of course, Bella – she needs a good-sized garden. And there's still Joseph's prize orchids that need a home too.'

Lili had been talking to Elspeth at the wake. 'It sounds to me as though you might have a permanent house guest, too. Elspeth wants to stay on for a bit, look after Joseph's plants and the garden.'

Lili leaned forward in her seat and moved the keys back along the coffee table in Nate's direction. 'I've already seen the solicitor. It's done. I signed the property over to you this morning before the funeral.'

Nate sat there speechless. When he found his voice, he said, 'Are you leaving?'

Alex had made his way down to the old cabin in the garden when he couldn't find Lili in the house. He stopped outside the door. His heart was pounding when he overheard the conversation and realised that Lili was hesitating. Why wasn't she telling Nate she was due to leave for Washington in the morning?

'Stay, Lili, please. There's going to be a vacant shop in Cobbler's Yard.'

'Is there?' Lili knew Nate wasn't talking about Joseph's antique shop. She had found out what was happening to his shop. Before Nate said any more, Lili replied, 'I heard what you did for Hannah.'

'Oh, it's nothing.'

Lili disagreed. She wasn't the only one giving away her inheritance. Nate had signed the shop over to Hannah. She would have to do some courses when she got out of prison, learn bookkeeping for starters, but by the sound of things, she was up for it. When Hannah had served her sentence, she was going to move into the flat above the shop and share custody of Maisie, who would live with her mother part of the week in the flat. It sounded as though the antiques side of things would be wound down in favour of expanding Maisie's budding amber jewellery empire.

Lili smiled. For the first time, Hannah would start taking responsibility for her life, and for Maisie's future. It was going to be a big change for her and Maisie, but all in a good way. Lili had visited Hannah in prison. She hadn't been the only visitor.

Hannah's parents had reached out to her. They had been visiting her too, building bridges, and were soon to meet Maisie. Lili was overjoyed at this unexpected outcome.

'Will you at least think about it?'

Lili stared at Nate. 'Think about what?'

'The vacant shop in Cobbler's Yard. Well, there're two. My mum is selling The Potting Shed, and Ray is giving up his shop too.'

'Oh, I'm sorry to hear that.'

Nate shrugged. 'Ray has too much work to do with his heir-hunting business now he has inquiries from all over the world. I think he only took on the shop because Mum was just across the yard.'

Lili had guessed that was the case. 'Sarah is leaving too?'

'Yes. I think she wants to retire properly, you know, have more time for other things she used to do – like painting, for one. She has two grandchildren to take up her time, and she wants to help Hannah set up Joseph's old shop and make a success of it.' Nate looked at her. 'You could run The Potting Shed. I know you enjoyed working in Cobbler's Yard.'

Lili bit her lower lip.

'Your best friend will be just across the yard, and you'll see Maisie all the time.'

Lili stared at Nate. She knew what he was doing – trying to persuade her to stay.

'What about William?' Lili asked. 'I'd want to see him too.'

'Oh, he won't be able to stay away. He loves amber-hunting and helping Maisie with her necklaces.'

'And Bella …' Lili ventured. 'I might need to come up to the house and take her for a walk from time-to-time …'

Their eyes locked. 'I'm sure that could be arranged.' Nate smiled. 'Perhaps you could stop for dinner. Oh, and if you needed a place to live, well, I know a super little cabin overlooking a lake …'

Lili looked around the old place.

'It's in good nick, but we could always spruce it up a bit.'

Lili shook her head. 'Yes, I suppose it could do with a new rug and some more furniture, but I'd want Alena's portrait left over the fireplace.'

They both turned to look at the portrait of Lili's great-grandmother.

'I think that could be arranged,' said Nate.

Alex was about to walk in and interrupt the conversation he wished Nate was not having with his girlfriend when a woman's voice behind him stopped him in his tracks. 'Excuse me.'

Alex turned around to find an old lady, small in stature, quite overweight and dressed all in black, leaning heavily on a walking stick.

The old lady said breathlessly, 'Do you know where I might find Lili? Someone told me to try the old summerhouse?'

Nate and Lili exchanged a glance when they overheard a woman with a thick Mediterranean accent outside. Lili shot out of her seat as Alex appeared in the doorway with the lady on his arm. He frowned at Nate before saying, 'Lili, I found her. I found Miriam.'

43

Leaning on a walking stick as she made her way around the room, Miriam took her time taking in the paintings covering each wall – the wonderful paintings by a talented artist, her father, Otto.

Lili watched her with bated breath, thinking of the paintings that had adorned her wealthy grandparents' mansion in Corfu decades earlier – paintings that were now sitting a vault in a London museum. She wanted her grandmother's blessing for what she wanted to do with them, but she needed her approval too. All along, despite the articles in the press calling her a wealthy young heiress of an art collection worth a fortune, Lili had known the truth. She was not the heir to the fortune. Miriam was. They had never been Otto's to bequeath; the provenance had shown that.

However, these paintings in the cabin – the ones that the press knew nothing about – did belong to Lili. He'd left them to Lili's mother. In the event of her death, they passed to Otto's great-granddaughter, Alena Lili Jones.

As she watched Miriam walking slowly around the room, staring at Otto's art, Lili guessed he'd had good reason not to leave her his private art collection. They had been estranged at the time of his death. He'd never met his grown-up daughter. Lili imagined that he'd thought there was a possibility that Miriam might just get rid of the paintings; destroy them. She watched her grandmother silently studying the paintings and wondered what she was thinking.

Miriam was thinking about a conversation she'd had up at the summerhouse before she'd found Lili. She'd had a long conversation with Elspeth. She'd discovered the human story behind the Nazi officer who had been her father, and it had dispelled all the assumptions she'd made about the skeleton in her closet; the person she'd seen as a war criminal. She'd found out that he'd been the gentlest, kindest man one could ever hope to meet.

Miriam stopped in front of the fireplace to stare at the portrait of her mother. She'd never known her late father had been such a talented artist.

She stood there for some considerable time before she turned and looked at her granddaughter. 'Remarkable,' she said. 'You look just like her. If there was any doubt in my mind that you were my grandchild …' she trailed off as they chose a seat on the sofa.

Nate, shooing Bella outside, took Alex with him. Lili caught the look on Alex's face as he followed Nate out of the door to give them some privacy. She wondered how long he had been standing out there and how much of their conversation he'd overheard. Lili was conscious of the fact that when Nate had asked her about leaving for Washington, she had been non-committal. Lili had surprised herself. Despite the playful banter with Nate over taking over Sarah's flower shop, and staying in the old summerhouse, it had been just that – playful banter. Hadn't it? She still wanted to go with Alex – didn't she?

As Miriam took a seat, she said, 'I wish …' Her wrinkled face crumpled as she looked around the summerhouse, tears flowing down her cheeks.

Lili had an idea what Miriam wished for; that she hadn't been estranged from her daughter or missed out on knowing her granddaughter. Then there were the years she might have spent getting to know her father.

'I wish I'd come with my daughter on her first visit to see Otto,' confided Miriam. 'Then perhaps we wouldn't have been estranged when you were born, and …'

Lili reached for her hand. 'It's all right. I'm here now. You're here now. And that's all that matters.' Lili stared at the portrait of Alena and imagined how happy Otto would be if he knew that his daughter had come back to him. Although she hadn't met him again in her lifetime, at least she knew him now – the kind-hearted artist who had saved her and a little English boy called Joseph.

Lili smiled. 'You know, I was in Corfu just recently, and my wonderful guide, Spiros, took me to a vineyard.' Lili glanced up at the portrait of her great-grandmother. It was the actual place where Alena grew up. I walked around the house. It was so wonderful to be there.'

Lili told her grandmother about the knowledgeable tour guide who had talked of the two brothers from the Greek mainland who had found the abandoned vineyard and derelict farmhouse, and how they had restored it.

'Have you returned to visit your parents' former home on Corfu since the war?'

Miriam smiled, although she shook her head. 'I haven't been back, but the couple who adopted me went. They knew I was the last living relative of the wealthy family who owned the biggest vineyard on the island. As my legal guardians, they acted on my behalf and sold the land to the brothers. You see, the tour guide does not know the full story. Some of the money paid for us all to resettle in Israel, but the rest, they put in trust for me.' Miriam shifted her gaze to the portrait of her mother.

'When I came of age, I chose to use that legacy to help other Greek Orthodox Jews, who had lost everything in the war, to resettle in Israel.'

Miriam turned to her granddaughter and smiled. 'I'd love for us to go there together, if you would like to visit the vineyard again.'

Lili nearly cried. 'Oh, yes! That would be amazing.'

Miriam squeezed her granddaughter's hand. She thought so too.

'Miriam?'

Miriam wiped her eyes dry and turned around at the sound of a familiar voice. 'Ah, this is Anita. She accompanied me to England.' Miriam held out her hand. 'Come sit with us.'

Lili turned in her seat to see a young woman, about her own age, hovering in the doorway. Lili stared at her as she walked into the summerhouse.

Miriam smiled at Lili. 'You notice the family resemblance. She is your cousin – one of your aunt's children.'

Lili looked at Miriam. 'My mum had siblings?' The idea had never occurred to her.

'Of course. I had five children.'

'Five?'

'There are many, many relatives waiting for you in Israel.'

'Waiting for me?'

Anita ran over and hugged Lili. 'Welcome to the family! This is amazing. You look just like me!' She giggled.

Her laughter was infectious. Lili laughed too.

'So, will you come?' Anita asked.

Lili looked at her. 'Come where?'

Anita sighed and turned to her grandmother. 'You haven't told her yet – have you?'

'I was getting to that.' Miriam took something out of her handbag.

Anita grabbed the plane ticket out of her hand and held it out to Lili. 'Here's a plane ticket for you to return with us to Israel. We all clubbed together to fly first class. Everyone is dying to meet you. All you have to do is bring your passport with you at check-in before we fly.'

Alex had returned, and he had overheard the conversation that was taking place in the summerhouse. Lili was just reaching for the ticket when she caught sight of Alex, standing in the doorway, raising his hands in the air in exasperation. 'Well, I guess Washington will have to wait,' he said.

Lili took the ticket, wondering when the right moment would be to tell Alex that she wasn't going with him after all. She wanted to take over Sarah's flower shop in Cobbler's Yard and move into the old summerhouse. But it was more than that; if she was thousands of miles away in Washington, she would miss Hannah and Maisie, William and Bella. And Nate. Of course, she would miss him; she'd been missing him every day since they'd been apart. She'd even miss his squabbling parents; they still hadn't signed the divorce papers.

Alex hovered in the doorway. He noticed Lili hadn't introduced him to her family. He guessed why. 'I suppose this is goodbye,' he said.

Lili walked over to him and took a deep breath. 'I'm sorry, Alex.' She cast her gaze around the summerhouse. 'This is where I belong.'

'I know.' He sighed heavily. 'I had a feeling this would happen if you returned. I guess I would have been more surprised if you said you were still coming with me.'

He glanced at Miriam and the young woman who bore a striking resemblance to Lili. 'I'm glad you found them, Lili,' he said earnestly.

'Thank you, Alex.' She smiled at the thought that they were parting on good terms and remaining friends.

'Let me know about your trip to Israel.'

'I will. Likewise, about Washington.'

He smiled. 'Ditto.'

Lili watched him go. Then she cast her eye around the cabin. Before she moved into her new home, and back into the lives of the family she had fallen in love with, first she had a plane to catch to meet the relatives she'd been searching for; she hoped they would become as much a part of her life as Nate's family had.

Lili joined Miriam and Anita, and followed their gaze around the old summerhouse, taking in Otto's paintings once more. Like Miriam and her family's art collection, Lili had a decision to make. Soon the secret of the summerhouse, Otto's real identity, would be revealed. It was inevitable that the truth would come out one day. Lili had to decide if his beautiful paintings should remain under lock and key in her private collection or if his legacy as an artist should be shown to the world. She had already made a decision. She wanted to give Otto's paintings to the museum, to put them on display for all to enjoy. She knew it was the right thing to do; above all, her great-grandfather had been an artist, and Lili knew in her heart that it was how he would have liked to be remembered.

Anita slipped her hand in Lili's and squeezed it tight. 'He was so talented.'

Lili turned to her cousin and smiled. 'I know.' She could only imagine, once the truth came out about Otto's incredible story, what they would be worth. Lili knew the press would be all over it, back to her rags-to-riches story, as soon they discovered there was another art collection. Lili wouldn't be surprised if she had no end of inquiries from art galleries, auction houses, and wealthy individuals, interested in acquiring her great-grandfather's artwork. But she couldn't sell Otto's paintings only for them to sit in another's private collection.

Besides, Lili didn't care how much they might be worth. That didn't matter to her. She already felt she was the richest woman alive, for she now had what she'd always craved, and what to her was priceless; something that all the money in the world couldn't buy. Family. That was the legacy Otto had left her. She couldn't wait to meet them all.

Anita turned to Lili. 'So, will you come with us to meet your family?'

Lili looked at the plane ticket, her eyes filling with tears of joy. 'When do we leave?'

The Sunrise Coast Series continues in

The Cottage by the Sea

Paperback and Kindle eBook available from Amazon

If you enjoyed The Secret of the Summerhouse I would be grateful if you would leave a review on Amazon.

For further details about the author and her novels visit

www.elisedarcy.com

Printed in Great Britain
by Amazon

19984217R00192